Praise f

Also by Sara Humphreys

The McGuire Brothers
Brave the Heat

The Amoveo Legend
Unleashed

Untouched

Undenied (novella)

Untamed

Undone

Unclaimed

Unbound (novella)

Dead in the City
Tall, Dark, and Vampire

Vampire Trouble

Vampires Never Cry Wolf

The Good, the Bad, and the Vampire

TROUBLE
Walks IN

SARA
HUMPHREYS

sourcebooks
casablanca

Published by Sourcebooks Casablanca, an imprint of Sourcebooks, Inc.
P.O. Box 4410, Naperville, Illinois 60567-4410
(630) 961-3900
Fax: (630) 961-2168
www.sourcebooks.com

Printed and bound in Canada.
MBP 10 9 8 7 6 5 4 3 2 1

For my grandmothers, Alicia and Amy…

*"The only way love can last a lifetime
is if it's unconditional."*
—Stephen Kendrick

Prologue

THE BOY HAD BEEN MISSING FOR TWELVE HOURS, AND Ronan McGuire knew better than anyone that if they didn't find the kid soon, the search could end in the worst possible way. It had been an unusually cold November, and when little David Newhart wandered away from his parents this morning in the park, he hadn't been wearing a coat. The sun had gone down hours ago, and the temperature was close to freezing.

Ronan's partner grew increasingly agitated as they climbed the steep incline of the hill near Turtle Pond, and hope fired brightly in Ronan's chest. He knew the dog's signals and could read him better than he could most people.

The boy was close.

Bowser whined loudly and tugged harder on the long leash, and Ronan swore under his breath. The enormous bloodhound had the best nose in the tristate area. Once he detected a scent, he rarely—if ever—failed to find what he was looking for. He tilted his snout to the air before spearing it back to the ground and turning left. Bowser's lanky brown-and-black-furred body quivered with excitement, the way it did whenever the trail grew stronger.

The scent article they'd given Bowser, the missing boy's hat, had given him a solid lead to follow, but this was more an art than a science. David had been missing for hours, and the gusty winds of late November had been blowing hard, making the search-and-rescue job that much more difficult. Well, for Ronan, it was a job. For Bowser, it was more like playing a big game of hide-and-seek. And there was nothing his dog loved more than finding what he was looking for.

Bowser kept his nose to the ground and trotted to the left toward a long stone wall. He followed the scent through the brush and dried leaves in an almost sideways direction along a wooded section of Central Park. Bowser was one of the most talented bloodhounds on the force and could detect scents up to a week old if he had to.

Tension settled in Ronan's shoulders, and his muscles bunched as he wrapped the leather lead tighter around his hand. He scanned the area ahead, and a tickle of panic glimmered in his chest as it sometimes did when he was searching for a missing kid. Faint memories from years ago bubbled to the surface. He knew exactly how this little boy was feeling. Alone. Terrified. Cold.

"David?" Ronan shouted. "I'm Officer Ronan McGuire with the NYPD. Your mom and dad are worried about you. David, can you hear me?"

The wind whistling by his ears was the only answer. The glimmer of hope began to fade right before Bowser whimpered and made a sudden turn to the right, his long, sword-like tail bouncing wildly as he picked up the pace. A bitter gust of wind whisked through the woods, sending a chill up Ronan's spine. *Shit. Please let the kid be okay.* Bowser dodged around a massive elm tree, and Ronan ran around behind him.

"David!"

That was when he spotted a dark lump...and it moved. Ronan's heart thundered in his chest. He shone his flashlight over the area, and the breath rushed from his lungs. *Got him*. David was curled up in a ball in a pile of leaves at the base of the tree. Bowser barked and went right over, sniffing and licking at the boy before sitting down beside him protectively.

"I wanna go home," David whimpered as he placed one quivering hand onto Bowser's paw. "I want my mommy."

"I gotcha, David." Ronan squatted down and took off his coat before quickly wrapping it around the kid. "Bowser and I are gonna get you back to your mom and dad. They're worried sick about you."

"I'm cold."

"I know, pal, but you're safe now. Everything's gonna be okay."

He started rubbing the boy's arms, but Bowser moved in and lay down right next to the kid, practically on top of him. David giggled through his sniffles and swiped at his eyes before snuggling up to the dog. Bowser was panting heavily, his long, pink tongue dangling from the side of his open mouth. The damn dog looked like he was smiling.

"Good boy." Ronan repeated the phrase a few times, scratched Bowser's ears, and gave him the praise he expected. "Nice job, buddy."

Bowser licked his hand quickly, as though returning the kudos. Ronan crouched next to his panting K-9 and radioed for the other officers in the area.

Ronan loved his job, especially when it had a happy ending.

Chapter 1

"I TOLD YOU THAT I'D BE THERE, AND I MEANT IT." Maddy Morgan pressed the iPhone harder against her ear. She was attempting to block out the sounds beyond her office door while her best friend pestered her to within an inch of her life. "I'm your maid of honor, for heaven's sake. What? You think I'm gonna bail after everything you and Gavin have been through? Hell no!"

"Okay, well, you can't blame me for double-checking, can you?" Jordan hesitated, her voice concerned. "We've hardly spoken. I mean, you haven't been home since... It's been over a year and..."

Maddy stared out the window that overlooked the hustle and bustle of Manhattan and sucked in a deep breath, her friend's unfinished thought hanging in the air. She nibbled her lower lip and fought the sudden, unexpected swell of emotion. It had been fifteen months since Rick died and a full year since she had been back to the town she'd always called home.

At least, she had until recently.

"I know," Maddy said quietly.

She swallowed the lump in her throat and refused to cry. She'd cried enough at Rick's funeral and during the weeks following. No more tears. If Rick were here, he would tell her to put on her big girl panties and get on with life.

"I'm not missing your wedding," she said firmly. "Jeez, Jordan. You and Gavin have waited sixteen years to finally get hitched. Hell, you two would have gotten married *last* Christmas if it weren't for me."

"That's not true," Jordan said firmly.

"Bull." Maddy laughed.

"Okay, well, it wasn't the *only* reason," Jordan replied. "Gavin's parents wanted to throw us a huge Christmas wedding, and four months wouldn't have been enough time to pull it all together. Deciding to wait a year has been a win-win. My future mother-in-law had plenty of time to do her thing, and we all had time to properly grieve for Rick. But I'm still worried about you…"

"I'm fine, Jordan, and I promise… I'm gonna be there to witness your dream coming true."

"Okay, but—"

"No buts."

"Yo, Maddy." The increasingly irritating voice of Chris Drummond shot into the room as he barged in. "That blond, the Brenda chick—are you gonna take her out to an open house this weekend, or should I? And what about those newlyweds? I know you've been slammed. I could take them out to see the new listings, if you want."

"Hang on, Jordan," Maddy said tightly.

She covered the phone with her hand and leveled an irritated gaze at her colleague. She knew that Terrence, the owner of the realty agency, had hired Drummond because he had an amazing reputation for selling and one of the best portfolios in the business, but he was a letch. A letch that thought anyone with boobs wanted him. Maddy had learned a long time ago that big talent usually meant even bigger egos.

Unfortunately, this *talent* was also turning out to be an asshole. She had already reported him once to Terrence for inappropriate advances on the young women in the office. Big talent or not, he was making her tired of him and his misogynistic bullshit. And lately, there had been attempts to steal her clients.

"Did you happen to notice that my door was closed?"

"Yeah." He leaned in the doorway with his usual casual arrogance. Tall, slim, well dressed, and always perfectly coiffed, he was considered good-looking by most. But the air of entitlement he wore like a cloak was a turnoff as far as Maddy was concerned. Besides, she would never date a colleague.

"I'm on a call."

"Right." He jutted his thumb over his shoulder. "Anyway, should I take that Brenda chick out and, uh, show her the ropes? We could take the newlyweds, the, uh…"

"The Bartholomews," Maddy finished for him. "No, I can handle my client list. Thank you."

"Fine, then let me take Brenda out."

The smarmy smile on his face gave Maddy pause. He'd been hitting on the assistants, who were savvy New Yorkers and more than capable of handling themselves, but now he was moving on to the young real estate agent. Brenda was a recent college grad from the Midwest. She was pretty, smart, and naive.

A prime target for a guy like Drummond.

"No," Maddy said firmly. "Terrence asked me to handle her training. Thank you, and please close the door on your way out."

His smile faded, and a hard, cold look settled in his

eyes. Maddy had moved up the ranks quickly since joining Cosmopolitan Realty House, and her rise hadn't gone unnoticed by Drummond. He hated not being number one, but she suspected that being second to a woman was a bigger insult.

"Sure thing," he murmured.

Drummond left but neglected to shut the door. Maddy crossed the room, pausing only to tell Sharon, her assistant, to hold her other calls before she closed her door once more.

"Sorry about that, Jordan." She caught a glimpse of her reflection in the window and grimaced before running one hand through her unruly brown curls. "I'm coming into town a week before the wedding so I can help you with whatever you need. Y'know, all that bridesmaid stuff. I mean, I'm not a real girlie girl, but it'll be fun to hang out. And tell Gavin he better not try to horn in on our girls' night out. It might only be the two of us, but there's a no-boys-allowed rule in effect for that event."

"I wouldn't worry about that," Jordan said through a chuckle. "All four of his brothers are coming in early as well. From what I hear, Ronan has quite the bachelor party planned. Speaking of Ronan, why don't you two ride back to Old Brookfield together? I mean, you're both in the city, and he *is* the best man."

"Yeah, that's not gonna happen. I'll take my own car, thank you very much. I'm staying at the Old Brookfield Inn, and Ronan will be at his parents' house, obviously." Maddy's eyes narrowed, and the smile on her face grew. "Your matchmaking scheme hasn't worked, Jordan. But I'll give you and Gavin an A for effort."

"What are you talking about?" Jordan asked with feigned innocence. "When you moved to the city last year, Gavin merely suggested that Ronan should look out for you. He's been a cop there for over a decade. Besides, I heard through the McGuire brother grapevine that you two have been going running on the weekends, so Ronan can't be all bad."

Nope. That was half the problem. He was exactly the right kind of bad.

They had gone jogging in Central Park almost every weekend for the past several months, but Maddy had made it clear from the start: she wasn't interested in dating. Not him, nor anyone else. Friends? Sure. Romance? No way.

Her heart couldn't take another turn through the shredder. Dating a cop, just because he also happened to be one of the sexiest men God ever put on this earth, would not be a smart move.

Besides, Ronan had a reputation as a total ladies' man.

Not that she could blame any woman for taking a ride on *that* handsome train. When he flashed that lopsided grin and his bluish-green eyes crinkled at the corners, it took superwoman strength for Maddy *not* to drop her panties. He was a combination of mischievous little boy and irresistible alpha male—a deadly pairing.

Ronan McGuire was wickedly sexy. The worst part was that he knew it.

"Well, yeah," Maddy said quickly. She sat at her desk and spun the chair to face the window so she could see the rest of the world. Living and working in this city made her feel like a rat in a cage sometimes. "Running around, getting sweaty, and panting in the cold is not exactly dating, Jordan."

"Sweaty and panting sounds promising," Jordan teased.

Maddy's face flushed. "That's not what I meant." She quickly added, "I was talking about Bowser."

"Sure," her friend said slowly. "Sure you were."

"You know Ronan doesn't go anywhere without that dog. Speaking of which, are you prepared to have a drooling animal at your wedding?"

"Oh fine, change the subject." Jordan sighed. "Any chance I can talk you into coming for Thanksgiving?"

"Sorry, babe. I'm slammed."

"Then how about staying for Christmas? The wedding is on the twenty-third. Come on. Please? The girls would love it," she said, referring to her two adorable daughters. "You're going to be here for a week, so what's a couple more days? You said they were closing your office between Christmas and New Year's anyway."

Maddy had never been part of big family holidays, and that had been fine with her, but the pleading tone in Jordan's voice was starting to make her rethink her decision.

"You know the holidays were never a big deal for me, Jordan. My mom hated celebrating them after my dad died, and then once she was gone, I didn't really want to. And besides," she added quickly, "Rick and I never even got a tree or anything. He was always working, and so was I."

"I know, but I hate to think of you alone in that big city on Christmas. *Again*. It's bad enough you wouldn't come last year. Please think about it?"

"I'm hosting a huge New Year's Eve party for my clients—it's at my apartment."

"You could leave on the twenty-sixth and still be

back in plenty of time to be party ready," Jordan persisted. "You and I both know your assistant already has the whole shindig tied up and ready to go."

Jordan was right. The party was a lame reason not to spend the holiday with them. Besides, it was all being catered, and the invitations had been sent. What did Maddy really have to do other than show up and schmooze? And what was here for her on Christmas? She didn't even have a cat or a fish to feed.

Ugh. She felt more pathetic by the second.

"Okay," Maddy said with a dramatic sigh. "I'll think about it. Jeez, when did you become such a nudge?"

"Since I had two children and learned that being a nudge can sometimes be quite effective."

A knock on Maddy's door sent a flicker of irritation up her back. But when she spun around, Sharon's tearstained face stopped her cold.

"Girl, I have to go." A knot of dread curled in her gut. "I'll see you in a few weeks. Give Gracie and Lily a kiss from Aunt Maddy."

Maddy hit End and set the phone on her desk. Her legs felt like Jell-O as she rose to her feet. Sharon was still weeping while she closed the door behind her, and before it shut, Maddy saw two of the other agents in the office crying.

"Sharon, what is it?"

"Th-they found her."

"Who?" Maddy asked shakily, her fingertips pressing into the mahogany desk. But she knew the answer before Sharon said it.

"Lucille Bowman." The young woman swiped at her eyes and let out a shuddering sob. "She's dead."

A haunting rendition of "Amazing Grace" spilled from the organ filling the small church, and Maddy wiped the tears from her eyes. The last time she'd heard this song had been at Rick's funeral. A new surge of sadness and grief welled up inside as the pallbearers carried Lucille's casket silently toward the open double doors.

The sounds of the city spilled in, buzzing beneath the mournful melody—a bitter reminder of how cruel life was. The world outside went on as though nothing had happened. While Lucille's death had barely been noted on the evening news, it was far more personal for Maddy and her coworkers. According to police, the last call Lucille had made was to her husband, saying she was going to meet a client at an open house. The client had called the office later that day to say Lucille had never arrived.

Lucille's husband kept his vacant gaze fixed to the ground. He lumbered silently behind his late wife's casket, seemingly unaware of anyone or anything around him. Grief and shock clung to him like an invisible shroud. Maddy knew that feeling all too well.

He and Lucille didn't have any children and, according to a few of the other real estate agents, had been married only a couple of years. People said that as though it would somehow make his loss less horrible. Did the amount of time he and Lucille had been together even matter? One year or ten, a loss was a loss.

The remaining mourners filed out, all of them in various states of grief, but Maddy remained quietly in the back row. She had spoken with Lucille only a few times, but that didn't stop her from wanting to pay her respects—but without overstepping her bounds. The little church in Old Brookfield had been full for Rick's funeral. Even though she couldn't possibly have said who was there and who wasn't, the presence of every individual was a comfort to her. The least she could do was offer the same to Lucille's husband.

After everyone had left, Maddy rose to her feet and slipped out of the pew. She could still go to the burial and reception afterward. The invitation had been extended to everyone at the end of the service. But those events felt like they were for close friends and family, and Maddy didn't qualify for either role. No, it was probably best if she dragged her butt back to work. After all, it wasn't like she had anyone waiting for her at her apartment.

Maddy tugged her black wool coat closed and tied the sash, bracing herself for the brisk air that awaited her outside. As she passed, she gave a polite smile and nod to one of the ministers rearranging some pamphlets in the vestibule.

Life went on, it would seem, even for the clergy.

When Maddy pushed open the heavy wooden door, a gust of brisk November wind rushed over her, making her suck in a sharp breath. Why did this city seem cruel and cold at every turn? The stubborn wind had pulled several strands of her curly hair free from her lame attempt at an updo. She pushed her unruly locks from her eyes and started down the stone steps, prepared to go back to her desk and stare at the computer. She had cleared her calendar today, but returning to an empty apartment was simply too depressing an option. At least at the office, she'd have the illusion of not being alone.

Maddy had made up her mind to hail a cab by the time she reached the sidewalk, but when she saw who was waiting for her, she stopped short.

Not much surprised her in Manhattan anymore— she'd seen just about everything in her year living here, including a woman walking a ferret on a leash, a naked homeless guy streaking down Park Avenue, and an old man strolling through Central Park with a squawking parrot on his shoulder.

But she never expected to find *this*.

Standing beside a lamppost, brimming with confidence and with his K-9 partner by his side, was Ronan McGuire. Dressed in his dark-blue NYPD uniform, he looked every bit the ruggedly handsome hero that he was. His cap obscured her view of his thick ebony hair, but those pale-bluish-green eyes peered at her from beneath a furrowed brow. His tall, broad-shouldered frame was covered from head to toe against the bitter air, and the bulletproof vest he wore only served to accentuate his size.

How did Ronan manage to look devastatingly gorgeous in a standard-issue uniform? She'd seen plenty of other cops in this city, but not one of them hummed with masculine sexuality the way Ronan did. He reeked of calm control and steely strength. On the surface, he was cool and steady, but beneath was a distinctly powerful energy. She knew, without a doubt, that he could burst into action in a split second.

The guys brushing past her on Park Avenue, the ones dressed in thousand-dollar suits, didn't look half as sexy as Ronan did in his uniform.

I bet he looks pretty good out of it too.

Bowser, an enormous bloodhound who seemed to delight in startling Maddy whenever possible, barked loudly. She flinched as Ronan's constant companion interrupted her naughty train of thought, and her face heated. How long had she been standing there staring at him? Based on the slight smirk curving Ronan's lips, it was longer than she'd like to admit.

"Hey," Maddy said, trying to collect herself. She crossed the sidewalk to greet Ronan but kept a healthy distance from the two of them. "What are you doing here? Did you just happen to be in the neighborhood? Because if I'm not mistaken, this isn't your usual haunting ground."

"This is most definitely *not* my neighborhood. Too rich for my blood," Ronan scoffed. He gathered Bowser's leash, wrapping it around his hand, before he pushed himself off the post and inched closer. "Our shift starts in a couple of hours. We came to check on you."

Her gaze flicked briefly to Bowser. He was staring at her as usual. She had never met an animal as tuned in to people as he was. But then, he was a search-and-rescue K-9, so tuning in was part of his job.

"Me?" Maddy stilled. "I'm fine, really," she said in a shakier voice than she expected.

Even *she* didn't believe it. *Nope. Not okay.*

"Your friend was murdered, and you just attended her funeral." Ronan leaned in and lowered his voice. "Don't give me that. There's not a damn *fine* thing about this whole crappy situation."

Something in Maddy's chest crumbled a little at the tenderness in his voice. How long had it been since someone had expressed concern for her well-being? It felt like forever. Still, she suspected there was more to it than that.

"You've seen things like this before," Maddy whispered. "Does it ever get any easier?"

"No," he said quietly. Bowser whined and licked Ronan's hand in a sweet, almost reassuring gesture. "Sucks every time. Nothing easy about it."

Ronan and Bowser had been part of searches that ended badly. He'd obviously been affected by those experiences, and knowing that he'd remained unjaded by the cruelty of his job somehow made him even more attractive.

Bowser, who was sitting dutifully at Ronan's feet, let out a low whine and snuffled loudly. Sometimes Maddy was convinced that dog was more human than half the people in this city.

"No...I don't imagine there would be." Maddy adjusted the purse slung over her shoulder, trying to squash a fresh swell of emotion. She pulled her leather gloves from her pocket and tugged them on while avoiding Ronan's inquisitive stare. "I mean, it's sad. It's beyond sad, the whole situation is horrible, but—"

"What are you doing now?" he asked abruptly. "Everyone else is gone. Since you're still here, I'm figuring that you opted not to go on to the burial. And knowing you, that means you're going back to work."

Maddy opened her mouth to argue with him but snapped it shut. He'd hit the nail on the head. Ronan's lopsided grin widened.

"I-I have work to do," she sputtered.

"Really?" He tilted his head and narrowed those beautiful eyes. They looked more blue today than green.

"Yes, really."

"Because if I had to guess, I'd say you were gonna go back to that fancy office of yours and stare at your computer or surf the Internet. Maybe play some solitaire or Candy Crush?"

Why, oh why, does he have to be so damn observant?

Maddy wasn't sure if it was comforting or irritating to have someone see her so clearly. Maybe it was both? She had started to get used to the anonymity of this city, the sense of disconnection from other people. She'd left Old Brookfield to give herself distance from Rick's memory and the well-meaning but meddlesome members of her small community.

No one here knew her past, or even cared enough to ask. Her life in Manhattan was strictly business, which made her feel safely cocooned, sheltered from painful memories. She remained insulated from having to dig past surface pleasantries. Ronan wasn't like that. He was a cop, and his desire to find the truth was evident in everything he did.

"Well, smarty-pants." Maddy folded her arms over her breasts, suddenly feeling exposed. "For your information, I don't play Candy Crush."

"Farm Heroes?" he asked playfully.

"No," Maddy said through a bubble of laughter. She swatted him on the arm and tried not to smile while avoiding his gaze. "I don't do any of that stuff."

"How about coffee?" He offered his arm and jutted his head toward the corner. "You do that, don't you?"

"Yes," Maddy said slowly. She flicked her gaze to his elbow and sighed dramatically. "You aren't gonna quit until I agree to go, are you?"

"Nope." His grin widened. "After all these years, you should know how persistent we McGuire boys are. Carolyn and Charles didn't raise any quitters."

"I can see that."

"C'mon, and I won't even try to pretend it's a date," Ronan prodded. He wobbled his elbow at her. "Don't make me look bad in front of Bowser."

"Well, I certainly wouldn't want to be responsible for that," she said dramatically. "Coffee it is."

Maddy slipped her arm through his and shivered, the warmth of his body seeping through the layers of wool. Her gut reaction was to snuggle deeper against him and his rock-hard body, but she resisted, straightening her back. She couldn't afford to dip beneath the surface and touch the raw emotions lingering there. That would get her nowhere, and she refused to be reduced to a weepy woman in the middle of the street. If Ronan noticed her subtle shift away from him, he didn't comment on it.

They walked in silence, arm in arm, with the bloodhound trotting dutifully at Ronan's side. They approached a Starbucks, but instead of crossing Fifty-Sixth Street, Ronan led her straight toward one of the street vendors.

"It'll have to be coffee and a walk." He jutted a thumb at his partner. "Starbucks isn't big on having dogs in their establishments. Besides, our squad car is parked around the corner. How about coffee and a ride home?"

"That's fine by me." Maddy sucked in a deep breath of cold air. "Sitting in a crowded coffee shop with half the population on their laptops doesn't sound appealing. But a walk sounds great."

"I thought you'd say that." He nudged her gently

and smirked. "But don't worry, I know you're not a cheap date."

"It's not a date. It's coffee." Maddy kept her tone light. "We've already been through this, McGuire. I'm not dating anyone, so don't take it personally."

"Can't blame a guy for trying."

They stopped at the truck, and she slipped her arm from his before quickly shoving her hands in the pockets of her coat. The cold air slithered under her clothes with surprising speed as the warmth of his body against hers became a memory. Ronan made quick work of ordering their coffee and, to her surprise, knew exactly how she took it.

"I know it's not that fancy French stuff you like, but it'll do in a pinch."

"Impressive," Maddy said, taking the steaming cup from his hand. "You nailed it."

"I pay attention." Ronan slid a sidelong glance at her while he handed money to the guy in the truck. "We've been going for a run followed by coffee almost every week for months. What kind of a cop would I be if I couldn't even remember how you take your coffee?"

"You love being right, don't you?" She tilted her chin, daring him to deny it.

"Yes." Ronan inched closer, cradling his cup in one hand and holding Bowser's leash in the other. Confident and in total control as always. "But *especially* when it comes to you."

She was about to ask him what exactly he meant by that, but Bowser started walking toward the corner. They strolled side by side, but she kept her eyes on the pedestrians ahead of them. If she looked at Ronan, he might get a peek at the conflicting swirl of emotions currently running through her.

"Okay, explain, please." Maddy shivered again, but not from the cold. "Why do you want to be right when it comes to me?"

"Because you're this big, bad businesswoman who acts like she's got it all under control."

"And I don't?" She let out a short laugh. "Gee, thanks."

"That's not what I said, and definitely not what I meant."

They stopped at the corner. Maddy was about to cross, but Ronan grabbed her arm, pulling her back just as a car blew through the light. If it hadn't been for him, she would have gotten hit.

"Shit," Maddy hissed. "Damn taxi drivers."

She turned her eyes to his, and his grip on her tightened, almost imperceptibly. Maddy's heart thundered in her chest. Was it from the near miss with the cab, or the feel of Ronan's fingers curled around her bicep?

"I like surprising you," he said quietly. Bowser made a snuffling sound and sat between them, but Ronan didn't take his eyes off hers. "How am I doing so far?"

"Today?" Maddy asked quietly. "Well, to be honest, you shocked the hell out of me by showing up at the church. Why did you come?"

"Are you serious?" His brows furrowed. "I thought that would be obvious."

"Not to me." Maddy shook her head slowly and studied him, clutching the cardboard coffee cup with both hands.

"I figured it would be a tough day for you." His mouth set in a tight line before he completed the thought she could practically see floating over his head. "Going to the funeral couldn't have been easy, and I thought you could use a friend. I didn't think you'd want to be alone."

"I didn't," she whispered. "Thank you."

The wind blew over them, sending her hair flying into her eyes. It was perfect timing, making the tears that welled up easy enough to explain away. Maddy tugged the strands of hair aside and nodded before turning her attention to the passing cars.

"See, Bowser?" Ronan scratched the bloodhound's head, which elicited a loud bark from the dog. "Right again."

Maddy burst out laughing in spite of the surge of emotion and wiped discreetly at her eyes. "No one likes a know-it-all, McGuire."

"Maybe not," he said with a wide grin. "But I still surprised you. Come on, the light changed. Let's cross before another taxi tries to run you over."

As they made their way to the safety of the other side, Maddy had a feeling that there would be more surprises where Ronan was concerned.

That was the part that frightened her.

Chapter 2

RONAN MCGUIRE LOVED WOMEN, AND UNTIL RECENTLY, he'd enjoyed a variety of them. All of that had changed when Maddy Morgan came roaring back into his life. The moment he'd laid eyes on her at his parent's anniversary party last summer, it had been like a kick in the gut. She was as gorgeous as she'd been back in high school, and just as unattainable. As far as she'd been concerned, he had merely been the pesky brother of her best friend's boyfriend.

Ronan would see her around town when he went home to visit over the years, but nothing had changed and she was still out of his reach. Maddy and Rick had been practically joined at the hip for years. Ronan was many things, but a home wrecker wasn't one of them. Rick had been a good guy and he seemed to make Maddy happy, so that had been good enough for Ronan. He had never considered himself the jealous type, but every time he saw the two of them together, the green-eyed monster would rear its ugly head.

When had he first fallen for her? If he had to nail it down, it was when she punched out Billy Hollibrand in the school parking lot. Maddy was feisty—a take-no-shit kind of girl—and if you asked Ronan's mother, that was exactly the type of woman he needed. Hollibrand had been the town bully, and when Maddy moved there in ninth grade, Billy made the mistake of trying to push her around. The jerkoff made fun of her curly hair and grabbed her ass. Two seconds later, the boy was on the ground nursing a bloody nose.

A smile curved Ronan's lips at the memory.

"Yo, McGuire." His captain's voice pulled him from his daydreaming. "You awake over there?"

Bowser was lying in his bed next to Ronan's desk, but he lifted his head and turned his brown eyes toward Ronan when the captain approached. If Ronan didn't know better, he'd swear the dog was laughing at him.

"Wide awake, Cap." Ronan adjusted his chair as Bowser settled his snout on his front paws again. "Can't say the same for my partner."

Bowser whined and made a snuffling sound before closing his eyes. Ronan couldn't really blame the dog—he was pretty beat himself. They had gotten back-to-back calls from two departments upstate. Not all of the counties in the state had K-9s, so he and Bowser helped out when necessary, lending a hand—or a paw—as needed.

Both cases had been high-stress with even higher stakes.

Luckily the little girl who had wandered away from her family's campsite was found safely, and so was the teenager who got separated from her friends on a hike. She must have been the only teen girl in the tristate area who didn't have a damn cell phone attached to her. Needless to say, it had been long days and longer nights, but both searches ended with happy parents.

Captain Jenkins strolled over, hoisting his uniform pants over his belly. The guy might be out of shape and only a couple years from retirement, but he was one of the best cops Ronan had worked with. Jenkins and his partner, Saratoga, a sweet bloodhound with wide, caramel-colored eyes, were in-house most of the time these days. Saratoga was retired, but like all K-9s, she would live out the rest of her days with her partner and his family. In Jenkins's case, that was only him.

"Why are you and Bowser here?" Jenkins settled his hands on his hips and pointed at Bowser just as Saratoga sidled over and lay down next to her friend. "You two have been goin' nonstop for the past three days. You should have taken today off, and you know it."

"No can do, Cap." Ronan hit a few buttons on the keyboard and printed out his report from the last search. "My brother is getting married in a few weeks, and I'll be out for a while. I'll be using up the rest of my time for the year, and I can't risk not being able to go because I didn't do my paperwork. I'm the best man after all."

"That you are, McGuire," Jenkins said through a snort of laughter. "But all work and no play, and you're gonna end up like me and Sara here. All we got is each other and this damn job. No wife, no kids. Just me and her." He smiled at the aging bloodhound who currently had her head nestled on top of Bowser's. "Ain't that right, sweetie?"

The old girl whined in response but didn't move.

"Seriously, McGuire," Jenkins said, sitting in the chair in front of Ronan's desk. "You coulda taken today, y'know. You sure as hell have enough time left over."

"Really, Cap." Ronan shook his head and held up one hand. "I'm fine."

"Right. You always are." Jenkins's mouth set in a thin line. "How's your friend? Didn't you say that your girlfriend, that real estate agent lady, knew the Bowman woman they found by the river?"

"She's not my girlfriend. Maddy's just an old friend from back home." Ronan went to the printer and grabbed the reports. "But yes, she knew Lucille Bowman, at least casually. Maddy's a broker, and they ran in some of the same professional circles."

"Well, tell your *friend* to watch her ass."

Ronan stilled and carefully placed the reports on his desk. A knot of dread curled in his gut, and the serious expression on the captain's face didn't do anything to ease it.

"They think the murder was somehow connected to Lucille's job?" Ronan let out a slow breath. "Shit."

"Don't know yet." Jenkins folded his hands on top of his round belly. "All they know right now is she was supposed to show an apartment on the West Side—an open house or something—and she never made it. Hell, those real estate people have all their contact info online now. It's easy to find someone and track 'em down, if you want to."

"What are they thinking?" Ronan's gut clenched.

"Husband ain't good for it," Jenkins said. "His alibi is airtight. No affairs, financials are in order. Whoever did this knew her though—or at least knew where she was going. Hell, she obviously didn't get dragged through the streets of the city kicking and screaming, so odds are that she knew the perp in some way. They're still waiting on toxicology. You know that shit takes forever."

"Damn it." Ronan ran one hand over his face and sat in his chair. "Maddy is always doing those open houses. Not to mention the running around she does for individual appointments. She works her ass off. You'd think that her life depended on it." He let out a slow sigh. "Hell, she lives and breathes it."

"You'd know somethin' about that. Wouldn't ya?"

"It's not the same thing, Cap. Those rich, fancy clients of hers love her because she drops everything to get them what they need. The woman is nothing if not tenacious."

"I guess that includes resisting your charms, eh, McGuire?" Jenkins laughed and wagged a finger at Ronan. "You *like* this broad, so don't even try to deny it."

"Of course I do. We're friends."

"Yeah but you wanna be more than friends." Jenkins raised his salt-and-pepper eyebrows. "You know how I can tell?"

"No." Ronan stapled the reports and busied himself, trying not to let Jenkins know how right he was. "Enlighten me."

"Ever since *she* came to town, you haven't been out on a *single* date." Jenkins hoisted his rotund form out of the chair with a groan. "And for a guy who seemed to have a different date almost every Saturday night for the past several years, that seems a bit odd. Don't ya think?"

"Careful, Cap." Ronan winked and extended the two finished reports to his superior. "You sound jealous."

"Some detective you are." Jenkins made a snort of derision and snagged the papers from Ronan. "Not jealous, more like impressed. I can't remember the last time I went out on a date…and believe me, it ain't for lack of effort. A good-lookin' guy like you could be out with any woman he wanted. And here you are, pining away for the *one* broad in this city who turned you down."

"See?" Ronan leaned back in his chair and laced his fingers behind his head. "You're working under the assumption that I've asked her out—for an actual date, that is. I'm still in the game."

"Sounds like you're on the bench." Jenkins narrowed his pale-brown eyes. "You haven't actually asked her out? You been joggin' with this woman all the freakin' time. What's the holdup?"

"I told you, man. We're just friends." Ronan shrugged. "Period. End of story."

"Bullshit," Jenkins snorted. "I may be old-fashioned, but men and women can't *only* be friends. Not really."

"Whatever, man." Ronan sighed and dropped his hands onto the arms of his chair. He would never win that argument with his captain. "It's complicated, okay?"

"You mean because of the dead boyfriend?"

"Real sensitive, Cap." Ronan gave him a sarcastic thumbs-up. "His name was Rick, and he was a firefighter in our hometown. He bought it on the job. I knew him, okay? He was a good guy."

"Right… That sucks," Jenkins said slowly. "But with all due respect, she can't date a dead guy, and his memory ain't gonna keep her warm at night."

"Come on, Cap," Ronan persisted. "They were practically married and were together for years, like almost a decade. It seems shady to be hitting on her so soon after something like that. I'm being her friend, which is exactly what she needs."

"Maybe, but it sounds like an excuse to me." Jenkins

snapped his fingers at his dog. "Come on, Saratoga. Let's go, girl. It's time to head home."

"Why would I need an excuse?" Ronan shouted after him.

"Easy," Jenkins barked over his shoulder. "If you don't ask, then she can't turn you down."

Ronan had no response to that. The son of a bitch was absolutely right. He hadn't come right out and asked Maddy on a date because he was pretty sure she'd say no. Plus, why would he want to make it weird between them, especially before the wedding? That wouldn't be fair to his brother and Jordan. The last complication they needed was awkwardness between the best man and the maid of honor.

He went to shut his computer down, and the Bowman case came to mind. A knot formed in his gut. Like the investigating officers, he suspected that Lucille knew her killer—at least enough to go off with him without raising an alarm. But on the other hand, the New York City real estate market was massive. The odds were probably slim that Maddy knew this guy too, whoever he was.

Slim chance or not, Ronan was going to have a chat with her about safety precautions. Bowser yawned loudly before stretching and rising to his feet.

"What do you think, buddy?" The bloodhound came over and laid his head in Ronan's lap, as though asking to get the hell out of there. "Think Maddy will listen to advice from me and take the proper precautions?"

Bowser snuffled loudly and sat on his haunches.

"Yeah," Ronan said, laughing softly. "Me neither. But that won't stop me from trying."

Maddy discreetly checked the time on her phone before turning her attention back to the young couple whispering with each other in the kitchen. Mrs. Bartholomew loved the place and Mr. Bartholomew wasn't entirely sold, but if Maddy had to bet, the wife was going to win.

While at an unorthodox time, the Friday-evening open house was turning out to be one of her busiest in the past month. Brenda was supposed to assist Maddy tonight to get a little more experience under her belt, but she'd never showed. The girl was new and eager to please, but flaking out on this event was not cool. Maddy loathed reprimanding people, but a lecture was coming Brenda's way. The beautiful blond was barely out of college. Might she have blown off work for a better offer and a hot date? The company had taken a chance with bringing someone so young and green into the office.

It looked like they had made a mistake, but Maddy hoped like hell the girl had a good reason for not showing up. A smile curved her lips. Terrence, her boss and the owner of Cosmopolitan Realty, would surely tell her to give Brenda another chance. His compassion and strong ethical code were the two main reasons she had signed on with his company. His business was about people, not just making the sale, which was unusual in the cutthroat real estate world.

Maddy had come to this city to live without emotional attachments, but time and again, she found herself getting suckered in. She couldn't help it. The city might be cold and unemotional, but no matter how hard she tried, she couldn't be.

Letting out a sigh, she checked her phone again. There was no answer to the text she'd sent Brenda, and no missed calls. *Perfect*. Managing staff and juggling personalities was Maddy's least favorite part of the business. She used to tell Rick she was fine not having kids, because she knew plenty of adults who acted like children. Maybe she was being too hard on the girl and too quick to judge.

She pictured herself scolding Brenda, but Maddy knew the fantasy would have to suffice. She'd never do it in real life. One look into Brenda's sweet, wide-eyed apologetic face, and Maddy would be telling the girl not to worry about it.

I'm a sucker.

Handling the open house on her own wasn't difficult. She could run events like this with her eyes closed. But it had been busy. The spacious Upper West Side penthouse had only been on the market for a week, and the owners were eager to sell. That typically happened with a divorce. Since they were so eager, Maddy had set up a Friday-night open house to go with the one on Sunday, but based on the interest tonight, the place could be sold by then.

God bless the Internet.

She'd done damn well in the Old Brookfield beachfront market, and many of those wealthy clients who'd bought summer property lived and worked in the city. Transitioning to the New York City market had been surprisingly easy.

Besides, her favorite part of being a real estate agent

was helping people find the place they would call home. The one space where they could kick off their shoes, snuggle up on the couch, and find shelter from the world and their worries. It was the most satisfying part of her job.

Maddy gave the wealthy young twosome the space she knew they wanted, loitering by the front door while they chatted quietly. Twelve other real estate agents had been through the massive apartment with their clients at last count, in addition to seven walk-ins. It had been a long and emotionally draining week, and there were about ten minutes left before she could go home and collapse.

Just as that thought rushed through her weary brain, the private elevator to the penthouse dinged. The doors slid open and a man stepped out. He was older, probably late fifties, good looking and distinguished in a Gordon Gekko way. He had Wall Street sleazeball written all over him and reeked of overcompensation. She'd be willing to bet he drove either a Porsche or Corvette— probably bright yellow.

Men like him dressed in expensive suits and carried themselves with shoulders back and head up, but the fear of discovery lingered behind their eyes. It was like at any moment someone might reveal them for the fraud that, deep down, they believed themselves to be.

Sucker or jaded bitch? Maddy forced a smile and extended her hand. *This city has already done a number on me.*

"Hello, I'm Maddy Morgan." She shook his hand briefly as he moved into the large foyer. His gleaming, polished shoes clicked on the tumbled marble floor. "You made it to our open house just in time."

"Thank you." He didn't look at her but scanned the foyer as he continued toward the open living room. "Peter Gregory."

"Did you have an opportunity to sign in at the front desk? The building's board insists upon it." Maddy strode up next to him. "The security here is top notch, which is, of course, one of the selling points."

"Of course." He gave her a tight smile and nodded toward the window bank on the opposite wall. "May I have a look around? I've just begun the process of finding a new home, and this one seemed perfect on paper."

"Absolutely." Maddy folded her hands in front of her and glanced at the yuppies. Still whispering. "Then you know that this lovely home has four bedrooms and three-and-a-half baths. The kitchen is state of the art, and you have a private garden terrace off the master bedroom."

"Yes. As I said, I've seen the listing." He tilted his head and strolled across the room with an air of arrogance about him. "Thank you, Ms. Morgan. I'll just take a quick walk through. I realize the showing time is almost over, and I wouldn't want to throw anyone off schedule. My wife will be joining me in a few weeks, and if I don't have something decent to show her, she'll be quite perturbed with me."

A wife? That was surprising. Maddy had thought for sure this man was a bachelor.

"I see," Maddy said as she scolded herself for jumping to conclusions. "Is there something in particular she's looking for?"

"I'll know it when I see it," he said quietly. He held his hands behind his back and surveyed the space. "Finding a new home, knowing when it's the right one, is more of a feeling. It's not something one can put on paper. Wouldn't you agree?"

"Yes, absolutely." Her lips lifted. She had definitely misread this man. "In fact, I couldn't agree more."

"Well then. I'll be just a moment."

"Take your time, Mr. Gregory." Maddy meant it too. She may have been tired, but time was money. Besides, if he and his wife weren't already working with another real estate agent, she'd be more than happy to help them. "I'll be right here if you have any questions."

"Excuse me, Ms. Morgan?" The young Mr. Bartholomew strode out of the kitchen with his wife's hand clasped tightly in his. Based on the excited twinkle in the pretty blond woman's eyes, she'd won the whisper war. "We'll be putting in an offer. We didn't officially sign the contract with you and Cosmopolitan Realty yet, but I'd like to rectify that immediately."

"Absolutely. I know you had to rush out to another appointment after our last meeting." Maddy smiled warmly. She pulled her card from her pocket and handed it to him. "This is my listing, and I'm happy to help you."

"Thank you," the young woman squealed with excitement. "I know you're not supposed to show how much you love a place, but I can't help it."

"Believe me, I understand." Maddy nodded. "I knew my apartment would be mine from the second I stepped through the front door. It just felt…"

"Like home?" Mrs. Bartholomew asked hopefully.

Referring to Maddy's apartment as *home* would be a major stretch. Nowhere in this huge, heartless city would ever be her home. Not really. Honestly, she'd begun to wonder if she'd ever feel at home anywhere again.

"You could say that." Maddy smiled. "It felt *safe*."

Yeah, safe for you to hide from your life and the rest of the world. Coward.

"Honey," her husband said warningly. "We still have to go over a few things. I'm sure if Ms. Morgan gets any offers between now and nine o'clock tomorrow morning she'll let us know, so we can jump into the bidding. Right?"

"Definitely."

Maddy showed the Bartholomews to the elevator and let out a weary laugh the instant the door slid closed with a dull thump. Their enthusiasm was refreshing—if not naive. They were first-time buyers and came from big-money families. Private schools and country clubs had been their playgrounds, and dropping several million on this apartment didn't seem like it would faze them in the least.

Really, though, what did Maddy know? They could have won the freaking lottery, or maybe the guy hit it big with some start-up company. At the end of the day, where they got their money didn't matter. It was none of her business, but that aside, she did like to speculate. It kept the process interesting and forced her to pay attention to details. Usually, the smallest detail gave the largest amount of information.

Like Ronan McGuire and the coffee, for example.

A smile curved her lips when she recalled the way he'd effortlessly ordered her coffee exactly the way she liked it. It might have seemed silly to some, but that small bit of knowledge showed his attentiveness. Her smile faltered, and she fished her phone out of the pocket of her suit jacket. In all the years she'd been with

Rick, the man had never remembered how she liked her coffee. He got it wrong so often that it had become a running joke between them. Then again, he'd always had a rotten memory and had even forgotten her birthday a couple times.

Details hadn't been Rick's strength.

"Ms. Morgan?" The voice pulled her from her memories and Maddy spun around quickly, feeling foolish for drifting off like that. "Are you feeling alright?"

Mr. Gregory stood behind her and was peering at her as though he was worried she was going to faint or something.

"Yes," Maddy said quickly.

"You're certain? Because my wife has been ill, and… well…she sometimes gets a faraway look on her face like the one you just had. It makes me worry."

"I'm so sorry, Mr. Gregory." Maddy's voice softened. "I hope she's on the mend."

"As much as one can be after a few rounds of chemotherapy." He dropped his gaze from hers and cleared his throat before turning his back to her. "I don't think she would truly love this penthouse, and given the circumstances, it must be exactly right."

"Of course." The broken tone of his voice tugged at her heartstrings. "If you decide to work with me, I promise you we'll find the perfect home for you and Mrs. Gregory."

"Thank you."

"Do you have any questions?"

"Yes and no." He turned to face her again, his cool demeanor once again in place. "I saw what I needed to see. Since I'm just starting my search, I'd like to go look at some other spaces. Do you have time on your schedule this weekend?"

"Of course." She squared her shoulders and grabbed a copy of the listing off the table before handing it to him. "I apologize. I should have given you this when you came in. The couple that just left said that they'll have a bid in by morning. No pressure, but I want you to have all the information you might need to make an informed choice."

"I see." He folded the paper lengthwise and slipped it inside his jacket pocket, and all the while his cool gaze remained pinned to hers. "I don't care for this particular apartment, so I'll want to see others. While I am not a man who normally makes decisions quickly, time is of the essence. For obvious reasons."

"Understandable." Maddy gathered the extra listing sheets into a folder. "If you're not already working with an agent, I'd be happy to help you."

"I was but…it didn't work out." He lifted one shoulder and waved his hand dismissively. "She wasn't a good fit. The woman seemed more concerned with her commission than finding me what I needed."

"I'm sorry to hear that you had an unpleasant experience."

"It's business," he said flatly. "I want the best, and based on everything I've heard lately, that would be you. You came highly recommended."

Maddy tightened her grip on the folder and held it against her chest.

"Really?"

"Yes." He nodded curtly. "I'm new to the city. Until recently, I operated out of our company's Chicago offices. After my unpleasant experience with the other real estate agent, I was told by our CEO, Bill Weinstein, that you are the best in the business on every level."

"I'll have to thank him for the kind recommendation." Maddy's chest puffed a bit with pride. The Weinsteins were one of her best clients and had rented houses in Old Brookfield from her every summer for the past several years. They had been persnickety about their new home in the city, but she'd stuck with them and found them a fabulous duplex that met every one of their needs. No small task, to be sure.

"If you know Bill," he said as a hint of a smile played at his lips, "then you know he's not one to pass out compliments easily. My wife, Helen, told me if I didn't take his advice I was a horse's ass."

Maddy's brows lifted, and her reaction elicited a small smile from Mr. Gregory.

"Thirty-five years of marriage and one learns to listen to one's wife. Especially when she refers to one as an animal's backside."

"Then I'll be sure I take the time to find out exactly what you're looking for." Maddy's lips lifted. "Perhaps we could meet at my offices tomorrow or Sunday. Just let me know what's best for you. I like to meet with my clients first to find out exactly what they are looking for."

She handed him her card, which he promptly slipped into his pocket without even looking at it.

"Sunday." He strode past her to the elevator and hit the Down button. "Your office at noon."

"Wonderful." Maddy smiled. "I'll see you then."

The door slid closed, and Maddy was left alone in the enormous apartment. She hoped that his *former* real estate agent wasn't anyone she knew. That could get awkward fast. This business was nothing if not cutthroat, but Maddy wasn't. Stealing clients was just plain wrong, and there was no way she would knowingly poach from another agent's list.

Gregory was uptight and bossy, but none of that mattered. Maddy had a new bee in her bonnet—finding a home for him and his ailing wife. Thirty-five years? Holy shit. That was a long damn time to be with one person.

She made quick work of shutting off all the lights and making sure everything was exactly as the owners had left it.

Her phone buzzed in her pocket as she stepped out of the elevator into the ornate lobby. She expected to see a voice mail or text from Brenda, explaining where she'd been.

But as Maddy glanced at the screen, a slow smile curved her lips. Her heartbeat picked up, along with a giddy fluttery feeling in her belly, making her feel like a swarm of butterflies had been let loose. Definitely *not* Brenda.

It was a text from Ronan.

> Meet you in the park for our Saturday morning run tomorrow? By the Alice in Wonderland statue. 9 a.m. Be there or be square.

Maddy bit her lower lip and started to type back, but her thumb paused above the screen. It hovered there like an indecisive squirrel in the middle of the street, choosing whether or not to get run over by the oncoming car. If she continued meeting up with Ronan, eventually

their platonic relationship would likely take a hefty turn
toward lusty.

Would that be so bad?

Before she could talk herself out of it, she typed back.

> Yes. See you then, and this time coffee is
> on me.

She went to put her phone back in her pocket, but
Ronan, the speed texter, texted back immediately.

> Good. You do know how I like it, don't you?

A wicked grin cracked Maddy's face because the
message was brimming with sexual innuendo. Before
she could come up with a witty response, he texted again.

> My coffee…I was talking about my coffee…
> really ;)

A delicious shiver flickered and got her blood moving.
How silly was it that a flirty text exchange could give
her such a thrill? Maybe *pathetic* was a better word, but
she didn't care. She was having too much fun, and it had
been far too long since she'd had any. Maddy puffed a
curly strand of hair away from her eyes and texted back.

> Sure, McGuire. See you tmrw.

Smiling and filled with almost schoolgirl giddiness,
Maddy tried to maintain her professional exterior. She
collected the sign-in sheet from the front-desk bell

captain and slipped it into her folder. Then she placed everything on the quilted bench by the desk and pulled on her wool coat, bracing herself for the dark, chilly night air. Her last message to Ronan was still on her screen, and without even thinking about it, she scooped up the phone and sent one more text.

And for the record, I bet I know exactly how you like it.

Chapter 3

"DAMN, IT'S COLD." MADDY'S BODY HAD WARMED during her run with Ronan, but she knew the minute that they stopped she'd be a shivering mess. "If it's this chilly now, what's it going to be like in February?"

"I'll take this over August." Ronan chuckled. "There's nothing more brutal than New York City in the summer. We don't get the relief of an ocean breeze the way they do in Old Brookfield. Bowser overheats pretty easily; I have to carry extra water for the poor guy. And he slobbers a lot when he's hot."

Bowser made a snort of derision, and Maddy couldn't help but smile at the agreeable floppy-eared dog as he ran next to them. Her curly ponytail was bouncing in unison with his tail, but only she and Ronan were there to see it. It was unusually quiet in the park today due to the overly chilly morning.

"I almost canceled," Maddy said through huffing breaths. She glanced at Ronan, who kept up a steady jogging pace on her left. "The rain from last night turned parts of this path into a freaking mess. There are icy spots everywhere."

"I figured it would be a rough run, but I knew you wouldn't cancel," Ronan said with a hint of arrogance. Bowser ran at his side and occasionally tilted his snout to the sky. "That's not your style."

She sent a sidelong glance at him, briefly catching

a glimpse of his square, stubble-covered jaw. Jeez, he was handsome. Rugged and manly. All rough angles and edges that looked like they could be carved from stone. What was it about a manly man that could get a girl's motor running?

"Is that so?" Maddy laughed. "Why so confident?"

"Well, aside from the fact that you aren't a quitter…" He pointed to a spot of black ice. "Watch out."

"I see it." Moving around the spot, Maddy kept her gaze straight ahead, the familiar curve of the path less distracting than the man next to her. That, and falling on her ass in front of Ronan was not an appealing idea. "And no, I'm not a quitter, but I sense more comments coming. What is it? Come on, spit it out."

They jogged quietly for a few strides, with only the sounds of their breathing filling the air. Maddy flicked her gaze to Ronan briefly when he didn't respond. A serious expression had set in on his handsome face, and muscles in his jaw flickered. Tension had settled where she'd expected to see humor, and his breath puffed out in white clouds when it mixed with the cold morning air. His broad, thick shoulders lifted and fell with the steady gait of his run. The man looked like he was about to erupt, but she wasn't sure why.

"Are you trying to come up with a witty retort, or did you forget the question?" she teased.

Ronan swore under his breath and slowed to a walk. Bowser instinctively matched his pace but it took Maddy a second or two to realize they'd fallen behind. She jogged in place and turned to find Ronan standing with his hands on his hips. His dark brows were knit together, and his mouth was set in a grim line.

"You're stubborn," he said flatly.

"And?" She kept jogging in place but nodded her head toward the direction they'd been headed. "Come on, you can keep pointing out the obvious while we run. We're almost at the end of our route."

"I mean it." Ronan strode toward her, his breathing still heavy. "I need to talk to you about something. It's been nagging at me for a while, and I've been trying to figure out how to approach you about it without pissing you off."

At six feet tall, he towered over her five-foot-four frame even when she donned heels, but when she wore only sneakers, he seemed positively huge. His tall, well-muscled body dwarfed her as he closed in on her, invading her personal space. Maddy stopped moving and held her ground, even though she wanted to run now more than ever.

Oh shit.

She knew what he wanted to talk about. The flirty text she'd sent him last night. Ugh. Why, oh why, had she done that? She was the one who shut down the possibility of anything more than friendship months ago. They'd always flirted a little; it was hard not to with a man like Ronan. But yesterday, she'd crossed some kind of invisible line.

When he didn't mention the text that morning, she'd figured it was for the best—even though she'd both dreaded and hoped he'd bring it up. But now it was time to face the music.

"Okay," she said after swallowing the lump in her throat. Her heart was racing now, and that had nothing to do with the run. Nothing at all. "What's up?"

"You need to take better safety precautions when you're showing properties."

Maddy's jaw dropped and she gaped at him. He might as well have suggested that next time, they should run through Central Park buck naked.

"What are you talking about?" She shook her head in an attempt to shake the stupid right out of her—or maybe it was the embarrassment. How could she have thought he was going to bring up the flirting? Damn it all. She was so out of her league. Dating. Men. Sex. She sucked at this whole single woman *thing*. She hadn't been on the market in so long that she had completely forgotten how to handle herself.

Not that she was on the market. Was she?

Thank God she hadn't *said* anything. That would have been totally humiliating. Her private mortification was more than enough.

"I'm talking about Lucille Bowman," he said, his tone gentler. The tension eased from his face and sympathy filled his eyes. "You need to be more careful."

"Oh, come on, McGuire," Maddy scoffed. "What happened to Lucille was horrible, but it's not unheard of in this city. What? Because one real estate agent gets killed, now all of us are in danger? That's crazy."

"See? Stubborn. Just like I said."

"Not stubborn, experienced. Look—I've been doing this for years, and I've *never* had an incident. I know how to handle myself."

"Is that so? Do you even know how to defend yourself?"

"Ask Billy Hollibrand," Maddy said with a smirk.

"He was a kid, Maddy." Ronan didn't flinch and his

expression remained humorless. "The guy they're looking for isn't an awkward teenager with grabby hands.
He's a killer."

"This is nuts." Maddy swiped at her sweaty forehead
with her arm. "McGuire, you're being overprotective.
Lucille was probably in the wrong place at the wrong
time. Besides, women are far more likely to be accosted
by someone they know. A boyfriend or a jealous
husband—neither of which apply to me. Now, can we
finish our run please?"

She turned to go, but Ronan linked his hand around
her bicep, preventing her exit. Maddy stilled. She looked
from his fingers—securely clamped over her arm—to
his face. Clearly, his stubbornness matched hers, and
they weren't going anywhere at the moment.

"It's not crazy, but I am being protective." He kept
his voice even but didn't let her go. "The detectives handling the case are almost certain that she knew the killer,
at least well enough to go off with him peacefully. And
given what she did for a living, odds are the perp could
be connected through her job. All I'm asking is that you
take precautions."

"I have Mace in my purse," Maddy said quickly.
"Jordan and Gavin gave it to me as a twisted going-away
gift before I moved here."

"In your purse? Oh, that's great," he said sarcastically.

Bowser started whining and shifting his weight rest-
lessly. Ronan dropped her arm and gathered Bowser's
leash around his palm, keeping the dog close. "I'm sure
the guy who attacks you will give you a minute to find
the Mace in that *suitcase* you carry around and try to
pass off as a purse. You and I both know that it weighs

about fifty pounds, and it takes you at least ten minutes to find anything in there."

Maddy opened her mouth to argue but snapped it shut quickly. He was right. She was constantly losing shit in there.

"Fine," she said quietly. "I'll give you that."

Bowser whined again and sat down before sticking his big snout in the air again. He was obviously tuning in to their little tiff.

"Keep it in your pocket, at least. Someplace you can easily get to it."

"Okay." She folded her arms over her breasts in an attempt to calm her now-shivering body. "Anything else?"

"Have your phone out and ready to use if you need it. But above all, trust your gut."

Ronan inched closer still and kept his voice low. He settled both hands on her shoulders and looked her square in the eyes. The heat of his palms seeped through the fabric of her running jacket surprisingly quickly, and Maddy had to stop herself from moving closer. Her gut instinct was to seek out more of him and his touch.

"If something or someone feels wrong, then you get the hell out of there. I don't care if you're meeting with a house full of nuns. If it feels wrong, then it probably is."

He squeezed her arms gently, and that fluttery feeling in her stomach came swirling back like a storm. Maddy forced herself to focus on his words instead of the nearness of him. His scent, a heady mixture of sweat and soap, filled her head. She swallowed hard and nodded, but staring into his eyes, dark with concern, she had trouble finding words. Ronan's protective nature was one of his most appealing qualities. As an independent modern woman, she probably should have protested more, but his concern for her was sweet.

And he was *all* man.

"I-I care about you, Maddy," he murmured, his voice quiet but rich with promise and purpose. "I don't want you to get hurt."

Maddy sucked in another deep breath to clear her head, but it had the opposite effect. Damn, he smelled good. The cold air seemed to make his scent stand out even more. As Ronan leaned closer, the fabric of his running jacket brushed against her folded arms, and his glittering gaze skittered over her face. She licked her lower lip but couldn't look away. For a brief, terrifying, exhilarating second, she thought he was going to kiss her.

Ohmigod. I'm not ready for this.

"I got it." Maddy abruptly stepped backward and out of his arms. "Mace in my pocket. Cell phone out. Trust my gut. Can we go now?"

She spun around and started jogging before he could answer her. Too bad she didn't look first, or she would have seen the thin layer of ice in her path. One second she was focused on getting distance between them, and the next she was flying through the air. A sharp pain shot through her left ankle, and she squeezed her eyes shut waiting for the inevitable impact. She would have landed flat on her ass if Ronan hadn't been there.

Instead of meeting the cold, hard pavement, Maddy was caught in the warm, firm, and unyielding embrace of Ronan McGuire. They were inches from the ground. Ronan's knee was bracing her body, and his arms were wrapped around her as though he'd just dipped her after an amazing dance. Pure unadulterated embarrassment kept her from moving, and the zing of lust from being pressed against him did little to slow her pounding heart. With her eyes still shut, her ankle throbbing, and her arms securely linked around Ronan's neck, it took Maddy a second before she could face him.

"I give you a ten on the dismount." Ronan's teasing voice floated around her and warmed her, along with the feel of him. "But you need to work on your landing."

She flicked her eyes open, and the second her gaze met his, any embarrassment melted away. Maddy burst into a hysterical fit of giggles and Ronan joined her, his body shaking with laughter as he helped her stand. But once she tried to put weight on her ankle, a fresh zing of pain shot up her leg.

"Shit," she said with a hiss. When she put all her weight on her right foot again, Ronan instinctively slipped his arm around her waist, pulling her against him. "I twisted it pretty badly."

"You aren't running on that anytime soon. Or walking, for that matter."

"I'll be fine," she said, not really believing it. At the moment, it freaking hurt. "Come on, let's go."

Maddy started hobbling away, wanting to retain some dignity, but before she could get far, Ronan scooped her up in his arms. He cradled her against his chest, and as she linked her arms around his neck, Maddy caught a glimpse of that cocky smirk.

"I can walk on my own, Ronan."

"No you can't." He stopped walking and let out some of the slack on Bowser's leash. The dog was whining again and pulling away, toward the wooded area to the

left of the path. "You're stubborn, just like I said before.
Bowser thinks you should stop complaining too."

"Right." Maddy rolled her eyes but couldn't stifle the
smile. "We aren't too far from the road. I can get a cab
from there."

"We," Ronan said firmly. "*We* can get a cab from
there. I'm taking you home and getting a closer look at
that ankle."

"You are persistent, aren't you?"

"You have no idea," he murmured. Ronan's fingers
dug into her leg. It was an almost imperceptible shift,
but it carried a wallop. "We McGuire boys have what
my mother calls 'tunnel vision.' Although she says I
have the worst case of it out of the five of us."

"What does she mean?"

Maddy's own voice sounded far away because the
sensations were beginning to drown out everything else.
Her fingers drifted over the nape of his neck, the strands
of his hair sifting tantalizingly between them. She swallowed hard and licked her lower lip as all of the words
went out of her head.

Tunnels? Visions? What were they talking about?

It took her a moment to realize that Ronan had
stopped walking. He held her tighter against him, and
those eyes remained pinned to hers, the bluish-green
conjuring up images of the ocean back home. Her heart
thundered in her chest, and she fleetingly wondered if
it would burst right out of her rib cage. Maddy stopped
breathing when Ronan flicked his gaze to her mouth and
then back again.

There was heat there and unmistakable desire, and
Maddy burned beneath the weight of it.

"Once we set our sights on something we want," Ronan rasped, "we don't quit until we get it."

She wasn't sure if he bent to her or she reached for him, but the end result was explosive. Ronan's mouth covered hers, and with a strangled groan, she opened to him immediately. His tongue sought entrance and lashed along hers with swift, furious strokes. Maddy's arms tightened around his neck as she met his greedy kiss with one of her own.

Devoured—that's how she felt—and she couldn't get enough.

Ronan's large hand cradled her head as he kissed her deeply, and she reveled in the wonderful warm expanse of his chest. The side of her breast molded against those muscles that grew harder with each passing second. It didn't matter that they were in the middle of Central Park in broad daylight or that anyone in the area might see them making out like a couple of teenagers.

All she could think about, see, or feel was *him*, and Maddy was lost in the rush.

Something tugged on them persistently, almost like a child yanking at a parent's sleeve, and Ronan slowly broke the kiss. He suckled her lower lip but didn't loosen his hold on her. Then he rested his forehead against hers. They stayed that way for a second, puffs of white from their hot breath mingling in the cold air between them.

A flood of conflicting emotions rushed through Maddy as she looked into Ronan's eyes. Guilt. Lust. Comfort. Longing. Sadness. Need. Fear. Betrayal.

"It's too soon." Maddy's eyes fluttered closed, and she cupped his cheek with one hand. "I'm sorry, Ronan. I-I don't know if I'm ready for—"

"How's your ankle?" he asked abruptly.

"Huh?" Maddy flicked her eyes open. "M-my ankle?"

That was the last body part she was tuned into at the moment.

"I bet it barely hurts anymore." He waggled his eyebrows and pressed a quick kiss to her forehead before casting a glance over at Bowser. "All I had to do was get you thinking about something else. You know? Get your mind off the pain."

"Oh really?" Irritation shimmied up her back, mixed with a healthy amount of embarrassment. "That's why you kissed me? To get my mind off my sore ankle? You know, McGuire, you are a piece of work."

Bowser barked, and the interruption only added to her aggravation.

"What is with your dog?" Maddy pointed at Bowser, who was standing at attention and pulling them toward the wooded area. "Is there an animal in those bushes, or is he trying to *distract me* too?"

"I don't think so." Ronan's body tensed, and all humor had left his voice. "He's gotten wind of something, and if I'm reading him right, it's not good."

"What is it?"

"I'm not sure. It could be a dead animal, but…" His voice trailed off, and his jaw clenched, a tiny muscle flickering beneath the stubble-covered flesh. "I should check it out. He's being pretty insistent."

Ronan strode over to a cluster of boulders along the edge of the path and set Maddy down. The ice-cold surface of the stone quickly seeped through her leggings, a stark contrast to the warmth of Ronan's embrace. She didn't have much time to register the loss, though; she was too concerned with Ronan's sudden shift from *regular horny guy* to *full-blooded cop*.

Maddy's breath hitched in her throat. For a moment, she'd allowed herself to forget what and who Ronan was.

A pit of sadness and a familiar ache of white-hot fear bloomed in her chest. Cops were never regular guys, just like firemen weren't. They were always on call, always on duty, and put themselves at risk every day. It wasn't merely a job for men like Ronan—it was a calling and a way of life. Being a policeman would always be part of who he was. It was woven through the fiber of his very soul, and there was nothing—and no one—that would ever change it.

She had already learned that lesson the hard way. So what the hell was she doing?

"Maddy, I want you to sit right there."

Ronan bent down and quickly retrieved his gun from the ankle holster hidden beneath his running pants. He wore a gun while they were jogging? That knot of apprehension tightened in her belly. Intellectually, she knew what he was and what he did. She'd seen him with the gun when he was in uniform, but it was never drawn. Somehow that made it seem less real.

Not anymore.

Ronan rose to his feet, and the shift in his body language was disturbingly vivid. The cocksure boy from Old Brookfield was gone, replaced by a man who had sworn to protect and to serve.

"Don't move a muscle." He held the gun at his side. Ronan's fierce gaze remained pinned to the trees on the small hill, the one that Bowser was itching to investigate. "Do you understand me?"

Maddy nodded and stared after Ronan as he and Bowser headed up the incline. Bowser had his nose to the ground, and his long tail bobbed behind him. Ronan was quietly reassuring the dog while he kept up with the bloodhound's pace. The two of them trotted up the hill, and it was evident that Bowser was following a trail.

But tracking who, or what?

A knot of fear coiled in Maddy's belly, and she shifted her position on the rock. She wasn't stupid. K-9 units like theirs looked for the missing—and the dead. Ronan's words of advice rushed through her mind, and she quickly took her cell phone out of her jacket pocket. She cradled the device in her lap but kept her gaze on the tree line at the top of the grassy hill. Dry leaves blew by and swirled in a tornado-like dance, but there were no other signs of activity from the trees.

"Ronan?"

She called him a few times, but no answer came. The city had never seemed as empty or silent as it did right this minute.

———※※※———

Ronan saw the woman's motionless body the minute he reached the top of the hill. Even if he hadn't seen it, Bowser's change in demeanor would have tipped him off. The bloodhound tensed and whined loudly before sitting down near the still form of the dead woman.

Pale-blond hair, with leaves and twigs tangled in it, partially covered her face, and her lifeless, vacant gaze stared out at nothing. She was on her stomach, and it looked like her blouse had been torn open. A pair of ripped stockings were tangled around her ankles, and one of her shoes was missing. It was in the area, no doubt.

Ronan swore under his breath and yanked his cell phone from his pocket after praising Bowser. Not all search-and-rescue K-9s would have picked up that scent without being instructed to do so.

The dog was one hell of a cop.

"Is everything okay?" Filled with uncertainty, Maddy's voice crushed the silence. "Ronan?"

"No, it's not. Stay where you are, Maddy," Ronan said firmly. He kept his gaze on the dead woman and pressed the phone to his ear. "This is Officer Ronan McGuire with the NYPD K-9 unit, badge number 1275-470. We have a female DOA in Central Park. We're gonna need a bus and a full crime-scene unit ASAP."

After giving them the location, Ronan moved back to the top of the ridge and caught Maddy's frightened gaze. His heart clenched in his chest. She looked scared shitless, and he couldn't blame her. Ronan glanced at the blond, sprawled amid the dry leaves and brush, and fought the fear that niggled at the back of his mind.

His gut told him she was connected to the real estate scene in the city, like Lucille Bowman.

And Maddy.

Seconds ticked by, and just when Maddy thought she'd scream with frustration, Ronan and Bowser reappeared at the top of the hill. Relief fired through her but dissipated quickly when she spotted the grim expression on Ronan's face.

"It wasn't a dead animal," he said quietly.

The sound of dry leaves crunching beneath his sneakers peppered the air.

"Wh-what was it?" Maddy squeezed her eyes shut and quickly held up her hand, preventing him from telling her what she suspected. "Don't. You don't have to say it. I-I think I get it."

"I'm sorry," Ronan said gruffly. "I know your ankle probably hurts like hell, but we have to stay here until the crime-scene unit and detectives show up."

"My ankle is the least of our problems," she said with a bitter laugh. Maddy shivered and hugged herself, trying to warm up. "Was he or she—?"

"She doesn't look like she's been there too long." Ronan squatted down next to Maddy, and Bowser moved in, mirroring his master's movement. "Luckily, Bowser picked up her scent."

Ronan's words tumbled through the cold around her, but Maddy barely heard them. She grew numb as the reality of what he was saying set in. Somewhere over that ridge, beyond the hustle and bustle of the city, lay the body of a dead woman. What would have happened if Bowser hadn't picked up her scent? How long would she have remained there, undiscovered and unseen in the center of a cold, uncaring city? Tears pricked Maddy's eyes and her vision blurred. Weeping for the woman who'd been killed and for all the things she never got to do, Maddy swiped at her cheeks with the sleeve of her running jacket.

"Luckily?" Maddy sniffled. "She doesn't seem all that lucky."

"Her family will know what happened to her," Ronan said quietly. He rose to his feet and gathered Bowser's leash around his hand. "Not knowing is worse than any-thing else. Trust me."

Ronan's tall, broad-shouldered form cut a striking figure, and with Bowser at his side, the two of them had an almost superhero-like air about them. They were resolute and unwavering in the face of a frightening and hopeless situation.

Man and beast, strong and steady.

The memory of Ronan's kiss still lingered in Maddy's mind and on her lips. It was too soon. There would be other chances. More time to explore the feelings she had or could have for him.

Sirens wailed in the distance, growing closer with each passing moment. No doubt they were headed here, answering Ronan's call for backup. As he and Bowser headed up the hill again, Maddy thought of the woman who lay in the woods just over the ridge. How much time had that poor soul believed that she had left? The number of years she imagined was undoubtedly longer than what she had. Maddy sucked in a shuddering breath and forced herself to give Ronan a reassuring smile.

When would she learn? The future was promised to no one.

Chapter 4

HAVING MADDY AT A CRIME SCENE MADE RONAN beyond uncomfortable. Even though he wanted to get her the hell out of there, they had to wait for the detectives to show up.

Bowser went right to Maddy and settled into an almost protective position. He sat right in front of her with his head up and his gaze alert while the cops milled about taping off the scene. After a few minutes, the dog nuzzled up against her legs and put his head in her lap seeking affection, which she was quick to give him. She scratched his ears and rubbed his flanks as though she'd been doing it for years.

Ronan had dated other women, but Bowser had barely paid them any mind. It was as if he knew they weren't going to be around long enough for him to bother trying to get to know them. But Bowser had been drawn to Maddy from the beginning, and the sight of them together was oddly...right.

Once they'd been given the all clear to leave, Ronan had tried to carry her, but Maddy had refused. She finally gave in and leaned against him for support, but he could tell it was killing her to do so. Her independent streak was matched by her stubborn streak. And damn if that didn't turn him on. He loved a woman with spirit.

By the time they got into a cab, Maddy was shivering and Ronan was relatively sure that it wasn't only because of the cold. His one comfort was that she hadn't seen the body. Looking at a brutalized homicide victim was tough enough for a seasoned cop, let alone a civilian. He didn't want her touched by that kind of ugliness any more than she already had been.

Maddy had hit the nail on the head earlier. He was being overprotective. But if he could shield the people he cared about from violence, then he damn well would.

Ronan stole a glimpse at her before getting out of the cab, and his heart clenched in his chest. She was staring out the window and absently stroking Bowser's head, which was once again in her lap. Her normally feisty air had been replaced by one of sadness and uncertainty, and all Ronan wanted to do was gather her into his arms and hold her, tell her that everything would be okay and vow that he'd never let anything happen to her.

Ever.

He did care about her, but that was more than he had admitted, even to himself. He had been doing his best to give her the space she needed, to be respectful of her wishes, but that had all gone out the damn window back at the park. Her kiss had been sweet and hot, cool mint with warm cinnamon. Right then, he knew that he'd gone directly past caring to fall into a swirling abyss of feelings that could only be classified as uncharted territory.

Ronan had never been in love before, so he wasn't even sure what it felt like. Whatever *this* was, this tangled knot of need and protective instincts that fired up every time he was near her, it scared the shit out of him.

He hadn't planned on kissing her, but she had been so soft and warm in his arms. When her delicate fingers tickled the back of his neck, it had been like a switch flipping—and he'd lost his damn mind right there in the middle of Central Park. She was injured, and he'd jumped her bones like some kind of horny teenager with no self-control.

Good move, McGuire. Real smooth.

The cab pulled to a halt in front of Maddy's building, the sudden stop bringing Ronan out of his self-imposed pity party.

Bowser, who was seated between Ronan and Maddy in the cab, lifted his head from Maddy's lap. He snuffled loudly and leaned against Ronan, his way of saying *I want to get out of the car now*. Not that Ronan could blame him. The three of them were stuffed into the backseat with little room to move.

"Alright, man. Keep your collar on." Ronan ruffled Bowser's ears before checking for oncoming traffic and opening the door. "We're going, you bossy, old dog."

"Don't be mean," Maddy chimed in. "I can't blame him. I'm ready to get home too."

Ronan and Bowser got out and went around to the sidewalk, but the doorman had already opened Maddy's door.

"You alright, Ms. Morgan?" The older man, probably late fifties, took Maddy's hand in his and helped her out of the cab. He cast a glance at the ice pack attached to her ankle with an Ace bandage. "You look like you took a tumble."

"Hey, David." A strained smile curved her lips. "It's not a big deal. I twisted my ankle but I'll live." Maddy stilled and braced herself on the door of the cab, letting out a short, bitter laugh. "Believe me, things could be a lot worse."

Her tone was light, but the sidelong glance she gave

Ronan was full of unspoken words. How could it not be? She obviously didn't want to share what had happened with the doorman. If Ronan had to guess, he'd bet that she wouldn't mention it to anyone. Like she seemed to do with most upsetting events, Maddy would squirrel it away and bury it.

"I should really be carrying you," he said, slipping his arm around her small waist as she tried to walk on her own. He dragged her arm over his shoulders and tugged her close. "But you're not going to let me, are you?"

"Nope." She was doing her best not to lean on him, but Ronan held on tight. "It's not that bad anymore, really."

"Humor me, okay?"

"Thanks, David," Maddy said to the doorman, her lips quivering. "I'm sure I'll be fine by morning."

"Let me know if you need anything, ma'am. I can have Vincent up to your place in a hot minute." The doorman held the enormous glass door open and stepped aside, allowing them entrance to the luxury building. He tipped his head to Ronan and looked warily at Bowser. "Sir."

"David, this is Ronan McGuire and his partner, Bowser," Maddy said. "They're two of New York's finest."

"Good to meet you, officers." David closed the door behind them and waved at the man behind the front desk. "Get the elevator for Ms. Morgan, Vincent."

Ronan surveyed the lavish, cavernous lobby of the building and hoped that he was hiding his shock. The floor was made of gleaming white-and-black marble, and the walls were detailed along the ceiling with intricate moldings. The entire place reeked of wealth and privilege. He knew Maddy had done well for herself, but he'd had no idea that she had *this* kind of money. Apartments in this building had to start at a couple million, and prices would only go up from there.

His entire crappy apartment in Washington Heights could fit easily in the lobby—with room to spare. Ronan was no stranger to wealth. His family had money; thanks to his great-grandfather, they held the patents on several handy-dandy inventions. But his parents had never allowed him or his brothers to become trust fund babies. Most of the money was tied up in investments, so there really wasn't a trust fund to be had and there weren't any cushy board positions to occupy.

They'd all been told, in no uncertain terms, that they had to go out and make their way in the world and, better yet, be of service to the community. His father had been in the military and so had his grandfather. It was a natural fit when Ronan and his brothers each donned a uniform of some kind.

Ronan had never really thought much about the way his apartment looked or the area it was in, but being here with Maddy certainly put it in perspective. He was making his way and doing what he loved, but he would never earn the kind of money that she did. He didn't know why that thought even occurred to him—or bothered him, for that matter—but it did.

They rode up in the elevator in silence, which was just as well, because having her soft, curvy body pressed against him was becoming a distraction. Her full breasts melded against his rib cage, and his fingers settled into the dip of her waist with comfortable and almost familiar ease. Even though he tried to think about anything other than the delicious feel of her, he couldn't. Without meaning to, he was quietly memorizing the way the swell of her hip fit perfectly against him. Add to that the brush of her thigh along his and her soft hands curled around his far rougher ones… Each sensation was more tantalizing than the last.

The elevator dinged and Ronan sucked in a deep breath, forcing himself not to look at her. If he did, he would want to kiss her again. That was all he could think about. Tasting her, drinking from her, and finding out if he made her half as crazy as she made him. But given the way she'd put on the brakes earlier, he was probably going to be crazy all by himself.

The doors slid open, and they stepped into a square foyer decorated almost exactly like the lobby. There were two enormous, white paneled doors, one on either side of the hall, and an antique-looking table with a huge arrangement of fresh flowers sat directly across from the elevator. Their sweet odor permeated the space, giving Ronan a much-needed distraction from Maddy's naturally alluring scent. Whatever her perfume was, it must have had some kind of pheromones in it or something, because it drove him wild.

"Mine is on the left." Maddy fished a key out of her pocket. "15A."

"Who's in 15B?" Ronan asked, hoping small talk would keep his mind off his increasingly dirty thoughts.

Before Maddy could answer him, the door of 15B opened suddenly, and Maddy's body tensed against Ronan's. He turned just in time to see a young guy with dark hair and glasses stick his head out quickly.

Bowser snuffled loudly and let out a low growl.

"Oh, hey, Maddy," the kid said. He flicked his gaze

at Ronan and Bowser but looked away a split second
later. "You okay?"

"Hi." The word escaped on a breathy sigh. "Yeah, I'll
be fine. I twisted my ankle when I was running."

"Okay, bye." The door slammed shut abruptly.

"Jeez," Ronan murmured. "Nice neighbor. What's
his deal?"

"He's an Internet whiz kid," Maddy whispered with
a giggle. "He's kind of a shut-in. Geeky and quiet.
Tim, or Tom? I can't remember. Anyway, I hardly ever
see him. Vincent and David say that he rarely leaves
his place. He's nice enough. We were in the elevator
together the other day, coming up from the laundry
room, and when I told him my computer was acting up,
he offered to fix it."

She hobbled over to her apartment, pulling away
from Ronan in the process, and slipped her key in with
the ease of experience. When he reached her side, he
held her arm and pushed the door open with his shoulder
before helping her inside.

"Your computer can wait. The ankle is more important at the moment."

"If you get me to the couch, I'll be fine from there."

"Mmm-hmm." Ronan kicked the door closed with his
foot. "Whatever you say, boss."

She tossed the keys onto a small table with a gilded
mirror above it, and they headed into the massive living
room. A bank of windows covered almost the entire
wall, but the drapes were drawn, and he fleetingly
thought it was a shame to close out the view she must
have had. Ronan let go of Bowser's leash, but as usual,
his partner remained by his side.

The walls had been painted in muted shades of gray, and the furniture blended in perfectly, almost seamlessly. A huge, white sofa faced the windows and was flanked on either side by overstuffed gray chairs, while a large glass coffee table sat at the center of it all. There were splashes of red in a few spots, and the bright pops of color were like blips of Maddy's bubbly personality busting out here and there. She had always been feisty and smart and full of life. Ronan had expected to see a home full of color, but what he'd found was the exact opposite.

It was a place to live, but it wasn't a *home*.

"I'm fine now, Ronan." Maddy bit her lower lip as he helped her ease onto the fluffy sofa. "Really, I'm sure you and Bowser have better things to do today than babysit me."

"Nope."

"And you say that I'm stubborn?" Maddy scoffed audibly. "Takes one to know one, McGuire."

Once she was settled, Ronan lifted her leg and propped a pillow underneath it, then slipped off her sneaker and tossed it to the floor. He knelt next to her and carefully unwrapped the bandage, removed the no-longer-cold ice pack, and peeled the sock from her foot, not moving it any more than he had to.

"It's probably sprained, but I don't think you broke anything." Ronan cradled her foot and inspected her ankle, trailing his fingers lightly over the swollen area. "Does that hurt?"

He locked gazes with her, and she stilled beneath his touch. Ronan stroked the graceful arch of her foot with his thumb, and a smile curved his lips when her eyes widened slightly. Some of her wild curls had come loose from her ponytail and perfectly framed her oval-shaped face. Those brilliant icy-blue eyes glittered at him, but unmistakable heat shimmered beneath the surface and reminded him of their kiss.

God, she was beautiful.

"N-no." Maddy shook her head quickly and tore her gaze from his. "It's fine."

Why did she insist on being so damn independent all the time? What was so wrong with taking help from him—or anyone else, for that matter? Jordan had warned him that Maddy would push him away and insist she was fine on her own. That was exactly what she had been doing. But he wasn't backing down.

"Stay put. I'll get some ice for that ankle and pop this in the freezer," he said, holding up the soggy ice pack. "Most of the swelling is down, so you'll probably be back to normal in a day or two."

Ronan unhooked Bowser's leash, snapped his fingers, and pointed to the floor next to Maddy. Within seconds, his partner lay dutifully by her side, his head up and his alert gaze fixed on her.

"Looks like I don't have any choice," she said through a nervous laugh. "He looks pretty serious, McGuire. Is he going to freak out if I try to get up?"

"Nah." Ronan winked. "But he might lick you to death. And besides, you're not gonna get up, because you are going to listen to me. I *am* a cop, after all, and you're supposed to obey the law."

With Maddy's sweet laughter drifting in the air behind him, Ronan headed toward the kitchen. The open floor plan of the apartment made it easy to spot. It was off to the left and just past the dining table and chairs that looked as though they had never been used. If he thought the living room looked unlived in, it was nothing compared to the kitchen, where gleaming stainless-steel appliances, all top of the line, were surrounded by bright-white cabinetry. The slick marble counters were void of clutter. No crumbs. No flowers. Not even a bottle of wine or an empty glass.

Nothing.

He stopped for a moment and looked around at the open, unfettered space.

No *living* happened in this apartment.

He turned slowly and leaned both hands on the island that divided the kitchen from the rest of the space. Maddy was lying back on the couch with her eyes closed and gently stroking Bowser's head.

That's when it hit him.

Maddy wasn't living in this city; she was hiding. Hiding from her grief over losing Rick and doing a damn good job of avoiding any kind of future. What better place to try to disappear? Other than him, no one here really knew her, and it was probably easy for her to simply exist, rather than live.

But that wasn't going to continue—not if he had anything to say about it.

Right then and there, Ronan made a vow. Maddy McGuire was going to start living again. She was too beautiful, vibrant, and smart to hide herself away from the world, and he sure as hell wasn't going to let her hide from him.

With his determination in place and a plan brewing, he grabbed some paper towels and a bag of frozen peas from the freezer. He couldn't help but notice that the only other item in there was a quart of Breyers mint chocolate-chip ice cream. Ronan smiled.

That was his favorite too.

He closed the freezer door and headed back into the living room.

"Okay, Bowser." Ronan shooed the dog out of the way. "Move it or lose it, man. I have business to attend to."

Bowser rose to his feet and shot Ronan a look of disapproval before trotting over to the front door and lying down. His partner may have been a dog, but he was still a cop. When all else failed, the bloodhound would park himself by the door. The strategic and protective move was never lost on Ronan and often made him wonder if his partner had been human in another life.

"He didn't look too happy with you." Maddy chuckled and adjusted her position on the couch. "*Someone* doesn't like being bossed around."

"Yeah?" Ronan knelt by the couch and slipped his hand beneath her bare ankle. "Well, that's something the two of you have in common."

"Very funny." Maddy folded her hands on her stomach. Her brows lifted when she saw the bag of peas in his hand. "You found those in my icebox?"

"Yup. It was either this or the ice cream, but the mint chip could get messy."

A smile tugged at his lips at the mental image of licking ice cream off her naked body.

"What are you grinning at?" She leveled a narrow-eyed gaze in his direction.

"Nothing I care to share…yet." He was in big trouble. "This is gonna be cold."

He gently placed the paper-towel-wrapped bag over her ankle, and a rush of air hissed through her lips when the makeshift ice pack made contact with her bare skin. She grabbed the cushions on either side of her and scooted back a bit. Ronan gripped her calf gently but firmly and shook his head slowly while holding the bag of peas in place.

"Ah-ah-ah," he sang. "Hold still. You know, if I hadn't become a cop, I probably would have been a doctor. Playing doctor was always one of my favorite games."

"Right." Maddy laughed and rolled her eyes. "So tell me, McGuire, what made you become a K-9 officer?"

"Because I get it." Ronan avoided her probing stare and adjusted the ice pack. "I know what it's like to be lost."

"You mean literally or figuratively?"

Ronan paused before answering her question and sat back on his heels as he studied her. He'd never told anyone why he'd chosen this job. His family knew, but no one else did. Not his captain or the guys he'd been with in the academy. It seemed too personal, and sharing it made him feel exposed somehow, or vulnerable. But staring into Maddy's big, blue eyes, Ronan knew he could share the story with her.

"My family was camping in the Adirondack Mountains when I was four. I woke up in the middle of the night and had to go to the bathroom. Gavin had been razzing me about being a scaredy-cat, so I didn't wake anyone up and went by myself. It was dark. I mean, like pitch-black. I thought I'd be able to go quickly and find my way back. I was wrong."

"You got lost in the mountains?" The concern in her

voice hit him like a kick in the gut, but when he turned his gaze to hers, the throb swelled to a burn. "Oh my God."

"I don't remember much," he said quietly. "It was dark and cold. Damn cold. I remember being terrified. The world had always been safe, you know? My family. Old Brookfield. It was a bubble. But when I got lost that night, the bubble burst and the big, wide world came crashing in. It was the first time I realized how small I was—how small we all are."

"Ronan, that must have been awful," Maddy whispered, her eyes searching his. "Your poor parents!"

"Yeah, from what I'm told, Mom was freakin' out, and my dad was ready to call in the National Guard."

"What happened?"

"A park ranger found me. He and his partner, an enormous German shepherd named Daisy Mae. Anyway, one of the things I do remember is Ranger Dave and Daisy Mae coming around a big pine tree. And ice cream." He grinned as the laughter bubbled up. "I got to have ice cream for breakfast for a week. Gavin was so pissed!"

"Now it all makes sense," Maddy said softly. "Why you do what you do."

He held her stare, and something in his chest squeezed. It was like the woman could see right through him to the core of who he was. *What the hell?* Ronan swallowed the lump in this throat and looked away.

"If you don't behave and stay off this ankle, you won't get your ice cream. As fate would have it, you just happen to have my favorite flavor, and I might go in there and eat it all up."

"Lots of people like mint chip," Maddy said quickly. "Besides, you're not the boss of me. It's my life, Officer

McGuire, and I'll have ice cream for dinner if I want to. So there."

"Your life, huh?" Ronan arched one eyebrow and loosened his hold on her calf, lightly trailing his fingers over the exposed flesh. "If you ask me, you haven't been doing much living since you moved here."

"What are you talking about?" Maddy stilled, and her cheeks turned pink.

"This apartment is more like a showroom than a home." Ronan adjusted the bag of peas and leaned his elbows on the edge of the couch. He shrugged. "It looks like you're never here, but I know that's not true. If you aren't working or out jogging with me on a Saturday morning, you're holed up in here like a hermit. You've been here for over a year, but this place barely looks lived in."

"Hey!" That feisty spirit was back, and fire burned in those blue eyes. "I am *not* a hermit. I am the top-performing real estate agent in the most successful real estate agency in this city despite having to deal with a staff of people who sometimes act more like children than functioning adults. Take last night, for example. I was supposed to be training one of our newest hires on how to run an open house, and the little blond dingbat never showed. No text. No phone call. Nothing. I have a full plate, McGuire."

Ronan stilled. Blond? The girl they had found in the park this morning was blond. She had no ID on her, but she was likely in her early to midtwenties, and based on the clothing she had left on her body, she was corporate. Not a pro or party girl, but a woman who had been at work or planning to go to work.

A knot of dread curled in his gut. The detectives had said the crime scene looked eerily similar to Lucille Bowman's. He must have been looking at Maddy funny because she had stopped talking and was staring at him with a puzzled expression.

"Hello?" She snapped her fingers in front of his face. "Are you listening to me? If you're going to insult me, the least you could do is let me rant at you a little."

"I'm sorry." Ronan shook his head. "I was thinking about work."

Damn it. He'd deliberately been avoiding any discussion of the woman in the park, but the topic was the undeniable elephant in the room. Silence settled between them, and Maddy folded her arms. Ronan let out a frustrated breath and looked past her to Bowser who was oblivious to it all, having fallen asleep on the floor in front of the door.

So much for guard-dog duty.

"Is that why you're giving me a hard time about *living*? Because of the girl in the park?" Maddy's voice shook. "Because don't think for *one second* that I don't know how fragile life is, okay? Believe me, I know. Life can change in an instant. One minute everything is normal and you're arguing about what to watch on television or what to make for breakfast in the morning…and the next…"

When he turned his attention back to Maddy and saw one tear fall down her cheek, he cursed under his breath. Without thinking about it, Ronan reached out and cradled her face with one hand, then swiped the tear away. Her eyes were closed, a fan of dark lashes resting on fair skin beneath them, and those full pink lips quivered.

"Ah, Maddy," Ronan whispered. He pressed a kiss to her forehead. His voice was gruff and strained, full of emotions he didn't quite have a name for yet. "I'm sorry. Look, sometimes I can be an insensitive asshole. Chalk it up to growing up in a house full of boys. But I'm worried about you. It's like you're hiding from the whole world...but please, don't hide from me."

When Maddy didn't open her eyes, Ronan settled his forehead against hers. She sucked in a shuddering breath and curled her hands around his wrists. For a second he thought she was going to push him away, but she didn't; she held him closer instead. He wasn't sure how long they stayed that way, nose to nose, heart to heart. No words were spoken, and yet he felt more connected to her than to anyone else in recent memory.

He flicked his tongue over his suddenly dry lips before brushing them over hers. A breathy sigh mingled with a needy whimper escaped her luscious mouth and the sound drove him wild. But Ronan fought for restraint. The last thing he wanted to do was scare her off.

Her lips reminded him of plums, soft and sweet, and he reveled in the sensation as they melded with his. Maddy tangled her fingers in his hair, and he groaned when her tongue sought entrance, pushing into his mouth gently but eagerly. Ronan tilted her head, taking control of the kiss, and dove deep. She sat up and he moved with her, wanting to savor every bit of contact while still being mindful of her ankle.

Maddy sighed into his mouth as her hands slipped beneath his jacket and shirt. When her fingers splayed over the flesh of his lower back and dipped beneath

the band of his running pants, all of the blood rushed
from his head to other parts of his anatomy. His body
started screaming for more—more of her touch, more
of her taste—but his brain told him to slow the hell
down. Emotions were running high for both of them. If
they took this too far too fast, whatever this *thing* was
between them could get snuffed out before they had a
chance to explore it.

She was vulnerable, so taking it any further right now
would be a shitty move. Ronan broke the kiss and pulled
back, her face cradled between his hands. Her heavily
lidded eyes were glazed with the unmistakable air of
lust, and her lips were swollen from his kisses. Maddy
tried to kiss him again, but he held her mouth a mere
inch from his.

Her brow furrowed and confusion flickered across
her face.

"What's wrong?" she said through heavy breaths. "I
thought this was what you wanted."

"It is," he rasped. "But I don't think—"

The shrill ring of the cell phone in her pocket cut him
off. Even if it hadn't, the annoyed look in Maddy's eyes
would have put an end to things. She let out a curt laugh
and removed the phone from her jacket before pulling
away from him.

"You surprise me, McGuire. I never thought that you,
the big stud I've heard about all these years, wouldn't
close the deal." She pressed her phone to her ear and
leaned against the cushions. "Maddy Morgan speaking.
How can I help you?"

Ronan rocked onto his heels before rising to his feet.
She avoided looking at him, but he couldn't miss the

irritated expression on her face. Great. He was screwing things up at every turn.

He ran both of his hands over his face and strode to the windows while Maddy took her call. Something about an appointment tomorrow and scheduling or rescheduling. The woman even worked on Sundays. Did she ever stop and breathe, or even take a moment to enjoy in the view from her own apartment? He pulled aside the drapes with one hand and looked out. The city was beautiful from up here. The windows overlooked the West Side and gave a partial view of Central Park.

Yup. It was easy as hell for her to hide up here, and why wouldn't she? Had anyone tried to stop her? Ronan glanced over his shoulder at her. The flush from their encounter still lingered on her cheeks, and in that moment, he decided enough was enough. She'd had the opportunity to grieve and regroup—plenty of it—but it was time to change things up.

When Maddy ended her call, silence filled the spacious apartment, and neither of them moved or said anything for a couple of minutes. The air was swollen with unspoken apologies and all the reasons why they shouldn't do what they had been doing.

"The wedding is coming up soon," Maddy said quietly. "I'm leaving for Old Brookfield about a week before, so I can help Jordan with the maid-of-honor stuff. And all that."

"Right." Ronan let the curtain drop, settled his hands on his hips, and nodded but didn't turn around. "Me too. Best man." He glanced over his shoulder at her and smiled. "And all that."

They locked gazes, and to his great relief, they both burst into laughter at the same moment. The tension between them eased, slowly and steadily but not completely.

"I'm sorry," Maddy said, her laughter fading. "This is…awkward. I'm not good at this. I never was and, well, I'm out of practice."

"Then we need to change that." Ronan pointed at her and grinned. "So, practice it is."

"What are you talking about?" Her eyes narrowed as he strode slowly toward her. "What kind of practice?"

"You're the maid of honor and I'm the best man. Right?"

"Right…" she said slowly.

"Are you bringing a date to the wedding?"

"A date?" Maddy blinked. "No."

"Me neither." He shrugged. "We can be each other's dates. As best man and maid of honor we kind of are anyway, but we wouldn't want to be selfish."

"What are you talking about?" she said through a laugh. He could feel her watching him as he strolled around the couch toward the front hall. "How exactly would we be being selfish?"

"Come on, woman. Think about it." He picked up Bowser's leash off the sofa table and snapped his fingers. The dog stretched, yawned, and rose to his feet before trotting over to Ronan. "We can't have our first date be at Gav and Jordan's rehearsal dinner or wedding. Now *that* would be awkward."

"Oh really?" Maddy sat up and rested one arm along the back of the couch. "Then what do you propose?"

"I'm not proposing yet." He hooked Bowser's leash

onto his collar. "Don't you think that we should date for a little while first?"

Maddy stared at him as though she couldn't figure out how much of what he'd just said was meant to be funny, and what was serious. The truth was, he didn't know what the percentages were on that either.

"You and me. A *real* date right here in New York City."

Maddy nibbled her lower lip and fiddled with the edge of the cushion as though weighing her options. Ronan played it cool on the surface, but his heart was thundering in his chest like a damn drum. What if she said no?

After what felt like forever, she finally spoke. "Okay."

Thank God.

"Great." He nodded and grabbed the doorknob of the front door. "Do you have plans for Thursday?"

"Um…isn't that Thanksgiving?"

"Whaddya know?" He smacked his forehead in an overly dramatic gesture. "It is!"

"Are you serious?" She let out a short laugh. "You want to take me on a date for Thanksgiving dinner?"

"Yup. And don't try to tell me you have plans because I know you don't."

"Oh really? And how could you—" Maddy's mouth snapped shut and her eyes narrowed. "You've been talking to Jordan and Gavin, haven't you?"

"When Gav called trying to get me to go home for the holiday, he might have mentioned that you refused their invitation and planned on staying home." He pointed around the room. "Not real festive around here."

"Are you asking me out or insulting me?"

"I'm teasing you…and asking you out." He grinned. "So what do you say? You and I will go out for Thanksgiving dinner. Provided you can walk by then, of course."

"I'm sure I'll be walking—or limping, at least, by tomorrow. It's feeling better already." She held up one hand before he could argue with her. "Where should we meet?"

"Woman, what kind of man do you think Carolyn McGuire raised?" He arched one eyebrow and tugged the door open. "I'll make a reservation and pick you up here at seven."

"What about Bowser?"

"He can get his own date. Besides, if I bring him a doggie bag, he'll forgive me." Ronan winked. "See you then."

The image of her smiling face filled his head all the way home. Maddy Morgan was going to start living again, and if he had anything to say about it, it would be with him.

Chapter 5

HER PHONE HAD BUZZED SOMEWHERE IN HER BAG SEVERAL times already, but Maddy made it a habit not to answer calls while showing a home. It was rude and could give the client the impression that they weren't her number one priority. Mr. Gregory was *definitely* one of those clients—finding him and his wife a new home had become her most important job.

Mr. Gregory took his time strolling through the fifth apartment of the day. Maddy gritted her teeth against the pain in her ankle but kept a polite smile plastered to her face. She'd already gone through the place with him once and was now standing by the front door, giving him the privacy to look on his own. Many real estate agents hovered over their clients, but that wasn't Maddy's style.

She leaned against the wall and gently rotated her ankle to loosen it up, but to no avail. The tall leather boots she wore had a low heel, and while they weren't as tough to walk in as her shoes with higher ones, she'd give just about anything for a pair of flip-flops.

Being a real estate agent in New York City was a far more formal venture than when she' had her business in Old Brookfield. Back home, she could wear her long, flowing skirts and peasant tops, and nobody would look twice. If she did that in this market, her clients would never take her seriously. Nope.

Gone were her trademark hippie-chic clothes, and her free-spirited lifestyle had vanished right along with them.

When Rick died, that part of her had died too.

She hadn't glimpsed that side of herself since that fateful August day—at least, not until recently. Something about Ronan McGuire brought that missing part back to life—or a glimmer of it anyway. Maddy pressed her fingers to her lips, a smile blooming there. The man could kiss like the devil. Hot, passionate, demanding. Holy hell. Ronan McGuire was a force of nature, and equally dangerous.

"Ms. Morgan?" Mr. Gregory's voice interrupted her memories. "I've seen enough. I'm afraid this won't do either."

"I see." Maddy forced herself to stand on both feet but kept most of the pressure off her sore ankle. "Unfortunately, these were the only listings on the market that met your specifications."

"Very well." Mr. Gregory's mouth set in a grim line. He was clad in a dark-gray suit, odd even for New York. Even here, most clients didn't dress that formally on the weekends, but this guy was definitely not "most clients." "Please keep me apprised of any new possibilities. My wife will be here soon, and I simply must have proper prospects to show her."

"Of course." She checked her watch. "If you have time—"

"I don't," he said abruptly. "I have a call with my wife in fifteen minutes, and I mustn't miss it. If anything new comes on the market that meets my criteria, I will see it immediately."

His dark eyes darted from her face to her ankle, and he gestured to her leg. "Is something wrong?"

"It's nothing," Maddy said with a wave of her hand. "I twisted my ankle on a run in the park yesterday."

"The park?" he said absently.

"Yes." Maddy limped over to the bank of light switches, not bothering to try to hide her injury anymore. "I run in Central Park most Saturdays with a friend. I'm lucky he was with me, or I would have had to hobble home all by myself."

"I see."

Mr. Gregory looked her up and down in a way that gave Maddy pause. It wasn't lascivious, but something about the way his gaze lingered made her uncomfortable. For a split second, the caring, dutiful husband vanished, and someone darker emerged. Ronan's words of warning flickered through her mind, and she realized that she hadn't put the Mace in her pocket like he'd told her to. She adjusted the huge leather bag on her shoulder. Nope, the little spray can was somewhere deep inside the disaster she liked to call a purse. Her phone was also buried in the abyss.

This was the penthouse.

No one would hear her if she called for help.

"Shall I walk you out?" Maddy held the folder with the listing details over her breasts. The man continued to stare at her wordlessly. "Mr. Gregory? Are you alright?"

"Yes. I'm sorry, I was just thinking about..." His voice trailed off, and he tugged the front door open. "Never mind. Do call me if any other listings are appropriate."

"I have to be honest with you. Because of the Thanksgiving holiday, there won't be much activity over the next week or so. I promise that I'll notify you if anything does come up."

"Of course." He gave her a tight smile. "Good day."

He left, closing the door behind him without another word. Maddy let out the breath she'd been holding and silently cursed Ronan McGuire for making her a paranoid crazy woman. Mr. Gregory was nothing but an uptight businessman who probably weighed twenty pounds less than she did. He was a rich man looking to buy a new home for himself and his ailing wife. The man wasn't a killer. She rolled her eyes and laughed at her foolishness. When she saw Ronan, she was going to give him a piece of her mind.

A shiver of excitement, along with a hint of dread, shimmied up her back at the thought of it. *When she saw Ronan.* A date. Holy crap. It had been years since she'd been on a first date, and now she was doing it with one of the biggest players she had ever known—and on Thanksgiving, no less! And not only that, but he was her best friend's future brother-in-law.

What the hell was she getting herself into?

Maddy shut off all the lights and locked the front door. She punched the button on the elevator inside the private penthouse foyer and leaned against the wall, waiting not so patiently for it to arrive. Her cell phone buzzed yet again. It was hidden in the cavernous reaches of her purse, and though she dreaded trying to find it, it was a necessary evil.

After digging around, and with a few choice curse words, she finally curled her fingers around the smooth case of her phone.

"Aha!" Breathless from her search, Maddy checked

the screen. She had four missed calls and two voice mails from Ronan, but the current call was from her office. "Maddy Morgan, how can I help you?"

"Maddy?" Sharon's voice was teary, small, and meek, and she was sniffling. "Hello?"

The doors to the elevator opened, and Maddy stepped inside. The line went dead almost instantly. Great. Her ankle throbbed, her client was displeased, and now her assistant was crying.

What else could happen today?

As soon as the elevator opened, Maddy hobbled into the lavish lobby of the Park Avenue building and checked the signal. Satisfied they wouldn't get cut off again, she called the office, and Sharon answered after the first ring.

"Hey, Sharon. Sorry about that. I had a crap signal. What's up?"

Sniffling filled the other end of the line.

"Sharon?" Maddy closed her eyes and sucked in a deep breath, searching for what little patience she had left. "What's going on? Did Drummond hit on you again, or did he yell at you or something?"

"It's not him," Sharon croaked. "It's Brenda. She's—"

"She's about to get fired, that's what she is," Maddy interrupted. "Tell her I want to see her in my office this afternoon. I don't care what she says. There is simply no excuse for blowing off her job the way she did. I've had it. If Terrence finds out what she's done—"

"No... She's dead," Sharon whispered.

Maddy stopped short. "Wh-what?" She swallowed the bile that rose in her throat. "Brenda's dead? What the hell are you talking about?"

"Yes. Someone killed her," Sharon said, sobbing loudly. "They found her body in the park yesterday. Just like Lucille."

"Central Park?" Maddy asked, her voice sounding wispy and weak. The woman in the park—the one that Bowser had found—had been Brenda. "Oh my God."

Somewhere in the middle of Sharon's explanation, the lobby seemed to tilt on its axis. Maddy could hear Sharon's voice, but she could no longer make out the words. She had to get out of here. *Get outside. That's it. Cold air.* If she breathed in cool air, then everything would be okay. It would be clear. The world would be steady again instead of completely insane.

Maddy burst out the front door, practically plowing down the doorman in the process. She choked on the frigid, late-November air when it hit her lungs. A sob escaped her lips, and she fought to stem the tears, but to no avail. She babbled a quick good-bye to Sharon and stood on the sidewalk for what felt like forever, with people rushing by and paying her little mind.

This city had claimed another victim. Once again, the world kept right on going, cruelly oblivious to the latest loss of life. Blinded by tears, Maddy hailed a cab, and one pulled up within seconds. Once inside the warm car, she stared blankly at her phone until the driver asked her for the third time where she was going.

Home? The office? Neither was appealing. What other choice did she have? Ronan?

Maddy shook her head and answered her own question before she even had the chance to ask it. No way. The last thing she should do now was go running to him for help. Their friendship was in a strange place as it was; using him for a shoulder to cry on would only make it more confusing.

"Yo," the cabbie grunted. "Where to?"

"Um, I'm not sure," she whispered shakily.

"You okay, lady?" The cabbie adjusted the rearview mirror and peered at her warily. "Where we goin'?"

"I-I don't—" Her phone buzzed in her hand, cutting her off. She answered it without even looking at who it was. "Maddy Morgan," she managed to croak out.

"Where the hell have you been? Jesus, I've been worried sick about you." Ronan's firm, steady voice washed over her, instantly putting her at ease. "Maddy, are you there?"

She let out a slow breath and squeezed her eyes shut, desperately trying to slow the awful feeling of spinning out of control.

"The girl you found in the park," she finally croaked. "It was... Ronan, she was only a kid. All this time... She's gone."

"I know." Ronan's tone was gentle and comforting. "Where are you?"

"In a cab. I'm going to work...to my office." Maddy swiped at her eyes and leaned toward the plexiglass divider. "The corner of Forty-Seventh and Tenth Avenue, please," she said to the driver.

"Maddy, you have got to be kidding me," Ronan scoffed.

"No, I'm not." She squared her shoulders, the tears finally slowing. "We have an office full of scared, upset people, and I need to get there and get it under control. Terrence is off-site with clients, so this falls to me. Not to mention Brenda's parents. Someone has to call them," she said, her voice wavering again. "So awful, and right before the holidays."

Maddy stifled a hysterical laugh after that comment. Would it be any easier on them if their daughter had been killed during a regular week? No, of course not. Rick had died on a normal summer night, and it had hurt like hell.

"They're already on their way," Ronan said quietly. "I spoke with the detectives handling the case early this morning, once she'd been identified. I tried getting in touch with you, but you didn't pick up. Probably because your phone was still buried in that suitcase of yours. Which *also* means you didn't listen to a damn thing I said about taking precautions."

A flicker of irritation shimmied up Maddy's spine at the hint of arrogance and outrage that edged his words.

"Well, excuse the hell out of me for not listening to your all-knowing pearls of wisdom, McGuire." Maddy stilled and watched the city go by through the window of the cab. "You know, I really don't think *now* is the time to lecture me."

"Really?" he scoffed. "Well, I think it's the perfect time."

"I have to go," she snapped. "I have responsibilities."

"You can't control this, Maddy, or manage it," he said bluntly. "And you sure as hell can't hide from it and pretend it didn't happen."

She bristled at that last comment because it hit too damn close to home. Facing the truth had never been her strong suit. Nope, she was much better at handling the details and moving on. She could compartmentalize her life like it was her damn job: there was no point in lingering on the good or the bad. "Hit it and quit it" had been her motto, and until Ronan came along, it had seemed like a perfectly acceptable way to live.

But not for him. He couldn't leave things alone. The man had to push and dig beyond the surface of everything, and it was making her crazy.

"Good-bye, McGuire."

Before he could utter another word or toss any more truth in her face, Maddy ended the call and threw the phone back into her purse. She sniffled and wiped beneath her eyes, knowing there likely were smudges of mascara firmly in place. She would go to her office and do her best to ease everyone's fears. Managing the details of a crisis was when she was at her best.

Nothing made her feel better than being in control.

***

Ronan hadn't spoken to Maddy since she hung up on him. Part of him, a big damn piece, wanted to go find her and shake some sense into her. But after a lengthy phone call with Gavin, he came to the conclusion that that would be a bad move. His brother confirmed what Ronan suspected: if he pushed her too hard or crowded her space, she would shut him down and cut him off.

So Ronan did the exact opposite of his instincts. He didn't call or text. He didn't push. He could give Maddy the space she craved, but when the time was right, he was going to dig deeper. Maddy Morgan had quickly become the riddle that Ronan not only *wanted*, but also *needed* to solve.

For the rest of that week, he kept his ear to the ground to gather every bit of information on the case that he could. While he wanted his Thanksgiving dinner with Maddy to be free of unpleasant conversation, he knew that at some point, she would ask about the police's progress in finding the killer. He couldn't discuss certain aspects of the case, but he could definitely tell her some others.

In his heart of hearts, though, he was hoping they could talk about anything except that. Life and living were on his mind, and getting Maddy back into both was his top priority.

On Thanksgiving, with a bouquet of flowers in hand, he climbed out of the cab and smiled at Maddy's doorman.

"Hey, David." Ronan gave a friendly nod as the man held the door open. "Happy Thanksgiving."

"You too, Officer." David looked at the cab as it pulled away. "No partner tonight?"

"No, sir." Ronan chuckled. Once people saw him with Bowser, they always expected to see the two of them together. The dog made quite the impression. "No wingman for this evening."

"You're here to see Ms. Morgan, I presume?"

"Yes, sir." Ronan held up the colorful autumn assortment, briefly wondering if he should have gone another way. Maybe roses? But that seemed too ordinary for a woman like Maddy. "Think she'll like 'em?"

"I'd say it's a safe bet." David tipped his hat before calling out to the man at the desk. "Vincent, Officer McGuire is here to see Ms. Morgan."

"Thank you, David."

Ronan went to the guest book and signed in, but the instant he stepped into the elevator, he started to sweat. Maybe he should have called to confirm their date? He had texted, and she responded, but was that enough? After what had happened with Brenda, perhaps Maddy would want to pass on a night out. The funeral services would be back in Ohio where the girl had grown up, and Maddy's office was closed for the holiday weekend.

She wouldn't change her mind, would she?

He quickly checked his teeth in the reflection of the gold trim on the elevator walls. All clear. His new black wool coat covered the navy-blue suit and white shirt. He'd managed to keep the whole outfit free of wrinkles, but that was probably only because everything he had on was brand-new. Except for the tie, a dark-red one with white paw prints.

He rarely wore neckties—hated getting dressed up or wearing ties in general—so if he had to do it, at least he'd have a little fun with it. His mom had given him one with dogs on it when he and Bowser graduated from the K-9 program, and the theme had stuck. Now they were the only ties he had. Hell, he hated clothes shopping in general and hadn't been in ages, even though he could clean up really nicely when he wanted to.

The salesgirl had found Ronan wandering the store helplessly and taken pity on him. She'd helped him pick out everything, including new shoes. His brother Finn was the clotheshorse in the family and usually ragged on Ronan for being lame about fashion, but this evening had certainly warranted a little retail torture. Even *he* had to admit that his boots and jeans weren't gonna cut it tonight.

The elevator dinged. He straightened his tie, and a smile curved his lips.

This was it.

He had wanted to take Maddy Morgan on a date since

he was in the eighth grade. She'd always been out of his
league and off the market.

But not anymore.

The timing was finally right.

Jeez. Why was he making such a big deal out of this?
Ronan wiped the sweat from his brow and let out a slow
breath. He almost laughed out loud at how nervous he
was. He'd been on dates with tons of women. If there
was one thing Ronan knew how to do, it was date.

Yeah...but none of them were her.

Ronan punched the doorbell and straightened his coat
one more time. Seconds ticked by painfully slowly, but
there was no response.

Holy crap. She forgot.

Ronan knocked this time, but instead of her door, he
heard the door of the other apartment open. He turned
around just in time to see the guy in 15B poke his head
out. The cop in Ronan did a quick rundown. Late twen-
ties. Brown hair with glasses. Thin build.

"Happy Thanksgiving," Ronan said. "Tim, right?"

"Tom," he said flatly. "It's Tom. You here to see
Maddy?"

"Yeah, I am. Happy Thanks—"

The guy disappeared inside and slammed the door.

"Okay then," Ronan murmured. "Nice to meet you too."

He rang Maddy's bell one more time. Was it possible
that she had forgotten about their date?

Son of a...

As that last thought whisked through his head, and
his ego began to shrivel, the door swung open. The sight
before him wiped every coherent thought from his mind,
and his mouth went dry.

She hadn't forgotten.

Her voluptuous curves were wrapped in a slinky black dress that hugged the delicious swell of her hips and breasts with wicked perfection. Her espresso-colored curls hung loose around her face instead of being tied up or tamed as they were most times he saw her. Instead, they drifted over her shoulders in wild waves, almost daring him to tangle his fingers in them. A long, silver chain hung around her neck, and an oval pendant dangled precariously in her ample cleavage.

Maddy smiled at him from the doorway, her brilliant blue eyes framed with impossibly long, dark lashes. Ronan was speechless. She was beautiful. He'd always known that, but tonight, there was something ethereal about her. A glow or a light that he hadn't really seen before...or maybe it had been so long ago that he'd almost forgotten it.

He didn't know how many minutes passed while he stood there staring at her, but he could have stayed that way forever.

"What?" She looked down at her dress and then lifted her injured foot. "Did I get something on my dress, or do I still have a cankle?"

"No." Ronan shook his head and let out a slow breath, taking in the delicious sight of her shapely legs. "Definitely no cankles. You're stunning."

"Thanks. So are you." Her cheeks turned pink, and she stepped aside. "Uh. Come on in. I just have to get my coat."

"I met your neighbor. Kind of," Ronan said with a smirk. "It's Tom, by the way. Not Tim."

He stepped into the foyer and closed the door behind

him. The wool overcoat had been a mistake because now he was sweating like a pig. Maddy wasn't limping anymore. Her ankle must have been feeling better, because she had donned a pair of sexy black heels. He couldn't help but get a good look at those gorgeous gams while she fished her coat out of the closet.

"Oh jeez," she groaned. "I've been calling him Tim. He came over the other day and fixed my laptop and was asking me all kinds of questions about real estate prices and said he might be moving. Anyway, now I feel like a jerk because I used the wrong name. No wonder he didn't take me up on my offer to get him some listings. I insulted the poor guy."

"Whatever his name is, he's not real friendly." Ronan stuck the flowers out at her like a dork. "Happy Thanksgiving."

"Thanks." Maddy curled her hand around the paper, her fingertips briefly brushing his. Her eyebrows raised, and she nodded with approval. "Very nice, McGuire. Orange roses, purple cushion poms, and burnt-orange lilies. This is an impressive autumnal assortment. Okay, fess up. Who helped you with this?"

"What? You don't think I asked for the pom-poms all on my own?"

"They're called purple cushion poms." She laughed. "Come on. Be honest. Did you call Jordan, or maybe Cookie and Veronica at the shop back home?"

"Absolutely not. That would be cheating." He took her coat and helped her into it. "I told the lady at the florist that my date and her mom used to own a flower shop. Obviously, I had to bring my A game. Like I said...I enjoy surprising you."

Maddy sniffed the bouquet, her blue eyes peering at him above the blooms.

"How am I doing so far?" he asked quietly.

"Well, you showed up," she said with a nervous laugh. "That's a good start."

"Are you serious?" He tilted his head and studied her closely. How could she think, for one second, that he wouldn't show up? "I've never stood up a woman in my life. And I certainly wouldn't start with you."

"After what happened to Brenda and the way I spoke to you on the phone the other day…" She looked back at the flowers and cleared her throat. There it was. The elephant in the room.

"Did you get a chance to speak to Brenda's parents?"

"Yes." She nodded, her shoulders lifting as she sucked in a deep breath. "The service will be tomorrow, back in Ohio. They never wanted her to move here in the first place. They were devastated, as you can imagine."

"I know. The guys on the case are keeping me in the loop." Ronan pulled her coat closed, but he didn't let go, tugging her closer instead. "They're gonna find the son of a bitch who did this."

"I hope so," Maddy whispered. Her lower lip quivered, and those blue eyes glimmered as she seemed to struggle with what she wanted to say. "Thank you, Ronan."

"For what?"

He grasped the lapels of her coat a bit tighter, as though that might stop the tears he feared were coming. Seeing any woman cry was awful, but watching Maddy cry might make him crazy. To see her hurting, and not be able to fix it, would be torture.

"For everything," she murmured. "Calling the other

day, being here tonight. Mostly for not giving up on me. After the way I bit your head off, I wouldn't have blamed you if you'd let me have Thanksgiving alone with the remnants of the lame pint of mint-chip ice cream for my dinner."

"Sorry, kid." Ronan tugged the lapels of her coat playfully and leaned a bit closer. "That's not my style. Besides, emotions were running high, and with everything you were dealing with, I shouldn't have pushed. That being said, backing down isn't my style either. I've got—"

"Tunnel vision," she murmured.

When her gaze slammed into his, Ronan's gut dropped to his feet. God, he wanted to kiss her again. But before he could say or do anything, she backed up toward the living room. The fabric of her coat slipped through his fingers, much like she was slipping into his heart.

Effortlessly and completely.

"*And* you brought me flowers. Like I said, you're off to a good start." She held up the bouquet. "I'm going to put these in water, and then we can get dinner. I hope you like a woman who can eat, McGuire. I'm starving."

As she vanished around the corner, he couldn't have agreed more. He was hungry too, but not for food. All he craved was more of her.

Chapter 6

MADDY COULDN'T REMEMBER THE LAST TIME SHE HAD laughed this much or enjoyed an evening the way she did tonight with Ronan. Whether he was making goofy faces while telling stories about the trouble he and his brothers had stirred up back in the day, or brazenly charming the waitress, Ronan was entertaining, sweet, and funny.

The restaurant he had chosen was a really cool little place in Hell's Kitchen, and the food was outstanding. She had never eaten a holiday dinner at a restaurant before, but based on the crowd of people, it was a popular idea. It certainly wasn't your traditional Thanksgiving dinner fare, but this hadn't exactly been a typical first date either.

Though Maddy had forgotten they were even on a date more than once already.

They were simply two people laughing, trading stories, and eating an incredible meal. There was no weirdness with Ronan. No awkward silences or uncomfortable getting-to-know-you conversations because they already knew each other. She didn't have to worry about having to explain the loss the she had suffered or everything she'd left behind.

Being with Ronan was effortless.

Maddy drained the last of the Malbec in her generously sized wineglass and peered at Ronan over the rim. Even when he was devouring the last of his molten chocolate lava cake, the man was absolutely gorgeous. When he'd shown up at her door tonight, she had been rendered momentarily speechless. It was the first time she'd seen him in anything other than jeans, his uniform, or running clothes—and boy, oh boy, did the man look good.

"Nice tie," she said, nodding at the dog-themed piece of silk. "You keep your partner with you no matter where you go, eh?"

"You like it?" He leaned back in the chair and picked up the end to look at it before letting it slip through his fingers. "I'm not a big tie guy, but if it has a dog theme, I'll wear it."

"That's it, huh?" Maddy arched one eyebrow. "Dog ties only."

"Yes, ma'am." A slow grin covered his face and his eyes danced. "Once I find something that appeals to me, I stick with it."

Oh boy. Maddy sucked in a shuddering breath and fought the swell of attraction. One flash of his cocky little smile, and she was practically moaning in the middle of the restaurant.

It wasn't the clothes he wore that set her heart racing, nor the adorable tie fetish. Not by a long shot. It was the look in his eyes that had her stomach in knots and tickled that part of her deep inside, the one that she'd thought died months ago. When Ronan trailed that sizzling stare over her, she shivered all the way down to her toes, to say nothing of other body parts. The man didn't even have to touch her and she was fired up. Something about the way he studied Maddy told her he wanted to uncover her secret desires, the ones she never dared utter to another human being. She had the strong suspicion that he would be happy to help her bring them to life.

"What's running through that beautiful head of yours?"

"I was just thinking what a nice Thanksgiving this has been," she said. That wasn't exactly a fib, more like stretching the truth. "Not the most traditional, but then again, I'm not a big one for traditions."

"No?" He eyed her skeptically. "You don't have *any* traditions?"

"Not really. Well, at Christmas, I usually make an apple pie from scratch. My mom always whipped one up when I was a kid, and then after she died, I took over the job. It was a way to keep her close to me, I guess. She had that *Better Homes and Garden Cook Book*, the one with the red-plaid cover that resembled a picnic tablecloth? Hers was beat up and covered in grease stains, but I still have it despite the fact that I have that pie and crust recipe memorized. Rick ate it every year, even though he hated apple pie."

She sucked in a deep breath and held it for a second before continuing. Maddy thought it might be strange to bring up her life with Rick, but the open, accepting expression on Ronan's face instantly put her at ease.

"Go on." He leaned both arms on the table, as if ready to soak up every word. "It's okay. I want to hear about it."

"Rick and I didn't have any family. Neither of us had any siblings. Our parents had all passed on, and with no children of our own…well…the holidays weren't really a big deal. Besides, he almost always worked them. The other guys in the squad had families, so he would offer to take those shifts."

"He was a good man."

"He was." She nodded and smiled at the fond memories. "We were both married to our jobs, which is probably why we never married each other. I never pushed for it, and he never asked. In fact," she said with a soft laugh, "we never even talked about it. That's funny, isn't it? We were together for almost a decade, but not once in all that time did we talk about getting married. We lived together and had a blast." Maddy smiled and quietly said, "I guess that was enough for us."

Ronan studied her intently and nodded slowly. Silence hung between them for a moment or two, and she was relieved not to see a look of pity in his eyes. Instead, there was acceptance and understanding.

At the moment, she was pretty thankful for that.

"How about you?" she asked brightly, desperately wanting to keep the mood upbeat. "Enough about me and my sad stories. Tell me about the McGuire traditions."

"Alright. Thanksgiving usually involves an enormous amount of food. Football on the television while Mom cooks. Then after dinner but before dessert, my brothers and Dad and I play a game of touch football that typically turns into tackle. Then, during dessert, we all go around the table and say what we're thankful for." Ronan picked up his wineglass and took a healthy sip. "So how about a little McGuire tradition tonight? What are you thankful for, Mads?"

"You first," she said quietly.

"My family, that's always at the top of the list, and our good health. I'm thankful Gavin and Jordan found their way back to each other." Ronan's gaze flicked from his wineglass to her mouth before traveling up to look her in the eyes. His voice was quiet and steady and sent a shiver over her flesh. "I'm also thankful that I've gotten to know you better, Maddy Morgan. Your turn."

She debated how honest she should be, but staring into his earnest, handsome face, she knew he deserved nothing less. A man like Ronan—one driven by duty, honor, and loyalty—earned far more than some prepackaged response from her.

"To be honest," Maddy began slowly, "if you had asked me this question a few months ago, I don't think I would have had an answer. Losing Rick and the grief that came with it almost swallowed me up. Hell, I had to move everything to try to get away from it, to shake it off. But you know, leaving Old Brookfield last year wasn't what helped me start to move on."

"What is it, then?"

"You," she said softly. Her fingers shook around the stem of her glass, and her heart raced as she admitted the truth to him and to herself at the same time. "You've been an incredible friend, Ronan. I don't know if I can ever repay you for that."

Her throat thickened with emotion and tears stung her eyes, but Maddy willed them away. She took another healthy sip of wine. All the while, Ronan's eyes stayed fixed on her. Oh jeez. Maybe she'd said too much. Her face heated and a hint of embarrassment crept in, but in true Ronan fashion, he diffused the situation with humor.

"Well, you *have* been politely laughing at my stories all night, and you haven't even mentioned how badly I've been hogging the conversation." He winked. "Consider us even."

"No," she said, laughing. "I'm serious."

"So am I. My brothers *did* call me Motormouth when I was a kid. In fact, Gavin said he thinks the reason I became a K-9 officer was so I could monopolize the conversations with my partner."

"I remember that nickname," Maddy said with a smile. She let out a contented sigh and ran her finger along the base of her glass. "But it wasn't your *only* nickname."

"Is that so?" His lips curved into a cocky smirk.

"Mmm-hmm." Maddy nodded. She leaned back in her chair and crossed her legs. "If memory serves, the girls in school also referred to you as 'Make-Out McGuire.'"

Her body warmed, recalling the two kisses they had shared.

The man had definitely earned that nickname, and she'd be lying if she said she hadn't replayed those moments over and over in her head. If Maddy was brutally honest with herself, she would admit she was hoping for more than a kiss tonight. She hadn't realized how starved she was for physical affection until she got a taste of Ronan.

Sex didn't have to mean love or commitment. It could just be sex—simply two adults taking comfort and pleasure in each other's arms. Easy. No muss. No fuss.

Her gaze skittered over the angles and planes of Ronan's strong jaw as the light of the table candle flickered, casting shadows and making the color of his eyes stand out even more than usual. They crinkled at the corners, and she couldn't help but smile with him.

"Never heard that one before," he said with feigned innocence.

"Really? I find it hard to believe that you weren't aware of your reputation. Let's be honest, McGuire.

You dated most of the girls in your class and half the girls in mine."

"That's interesting." Ronan leaned both elbows on the table and leveled a knowing gaze at her.

"What is?"

"I thought you barely knew I existed back in high school."

Silence hung between them, and Maddy's heartbeat picked up. She probably should have played it cool, but why bother? She wanted him. And if she were going to be really honest with herself, a part of her always had. But even when they were kids, there was something dangerous about Ronan. It was like she knew, deep in her gut, that if she allowed herself to get too close, there would be no going back.

Nope. Nope. Nope.

What the hell was she thinking? The sex-only idea was a colossally bad one. She couldn't compartmentalize with a man like him. Men like Ronan McGuire didn't fit neatly in one little spot; he couldn't be contained. There was pervasiveness about him. It was the same quality that allowed him to fill a wide-open space simply by stepping into it. If she allowed it, Ronan could consume her and obliterate all the neat little boundaries she had built around her heart.

No sex. Just friends. That's it, Morgan. Be smart.

"You're not an easy man to ignore, and you know it." A smile touched her lips. "Believe me, I've tried. But you are one tenacious son of a gun, and you've only gotten more so as the years have passed. Let's just say…I noticed you."

"Good to know," he murmured, his gaze skittering

over her face. "I noticed you too. More than that, honestly. You were the one girl I wanted who wanted nothing to do with me."

Oh boy, so not smart.

Her breath hitched in her throat, and her blood began to hum. Maybe it was the wine? She bought that lie for about three seconds—right until Ronan reached across the table and covered her hand with his. His long, strong fingers curled around hers, and the heat of his flesh seared over Maddy's with wicked promise. She sucked in a shuddering breath and imagined him running his hands over far-more-sensitive areas.

Holy crap; she was in big, fat, stupid trouble.

Her cheeks heated.

"Who gets the bad news?"

The waitress's playful but poorly timed interruption broke the moment. Maddy swiftly pulled her hand from Ronan's before reaching for her small evening bag. A shadow passed briefly over Ronan's face but he recovered, flashing that charming smile to the young woman before taking the check.

"That's all mine," Ronan said, placing the leather folder next to his plate. "Thank you."

"Don't be silly," Maddy said quickly. She fished through the small zipper compartment for her credit card. "This isn't the fifties. Let's go dutch. What do I owe you?"

When she finally looked back up at Ronan, the annoyed expression on his face stopped her cold. He slipped his card into the folder and held it up for the waitress without taking his eyes off Maddy's.

"Like I said...I got it."

"Ronan," Maddy said, flicking an embarrassed glance to the waitress. "This place is really expensive. Come on, let me pitch in."

"No way." Ronan leaned back in his chair and waved at the waitress while staring Maddy down. "Just bring me a receipt, please."

The waitress lingered for a few seconds before finally scurrying away with the check and Ronan's credit card.

"Ronan," Maddy said with a warning tone. "Our bill had to be at least two hundred and fifty bucks. Stop being such a guy and at least let me leave a tip."

"No." He smiled and finished off his wine. "In case you forgot, we're on a date. In my world, that means the *guy* picks up the check."

"I know we're on a date but—"

"I'm not finished." He placed his glass on the table and leaned closer, lowering his voice to barely above a whisper. "Now, I may not be able to afford a fancy West Side apartment like you and your clients, but I can certainly manage to take a beautiful woman out for a nice Thanksgiving dinner."

Oh shit.

Ronan thought she was implying that he was too poor to pay for it? Embarrassment flickered up her spine, and in that moment, all she wanted to do was crawl under the table and disappear. They had been having a lovely evening, and Maddy had managed to ruin it by insulting him. She didn't care how much money he made or didn't make.

She rarely gave much thought to money at all.

"I didn't mean it like that," Maddy said quickly. "I was only saying—"

"That some poor old cop can't afford a fancy joint like you can."

"Hey!" Maddy shoved the credit card back into her evening bag and snapped it shut more harshly than necessary. "That is not what I meant, okay? Look, I warned you. I'm not good at this dating stuff. I offered on instinct. Rick and I always split the check, and I guess..."

Her throat tightened with a tsunami of unexpected emotion, and she stopped talking for a split second because she thought she might cry. Regret lingered in his eyes and they sat there in silence, a swell of unspoken apologies swirling between them.

"Shit," Ronan whispered. He ran one hand over his face and let out a slow breath. "I'm sorry, Mads."

"No, I'm the one who's sorry, Ronan. Look, this whole *date* business was probably a mistake. It will only make everything really messy between us. We're both adults, and we won't let any of this interfere with Jordan and Gavin's wedding. Let's forget it." She waved one hand and pushed her chair back before rising to her feet. "I'm going to the ladies' room. I'll meet you at the coat check, and then I'll get a cab home."

She hurried toward the safety of the restroom before Ronan could stop her. Maddy slipped inside the lavish lounge and tossed her bag on the marble counter. How long had it been since she'd felt so totally unsure of herself? She'd been working like a dog since last year to put her life back in order and feel safe. Now, here she was, dallying with Ronan McGuire, and it was like attempting to walk through a bed of quicksand.

No matter what she did or said, it was a wrong move, and she only sank deeper.

She placed both hands on the counter and closed her eyes, struggling to get herself together.

Nice going, Maddy. So much for not making it weird.

Her bag started to buzz. Maddy gave the attendant, who was standing at the ready with hand towels, an embarrassed glance. She took out her phone, and a smile bloomed when she read the text from Ronan.

> Glad we got the awkward part of the date out of the way. Shake a tail feather, Mads. The night is just getting started.

Mads? The sweet nickname hadn't been lost on her when he used it back at the table, and the easy, familiar way it tumbled from his lips was surprisingly wonderful. No one had ever called her that, but somehow, coming from Ronan, it seemed as though *he* always had. Maddy cradled the phone in her hands and bit her lower lip, debating what to text back. Finally, after tossing around various responses, one cheekier than the next, she simply sent back:

> Be out in a minute.

The guy was incorrigible, cocky, proud, and playful. Maddy let out a sigh and gave her reflection one last look before heading out. Ronan was exactly the type of man she could fall in love with, and that's what made him dangerous. She really should put a stop to this whole thing before it got messier than it already was.

Maddy wove her way through the crowd in the bar area, but she had her sights on Ronan the entire time.

His tall, broad-shouldered frame stood out amid the sea of people milling near the entrance, but the draw was about more than his size. Ronan had an air of authority: he gave the impression of a man in total control of himself and his surroundings. His careful, intelligent gaze scanned the crowd, not in a weird Terminator way, but subtly and consistently. It was the cop in him. No matter where he was, Ronan took note of what was happening in the immediate vicinity.

When his penetrating stare met hers, her stomach swirled and she caught her breath. It was unsettling to know that when he looked at her, he was seeing *her* more than anyone else had in a good, long while. Ronan had been right on the money when he called her out for hiding in her apartment and in this city.

In some ways, it was a relief to have someone simply know where she was coming from, and in others, it was terrifying. With that one revelation, Ronan had stripped away the protective blanket she'd thrown over herself, leaving her naked and exposed. Maddy let out a short laugh and shook her head. If Rick had been there for that conversation, he would have slapped Ronan on the shoulder and congratulated him for calling Maddy out on her bullshit.

"Mind if we walk awhile?" Ronan asked as he helped her into her coat. "It'll probably be a bitch to get a cab around here anyway."

"Sure." Maddy nodded and avoided looking at him while she tied the sash tightly. The embarrassment of insulting him lingered. "Let's go."

She hurried ahead of him and started walking toward the corner.

"Hey," Ronan called after her. He caught up easily and linked his arm around her bicep. "Mads, what's wrong?"

Maddy stood on the corner and stuffed her hands into the roomy pockets of her coat. She paused long enough to suck in a deep, cleansing breath of cold air. Being around Ronan was quickly becoming a real-life roller coaster ride. One minute it was easy and fun, the next, awkward and fumbling. Through it all, however, no matter what part of the ride she was on, she had no desire to stop. Maddy was intensely attracted to Ronan. It was carnal and primal and made her feel completely out of control.

She wanted him, but she didn't *want* to want him.

Ugh. She was a hot mess.

"I'm sorry about before." She forced herself to look him in the face. Curiosity and a touch of humor lingered there. "I didn't mean it the way you think I did."

"I thought we were past that." Ronan tilted his head and flashed her that devastating smile. "Didn't you get my charming text message?"

"Yes." She couldn't stop the laugh that bubbled up. "But I want to be clear that I wasn't implying you couldn't afford to pay for dinner. In all honesty, I'm feeling really nervous about this *date* and sorely out of practice."

"Oh! We're being honest?" Ronan's lips tilted. "Well, in the spirit of honesty, I should fess up about something too." He gathered both of her hands in his. "My male ego took a hit when I saw your building, and then when I saw your actual apartment...I guess I was feeling a little inadequate."

"Why?" Her brow furrowed. "Your parents' house is

one of the largest in Old Brookfield, and it's no secret how wealthy they are. It's not like you grew up without money. Didn't your great-grandfather invent the shoe-lace or something?"

"The seat belt, among other things." He laughed. "And yes, my *family* is wealthy, but *I'm* not. I'm a cop, Maddy. I make a cop's salary. Let's just say that my entire place could fit in the lobby of your building. Twice." He shrugged. "Hell, I was worried Bowser wouldn't want to come home with me after seeing it. He might be a dog, but he has expensive tastes."

"Very funny." Maddy rolled her eyes.

"I am sorry for jumping to a stupid conclusion, but I won't apologize for being old-fashioned or for insist-ing that this is a real date." He tugged her closer and lowered his voice, a wicked glint in eyes. "Speaking of which, we aren't finished."

"Ronan," she said in a warning tone. "What are you up to?"

He raised his arm and tried to flag an oncoming cab that scurried by.

"Do you plan on telling me where we're going?" Maddy tugged her coat tighter against the bitter gust of wind. "Because I'm obviously not going home."

"Nope." Ronan took her hand in his and hailed another cab. "You aren't the boss tonight, Mads. I know you love being in control and calling the shots, but let it go for now. I told you I was gonna take you out on a real New York City date, and I meant it."

"Fine," she said, feigning annoyance.

By some small miracle, a cab barreling down the street toward them pulled over. Ronan opened the door, and Maddy scooted in quickly. Ronan slipped in behind her and whispered to the driver.

"You got it, man." The cabbie hit the meter and pulled away.

"I have a love-hate relationship with surprises." Maddy shivered and adjusted the scarf around her neck. "I don't even get a hint?"

"Nope." Ronan sat on his side of the backseat with a smug smile on his face and his hands folded in his lap. "No hints."

Maddy adjusted her position and pressed her body into the corner, a move meant to keep distance between them but also to allow her to study him. Except that her coat fell open when she did, and since the hem of her skirt had ridden up to precarious heights, it offered a generous view of her legs. She went to cover them but quickly recalled the way she'd caught him staring at them back at her apartment.

The emotional roller coaster had Maddy feeling more adventurous and alive than she had in a good, long while. She could blame it on the wine, but that would have been a lie. It wasn't booze or loneliness. It was the man in the cab next to her that had her head spinning and her body burning.

He was spot-on. She did love being in control. If she had to be at the mercy of her overheated libido, then she would grab the wheel.

"That's a damn shame." Maddy sighed. "I do love a good…hint."

Ronan, who had been looking out the window, turned—to argue with her, no doubt. But when he caught sight of her bare legs, Maddy shivered beneath the weight of his heated stare. His eyes, which had seemed greener in the restaurant's lighting, now gleamed smoky gray as they drifted slowly over her. She couldn't move. He pinned her there with his gaze, and in that instant, there was nowhere else on earth Maddy would rather have been.

"Something wrong, Ronan?" Maddy lifted her knee, gently adjusting her legs and doing nothing to cover them. "You look a little pale. Are you feeling alright?"

"I'm feeling a few things"—his voice was gruff and strained—"but none of them would be classified as *alright*."

His heavy-lidded stare slammed into her, and the force of it drove all the air from her lungs. Maddy couldn't move. A hungry, almost feral look was carved into his features. The lights of the city outside flickered over him and highlighted the sharp angles of his well-chiseled jaw, wide cheekbones, and firm, full lips. But what stood out were those intense, glittering eyes peering intently from beneath jet-black brows.

"That so?" Maddy's tongue flicked out and moistened her lower lip. "Then how would *you* classify them? What words would you choose?"

Ronan's hand shot out with the same lightning-fast reflexes he'd used to catch her in the park, but this time his touch carried a far different purpose. It wasn't safe or comforting. It was hot and demanding.

His wide palm seared along the exposed flesh of her bare calf, and his fingers fluttered lightly beneath the crook of her knee. She gasped and bit her lower lip when he leaned closer and rested his arm along the top of the seat, closing in on her. He studied her intently, and

Maddy fought the urge to moan when his thumb brushed over her kneecap. Ronan lifted her leg ever so slightly and ran his hand along the inside of her lower thigh.

She was cornered. Trapped between him and the door of the cab. Her breath came in short jags, and her hands were clamped around the small evening bag in her lap. Maddy was afraid that if she moved even one inch, the exquisite sexual tension between them—the rising, burning swell of lust and need—would shatter her into a million pieces.

"I've never been great with words," Ronan murmured. "I'll have to show you instead."

His hand moved higher up her thigh, and his hot breath, infused with a hint of wine, fanned over her cheek and made her dizzy. His fingers pressed into the sensitive flesh of her leg, gently but insistently, and Maddy moaned. When he brushed his firm lips across the corner of her mouth, the dam broke.

On a groan filled with desperate carnal need, Maddy grabbed his face and kissed him. His arm slipped behind her and held her close as his tongue sought to possess hers. The kiss was rough and edged with passionate desperation, as though neither of them could get close enough. She tangled her fingers in his dark hair and uncrossed her legs as he deepened the kiss, his hard, muscular body pressing her deeper into the seat. She reveled in the weight and feel of him. All she wanted to do was get lost in the all-consuming force that was Ronan McGuire.

Neither of them realized the cab had stopped.

"Yo, lovebirds," the cabbie shouted. "You want I should keep the meter running or what?"

Both of them were breathing heavily when Ronan broke the kiss. He didn't let her go. One hand remained curled possessively around the top of her inner thigh, and the other was pinned behind Maddy's back.

"Where are we?" Maddy said in a shaky voice. She slid her hands down to his chest and grabbed the lapels of his coat before looking past him to the window. "You planned on taking me to the Plaza Hotel?"

"Not the hotel! I was going to take you on a carriage ride," he said between heavy breaths. "But—"

"Driver?" Maddy's lips curved into a smile. She was going to do exactly what she'd told herself she wouldn't. "Change of plans. Take us to 115 Central Park West."

"You got it, lady."

Ronan pressed a kiss to her lips as the cab pulled away from the curb. Then he sat up and adjusted her coat to cover her legs.

"I guess I do like being in control," she whispered.

"I just discovered something, Mads." Ronan curled his arm over her shoulders and pulled her against him. "There's only one thing I enjoy more than surprising you."

"What's that?" She snuggled into his embrace and rested her head on his chest. "Living up to your nickname?"

"No," he said through a short laugh. Ronan kissed the top of her head and murmured, "When you surprise me."

Chapter 7

RONAN AND MADDY DIDN'T SAY A WORD THE REST OF THE ride. They didn't have to. The taste of her lingered on his lips, slowly driving him wild. The cab ride might have been the longest one of his life, because all he wanted to do was gather Maddy's curvy little body into his arms and peel that dress off her one inch at a time. But they had already given the cabbie enough of a show, and Ronan wasn't going to share that part of Maddy with anyone. He did his best to be a gentleman and keep his hands to himself.

It wasn't easy.

"Good evening, ma'am." A doorman Ronan hadn't met yet tilted his cap. "Happy Thanksgiving."

"Happy Thanksgiving," Maddy said sweetly.

"Did you have a nice night?" The older gentleman held the door open for them. "Eat a lot of turkey?"

"We had a lovely dinner, but I'm still a little hungry." She shot a sly glance at Ronan before tangling her fingers in his. "Not quite sure what I want, though."

"Could've fooled me," Ronan murmured.

The door shut behind them and Ronan squeezed her hand, brushing his thumb along the inside of her wrist. Maddy's lips curved into a saucy smirk, and she nodded politely at Vincent, the concierge, artfully avoiding Ronan's gaze. She was toying with him, which was a hell of a turn-on. There was nothing he loved more than a woman who knew what she wanted, and even better when she wasn't afraid to go after it.

If Maddy was half as daring in the bedroom as she was in her professional life, he was a dead man.

Ronan punched the button for the elevator with more ferocity than necessary. Maddy undid the belt of her coat and let it fall open, a seductive sigh escaping her lips. He was greeted with a perfect view of her cleavage, and every inch of him hardened at the sight of it.

"It's warm in here." She kept her bright-blue eyes on the elevator doors and brushed the long curls off her neck. "How about it? Are you getting hot, McGuire?"

He tightened his grip on her hand and hit the stupid button again.

"Where's the damn elevator?" he growled.

"Apologies, sir. It's been acting up tonight, Ms. Morgan," the concierge said. "The service company will be here first thing in the morning to take a look at it."

"Is the camera still out of service?" Maddy flicked her seductive blue eyes to Ronan. "David said it wasn't working yesterday."

Ronan's mouth went dry and he swallowed hard. Was she suggesting what he thought she was? God, he hoped so.

"No, ma'am. We've been having trouble with the security cameras. The entire computer system is having issues. We couldn't get anyone here due to the holiday, but they assured us that they would have an attendant here first thing tomorrow."

"Computers, huh?" Maddy shot a glance at Ronan and smirked. "What about my neighbor..."

"Tom," Ronan murmured.

"Right." Maddy giggled. "Maybe Tom could help you with it. Isn't he a technology whiz kid?"

"I hadn't thought to ask," Vincent said nervously. "I hate to bother one of the residents with something like this. The emergency phone is functioning properly, however. If you have a problem just pick that up, and it goes directly to the front desk."

"Good to know," Maddy murmured. "Well, if we get into trouble in the elevator, I'm sure Officer McGuire can handle *things*."

Ronan tapped his fingers impatiently and was about to push the button again when the damn thing finally dinged and the doors opened. Maddy slid her hand from his, stepped into the elevator, and leaned against the back wall with a smile curving those sweet lips. The doors closed behind Ronan, and he hit the button for the fifteenth floor.

"Camera's broken, huh?" Ronan asked quietly.

"Seems so." Maddy sighed. "I'd like to add that to my list of things I'm thankful for."

Without taking his eyes from hers, Ronan reached behind him and pressed the red emergency stop button. The shrill alarm rang three times announcing the elevator's sudden halt. Maddy's lips tilted, and she rested both hands on the brass handrail behind her. She raised her eyebrows and murmured, "Uh-oh. It looks like we're stuck."

The emergency phone rang and Ronan spun around, picking it up immediately.

"Hello, Vincent." Ronan took a couple steps back so that Maddy was directly behind him and the phone cord was stretched to its limit. "It's my fault. I wasn't looking where I was going and bumped into the emergency button. The damn thing is jammed."

Reaching his left hand back, he found the hem of Maddy's skirt. He slid his fingers beneath and curled them around the crook of her knee. A breathy whimper escaped her lips and she adjusted her stance, giving him better access.

"I see, sir." Vincent's nervous tenor came through the crackling line. "We'll get someone up there to try to fix it as soon as possible. B-but with the holiday…"

As Ronan listened to the concierge, he slid his hand higher along the soft swell of Maddy's inner thigh. He felt her shudder and moan softly when his fingertips brushed the damp heat between her legs.

"Not a problem," Ronan said firmly. "Ms. Morgan is in good hands."

Ronan leaned forward and hung up the phone before Vincent could protest further, keeping his hand on Maddy all the while. Moving slowly and with purpose. Ronan turned to face her. Her heavy-lidded gaze and parted lips told him more than any words she could possibly utter. He saw need and desire that matched his own.

"Looks like we could be stuck here for a while," Ronan whispered.

He moved his hand higher, and she sagged against the railing when he slipped one finger beneath the damp edge of her panties. He brushed lightly over her sex, and she gasped and gripped the rail tightly. He loved seeing her let go, even if it was only for a moment. If he had anything to say about it, it would be for far longer.

"Is this how most of your dates end up?" Maddy asked through a shuddering breath.

"This isn't just *any* date." Ronan cupped her neck and tipped her chin with his thumb. "Tonight isn't some getting-to-know-you snooze fest with a woman I doubt I'll ever see again. This evening, and every night from now on, I plan on finding out how many different ways I can get you to make that sound."

"What sound?" Maddy asked absently.

Ronan withdrew his hand from her beneath her skirt and trailed his fingers up her rib cage to the generous swell of her breasts. He pressed a soft kiss to the corner of her lips and ran his thumb over her nipple, which poked insistently through the thin fabric of her dress. She shuddered against him and her eyes fluttered closed, a breathy moan sounding beside his ear.

"That's the one, Mads," Ronan said between butterfly kisses along the delicate flesh of her neck. "I could listen to that for the rest of my life."

Moving with surprising speed, Maddy grabbed his face with both hands and forced him to look her in the eyes. Urgency simmered beneath the burgeoning tide of lust and Ronan wrestled for control, but when she lifted her leg and hooked it over his hip, a smile curved her lips.

She was toying with him again.

"You're living up to your nickname." She flicked her tongue over his bottom lip and tugged him tighter against her with her leg. "Motormouth."

Ronan's eyes narrowed, and he placed both hands on the wall on either side of her, caging her in. "Tell me what you want, Mads."

He tilted his hips, making no effort to hide his arousal. He wanted her to know what she did to him, to be fully and totally aware of the savage effect she had on his body. But it wasn't only physical. Everything about this woman turned him on, inside and out. She was smart, funny, full of surprises, and at the moment, completely open to him, which revved him up more than anything else.

Or anyone. Ever.

"This," she whispered.

Maddy brushed her lips over his. The touch, brief but electric, sent a shock directly to his crotch. Two could play at that game. Ronan shifted his stance and slipped his thigh between her legs, pressing it against the heat of her sex. His gut clenched when her eyes widened and that breathy little sigh escaped her lips again.

"I want you to touch me, Ronan." Maddy slid her hands up his arms until her fingers tangled with his, resting along either side of her head. She arched her back, her full, soft breasts pressing against his chest, and he groaned. "Make me feel again," she pleaded. "I've been numb for so long... You woke me up, Ronan. I want to feel *you*. It doesn't have to mean anything. It can just be tonight."

Between the weight of her body pressed against his and the needy plea in her voice, Ronan couldn't hold back any longer. He cursed and his lips covered hers, his tongue pressing deep inside the warm cavern of her mouth. The kiss was demanding and rough, but she met his challenge eagerly. Her tongue lashed along his with the same urgent sense of possession and need. The kiss was laced with wine and spice, and he fleetingly wondered if he could get drunk simply off the taste of her.

Ronan held Maddy's hands overhead and kissed her

deeply, but he craved more. He suckled her lower lip and covered her wrists with one hand before dragging the other down to the nape of her neck. He tilted her head, giving him better access, and took total control of the kiss. She arched her back and moaned, the sound reverberating along his lips and intensifying the experience. In that moment, she surrounded him completely. Still, he wanted more.

Breathing heavily, Ronan held her lower lip between his teeth briefly before releasing it. Her breath came in jagged gasps, and her mouth, only an inch from his, was red and swollen from their kiss. The mane of dark curls framed her lovely face, and those brilliant blue eyes were glazed with stark, unabashed lust.

He'd never seen anyone more beautiful or sultry in his life.

"Don't move," Ronan ground out. "Keep your hands over your head, and don't move an inch."

She opened her mouth to respond, but he silenced her with a deep and savage kiss. When he lifted his head and finally came up for air, she gasped, as though trying to catch her breath.

"Not an inch," he murmured.

Maddy gave a short nod, and when he released her wrists, she kept them high above her head. Ronan trailed kisses along her neck as his hands found their way to the dip of her waist. He flicked his tongue in the valley of her cleavage and dropped to his knees, worshipping the electric, vulnerable woman in front of him. His mouth covered one breast, the thin fabric of her dress and lacy bra the only barrier, and he captured her nipple between his teeth, biting down gently.

Maddy twitched and moaned but he held her still. His large hands easily spanned her waist before slipping behind and slowly gathering up the fabric of her skirt. She shivered against him and sighed when he palmed her bare ass cheeks. She must have been wearing one of those thong things, and damn if he wasn't grateful for it. Ronan groaned when her heated skin filled his hands, but when he peered up at her, he almost came from the vision alone.

Eyes closed, lips parted, with a flush of pink in her cheeks, she looked like the goddess Aphrodite come to life. Her espresso-colored curls tumbled over her shoulders, and her breasts heaved with each labored breath. Maddy looked primed and ready for whatever came next, and that might have been more of a turn-on than anything else. He pressed a kiss to her quivering belly, the smooth fabric of her dress covering the rest of the as-yet-undiscovered bounty.

God, he wanted her.

But was an elevator really the place he wanted to make love to her for the first time? The answer was a resounding and surprising no. He rested his head against her hip and pressed his fingers into the soft dip of her waist.

He could have her right here and right now, but for the first time in his life, Ronan wasn't thinking about his own sexual satisfaction. Maddy deserved more, and he wanted more from her. No matter how tough she pretended to be, she was in a vulnerable place. He had to tread carefully and take it slow, or there was a good chance she'd count their date as nothing more than a hookup.

Her words haunted him... *It doesn't have to mean anything.*

Bullshit. Deep in his soul, buried in the recesses of his heart, a place he never thought he would share with anyone, Ronan knew that wasn't true.

When he made love to Maddy, it would mean *everything.*

He rose to his feet without another word and reached over her head, taking her hands in his. Ronan drew them to his mouth and pressed a kiss to each palm. Maddy's eyes fluttered open, glimmering pools of blue rimmed with a hint of confusion. Ronan gently tugged her coat closed, covering that gorgeous cleavage, and tied the sash tightly, all while avoiding Maddy's inquisitive stare.

He stepped back and released the emergency button. A second later, the elevator car jolted and continued its ascent toward Maddy's floor. Ronan grabbed her by the arm when the sudden movement of the car made her stumble. Her hands curled over his shoulders as she steadied her stance. Her breathing had slowed, but the confusion in her eyes increased.

"I-I don't understand... I thought that..."

"Not like this," he said quietly. "I am going to give you everything you want, need, and deserve, Mads. But not in an elevator." A smile curved his lips. "At least not tonight."

"Right." Maddy's cheeks reddened and she looked away, quickly dropping her hands. "Whatever. Let's just forget it."

She tried to step away, but Ronan linked one arm around her waist and tugged her against him. Maddy's

hands flew to his chest, and she gaped at him like he'd
lost his mind. Maybe he had.

"I will not forget it," he growled. Ronan cupped her
neck with his other hand and brushed his lips lightly
over hers. "I want you, Maddy. I want you more than
I've ever wanted any woman in my life."

"Then why put on the brakes, McGuire? Things were
just getting good." She curled her hands around his tie
and pulled him against her. "How about we continue this
in my apartment? Don't be scared. Making out doesn't
mean we're going steady or something. We aren't kids
anymore. It can just be sex. No strings."

Before the words had escaped her lips, the elevator
dinged and the doors slid open. Ronan arched one eyebrow and stepped back, holding the doors open with one
arm but keeping the other securely around her waist.

"Because you and I aren't just gonna hook up." He
kissed her quickly and released her from his grasp. "I
want more from you, Mads. And I promise you something—it will never be *just sex* with us. My gut tells me
that if you and I go to bed tonight, then you're going to
cross me off your list."

"My list?" Maddy slipped her hands in the pockets
as she moved to the open doorway. She narrowed her
gaze and studied him curiously. "What are you talking about?"

"You know exactly what I'm talking about." Ronan
leaned close and lowered his voice. "That neat little list
you keep, the one that you've been following ever since
Rick died. The one that prevents you from really *living*
your life. You put everyone and everything in an appropriate place. Like your apartment, for example. Neat,

orderly, and in total control. It's funny because that's nothing like the girl I remember. If we take this any further tonight, I think you're gonna write me off and consider us finished. But we're only getting started."

"Is that so?" she asked haughtily. "Well, maybe that's because I'm not a girl anymore. We aren't children, Ronan. Jeez. Where *exactly* do you think your place with me is, McGuire? Because it obviously isn't in my bed."

"I didn't say that." Ronan brushed a stray curl from her forehead, and she batted his hand away with a scoffing sound. He couldn't suppress the grin that curved his lips. "In fact, I'm the *only man* who belongs in your bed from now on."

She opened her mouth to argue with him, but before she could utter a sound, he grabbed her face with both hands and kissed her deeply. She stiffened at first, but a second later she opened to him, returning his affections with equal fervor. He pressed her against the other side of the elevator door and devoured her, branding her with every stroke of his tongue.

She was his. There was no doubt about that. Not anymore.

The alarm blared again as the doors protested. Ronan broke the kiss but kept her cheeks cradled in his hands, his mouth an inch from hers and both of them breathless.

"You've kept me in the friend zone, and now you want to put me in the friends-with-benefits category," he rasped. "I don't know if you've noticed, but I'm *not* that guy when it comes to you. I want more than one date with you, Mads, and I want a helluva lot more than a quick hot-and-heavy hookup in an elevator."

The alarm rang loudly again. This was a risky move. She could get pissed off and tell him to go screw himself. A few more agonizing seconds ticked by, and for a moment, Ronan thought he'd made a colossal mistake.

"Well," she murmured, "you sure do know how to show a girl a good time…if a confusing one."

"Like I said"—Ronan kissed the tip of her nose and released her from his embrace—"I enjoy surprising you. And if you think Thanksgiving has been fun, just wait until Christmas."

The doors buzzed again and tried to close, but he continued to hold them open, wanting to squeeze out every last second with her that he possibly could.

"What? You want to take me out for Christmas too?"

"Maybe." He winked. "I want to try your apple pie."

The emergency phone in the elevator rang, and a smile bloomed on Maddy's lips.

"Looks like you have a call." She slipped past Ronan and went to the door of her apartment, opening it quickly.

Ronan ignored the phone as Maddy tossed a glance at him over her shoulder, her wicked gaze flicking to the erection he was doing nothing to hide.

"Just remember," she purred, "turnabout is fair play. I might have a surprise or two in store for you."

"Are you kidding?" Ronan dropped his hand, and the elevator doors began to close. "I'm counting on it."

The doors slammed shut with a muffled thud, and all he could think about was the revenge she could be planning. He'd never looked forward to anything more in his life. "Game on."

Chapter 8

THE PAST THREE WEEKS HAD GONE BY IN A BLINK, BARELY leaving Maddy time to breathe, let alone explore any more dalliances with Ronan—even though that was almost all she could think about.

The holidays were usually slow in the real estate market, but not this year. Suddenly, the holidays were prime time for showing million-dollar apartments. She had been going nonstop since the Monday after Thanksgiving, and the rush didn't look like it was going to let up any time soon.

The inherently high-energy nature of their industry had become even more intense lately, every meeting laced with tension and a hint of fear. Lucille's and Brenda's deaths were on everyone's minds, but oddly enough, nobody spoke about them openly. Oh, their deaths were whispered about by the watercooler but not freely discussed. It was almost as if the danger wasn't real if nobody talked about it. Nothing else had happened since Brenda, thankfully, though that meant most people were beginning to believe the two crimes weren't connected.

And on top of all that, Maddy had to contend with demanding Mr. Gregory. The man had seen virtually every available apartment on the island of Manhattan, some of them twice, but none were acceptable. She loved a challenge, but this guy was seriously on her last nerve.

Maddy leaned against the elevator wall and stared at the changing numbers along the top as they crept slowly toward the floor for her office. She only had to hang in there for two more days, and then she was off to Old Brookfield for Jordan and Gavin's wedding. She flicked her gaze to the red emergency button, and her face heated.

The memory of that stolen moment with Ronan had kept her going through the past couple of weeks. A few times since, they had made plans to get together, but either his job or hers kept intruding. Their busy schedules and her sore ankle had even kept them from their Saturday morning runs. They had texted, mind you, and each of his texts had been flirtier than the one before.

She nibbled her lower lip but couldn't squelch the smile that emerged. She had been confused at first when he put the brakes on their dalliance, but once he confessed why...that had turned her on more than ever. But it scared her too. Maybe that's why her attraction to Ronan was so intense. She was exhilarated and frightened by the possibilities at the same time.

He wanted more than a quick hookup, but what if she wasn't prepared to give him that? What if she wasn't even capable of more? The night of the episode in the elevator, she'd lain awake alone in bed and started to freak out about how they would handle things once they got back home. Talking herself off the ledge had been easier then, knowing they had three whole weeks to sort things out. But now that time had evaporated.

So much for that stupid plan.

While Maddy was excited about the wedding, she would be lying if she didn't admit that she was mostly looking forward to seeing Ronan again. Of course, that also meant going home for the first time since Rick had died. Ugh. Her stomach twisted in a knot as guilt swelled, immediately squashing her excitement. She was a conflicted mess. One minute she couldn't wait to see Ronan, and the next she was listing all the reasons why she should stay away from him. Keep him in the friend zone:

1. Getting involved with him was too intense and fraught with complications.
2. It was too soon after losing Rick.
3. His job was too dangerous.
4. Her heart couldn't take another beating.

But still…

The elevator doors slid open, and Maddy trudged forward along the carpeted hall toward her office suite. She pushed the door open and was met with the familiar sounds of the staff members at work. The four assistants were clacking away on their computers, and the office doors of the agents were all closed, except for Drummond's. Maddy rolled her eyes. He always kept his open, and she was convinced it was so he could ogle any attractive women who might be in the vicinity.

She hoped to slip by without having to deal with him.

"You look like shit."

No such freaking luck.

"When was the last time you got any sleep?" Coffee mug in hand, Chris Drummond leaned in the doorway to his office. "Been keeping late hours?"

Maddy puffed the hair from her eyes and adjusted her massive shoulder bag before shooting him a strained smile and continuing toward her corner office. Unfortunately, he followed her. He wasn't wrong, and that was more annoying than anything else. She *hadn't* been sleeping well, and how many of those sleepless nights she lay awake thinking about Ronan, the wedding, and the trip she couldn't avoid?

The answer: Most of them.

"I hope that's not how you greet your clients, Chris." Maddy smiled at her assistant. "Sharon, can you come into my office in about fifteen minutes? I want to go over the plan for while I'm away. Bring me everything on the New Year's Eve party RSVPs as well, and make sure the caterer has been read in on everything. Okay? I may stay in Old Brookfield a few days longer than I originally planned, so the timeline will be a bit tight."

"Sure thing, Maddy." Sharon's smile faltered when she looked past Maddy. Her shy gaze flicked back to the papers on her desk. "Good morning, Mr. Drummond."

"Hey, babe." Chris sat on the edge of Sharon's desk. "You're looking lovely this morning."

Maddy stopped short in her office doorway and turned slowly to face the increasingly offensive broker.

"Her name is Sharon," Maddy said overly politely. "It's right there on her desk. See the nifty nameplate? It's Sharon. Not 'babe' or 'honey' or 'sweetie.' Got it?"

"Whoa." Drummond held up one hand as if in surrender before sipping his coffee. He wore his usual slick-looking gray suit and was perfectly manicured, but none of that hid his glaring sense of inadequacy. "Sorry, *Ms. Morgan*. I was only being friendly. Speaking of which, I'll RSVP to your big New Year's Eve bash now. You can put me down for one, *Sharon*."

"Really?" Maddy's eyebrows flew up in mock surprise. "I'm shocked you don't have a date. A man like you must be beating them off with a stick."

"I *could* bring a date," Chris said, rising to his feet from the edge of the desk. "I choose not to. It is a business gathering, is it not?"

"It is," Maddy said smoothly. "But it's also a party. Brenton, Susan, and Maureen are bringing their spouses. I extended the same courtesy to the unmarried staff, but feel free to fly solo. I've invited all of our clients, including the brand-new ones, so there will be plenty of people to mingle with."

"What about our fearless leader?" he asked, referring to the owner of Cosmopolitan Realty. "Will Terrence and his wife be there?"

"No. They'll be in Milan. Remember? They go to Italy every Christmas to see her family."

Maddy went to close the door to her office, but Drummond pressed his hand against it and held it open. Now he was really starting to piss her off. The man who had been mildly irritating was turning into a full-fledged creep.

"What about you?" He sipped his coffee again and peered at her over the rim. "Will you be bringing a date? If not, we could be each other's dates. Unless you're seeing someone."

She almost laughed out loud at the ludicrous nature of his suggestion. Ronan had said almost the same thing about the wedding, but her reaction to him had been far different. Then again, Drummond and McGuire couldn't have been more opposite if they tried.

"I'm not interested." Maddy rolled her eyes, let go of

the door, and headed back toward her desk. "Besides, you are well aware that there is a standard no-fraternization policy firmly in place within the company. Like most places of business. We've had this conversation before. I'm unclear why it needs to be repeated." She hung her coat in the closet on the far wall and shut the door with more force than she'd intended. "Secondly, who I date, if I date, and when I date is not, and never will be, any of your business."

"No need to get defensive." He sighed. Drummond strolled to the chair in front of her desk and sat down. "I just thought we could present a united front. You know, for the office."

"Right," Maddy said under her breath. "The answer is still no."

"How about another night then?"

She stood behind her desk, grateful for the distance, as she pressed her fingertips to the surface and returned his stare. It irked her to no end that she was having this conversation with him. Again.

"You aren't getting it, are you? We are colleagues, Chris. That's all. Since you don't seem to know when to quit, I'll repeat that the no-fraternization policy applies to *everyone* in the office. A fact you seem to forget. Repeatedly."

"Funny." Drummond stood up and leered at Maddy. "I didn't peg you for an uptight ice queen. Do you even like guys?"

Maddy was about to share some choice words with him when her assistant knocked on the open door.

"I'm sorry to interrupt." Sharon slipped past Drummond and handed Maddy a file folder. "Here are your updated client contracts."

"Thank you, Sharon." Maddy flipped it open and quickly perused the running list and immediately noted one name missing. "The Bartholomews aren't on here."

"I'm sorry, Maddy." Sharon shot a wary glance at Drummond. "I didn't—"

"They're working with me," Drummond said smugly. "The newlyweds? They came by yesterday, and you weren't here. I was. End of story."

Maddy was seething. She slammed the folder onto her desk. "You knew damn well they were working with me."

"You snooze, you lose."

"Are you for real? That is not how we do business here. Our way of operating doesn't involve stealing another agent's clients. You unethical son of a bitch."

"Screw ethics," Drummond scoffed. "This is business, and you're a sore loser."

"Drummond!" The sharp baritone of Terrence Sterling cut into the room.

The stunned expression on Drummond's face as he paled almost made Maddy laugh aloud. Chris turned around slowly, the sweat beginning to bead on his forehead, and faced their boss. Looking furious, Terrence stood in the doorway of Maddy's office glaring at Chris.

"Madolyn is correct. We have a code of ethics here at Cosmopolitan Realty—one that you seem unable to adhere to."

"Terrence, this is a misunderstanding," Drummond said with a shaky laugh. He glanced over his shoulder at her with a pleading look in his eyes. "Right, Maddy?"

"No." Maddy simply shook her head. "There's no misunderstanding. Terrence heard everything correctly."

"Drummond," Terrence barked. "In my office. Now."

"Don't bother." Drummond kept his stony stare locked with hers. "I quit, and I'll be taking my clients with me."

He stormed out of the office past Terrence, practically knocking over the distinguished older man.

"Check your contract, Mr. Drummond, and those of Cosmopolitan's clients," Maddy said calmly.

She moved slowly toward her boss and kept her eyes on Drummond. Chris stopped dead in his tracks but didn't turn around.

"When the Bartholomews signed those documents, they were committing to work with this company, *not* solely with you. The same goes for all of the clients you acquired here. And if you have a close look at *your* contract, you'll see a clear non-compete clause. Cosmopolitan Realty House clients are off-limits to you for at least the next twelve months. With Terrence's permission, I'll personally contact each of them and let them know who will be handling their files moving forward."

"Thank you, Madolyn," Terrence said quietly. "It's easy to see how you've advanced in my company so quickly."

"You bitch," Drummond said, seething. He spun around as his normally calm demeanor shattered. The facade had finally come down, and the real face of the man emerged. "I'll sue your ass off. All of you."

Maddy folded her arms. It was a defensive posture, but she couldn't let him see that her hands were shaking. Thank God her boss was such an ethical man. He chose people over money, which was exactly why Maddy chose to work for his agency.

"I'd like to see you try, Christopher." Terrence's voice was cold and steady. "Do you really think I built my reputation and my business by being careless? You can attempt to sue me, but you'll be wasting your time and energy. I have ironclad contracts. You're a good real estate agent, and so far, you have a decent reputation." He delivered a wicked smirk and quietly said, "I'd hate to see that change."

"Are you threatening me?" Drummond was shaking, and his hands were curled into fists. "What is this? Blackmail?"

"I'm sure you're aware that Terrence doesn't make threats he won't follow through on," Maddy said.

"If you go quietly," Terrence interjected. "I'm sure you'll find a new agency in no time."

"This isn't over," Drummond bit out.

"Madolyn, call security."

"Yes, sir." Maddy went to her desk and dialed the number with quaking fingers. "I need security up here, please. Cosmopolitan Realty. Suite 400. Mr. Drummond has to be escorted from the building. He no longer works here."

Before the call was over, Drummond had vanished from the doorway. Maddy collapsed into her chair with a shaking breath and hung up the phone just as Sharon appeared behind Terrence. The young woman looked as unhinged as Maddy felt, and she could still hear Drummond pissing and moaning down the hall in his soon-to-be former office.

"Madolyn, are you alright?" Terrence asked gently.

"Yes, sir." She nodded and fought to maintain her composure. "I'm sorry that—"

"Stop." He held up one hand and shook his head curtly. "You are not the one who should apologize. I should have let him go months ago."

Without another word, Terrence stepped out of Maddy's office and strode toward Drummond's.

"Are you okay?" Sharon asked, looking from Maddy to the hallway. She was fiddling with a pen and reminded Maddy of a frightened little girl. "Should I call security again?"

"No." Maddy sat back in her chair and gripped the armrests in an effort to maintain a calm facade. "Stay clear of him. He won't pull anything else with Terrence here. Rocket should be up here any minute," she said, referring to the behemoth who worked daytime security in the building. "I'm sure Drummond will calm down as soon as he sees Rocket's on the case. Leave my door open, and let me know as soon as security—"

The ding of the elevator floated in the air, the sound a reminder of the bells Maddy had heard during boxing matches. She scrambled out from behind her desk and stepped into the hall just in time to see Rocket, all six foot four inches of him, holding the elevator doors open for Drummond. He had stopped shouting but was muttering furiously under his breath, while still shooting a hateful glare in Maddy's direction.

"Thank you, Rocket," Maddy shouted. "I'm sorry for the trouble."

"Oh, you'll be sorry alright," Drummond barked at her as he stormed into the elevator. He went back to muttering when Rocket turned around and shot him a look.

"Anytime," Rocket said firmly. He nodded, and light

flashed off his smooth, bald head as he punched the lobby button. "And it's no trouble at all."

The doors slid closed, and Maddy breathed an audible sigh of relief. After dealing with that jerk, going to Old Brookfield didn't seem anywhere near as daunting as it had a little while ago. In fact, now more than ever, she wanted to see Ronan and that naughty grin of his.

"Are you okay, Maddy?" Sharon asked quietly.

"Yes. It's done."

Maddy gave Terrence a tight smile as he headed to his corner office.

"You will see to his client list, won't you, Madolyn?" Terrence called to her.

"Absolutely, sir."

"Do you still want to go over that party list?" Sharon asked. She had a notebook in her hands and was fiddling with the pen again. "Or should we do it later?"

"Let's hold off on that. Please pull Drummond's current client list and email it to me. All sales—active, completed, and pending. I want to beat the smarmy son of a bitch to the punch." Maddy gave Sharon's arm a reassuring squeeze and looked around at the rest of the staff who had gathered to watch the previous shit show. "Back to business, everyone."

Amid a flurry of whispers, everyone retreated to their respective desks, but Sharon remained next to Maddy.

"I think we should call a meeting before we close for the week," Maddy said quietly. "I'll clear it with Terrence. Check the booking calendar, and find a time when everyone is in-house. All brokers and support staff in the conference room... We should tie this up before the holiday. I leave bright and early on Saturday, so that only gives us today and tomorrow to put a bow on this mess. I'll be able to stay on top of everything else via email and so forth while I'm gone, at least. God bless the Internet."

With the suite quiet and calm once again, Maddy disappeared into the sanctuary of her office and closed the door tightly. Part of her, a really small part, wondered if she should be leaving town after all this, but she quickly shoved that notion aside. She had made a promise to Jordan, and there was no way on earth she would break it.

Besides, what could Drummond really do to her anyway?

⁓

Ronan tossed his toiletries bag into the suitcase and zipped it closed, the noise immediately capturing Bowser's attention. After assessing the situation and finding no imminent threat—or snack—the bloodhound settled his snout back onto his paws in his well-worn bed and drifted right back into sleep.

"Lucky bastard," Ronan groused. "I don't envy much about being a dog, but the ability to sleep on demand is pretty awesome."

He wasn't exaggerating either.

Thanks to the six different searches they'd executed over the past three weeks, Ronan *should* have been able to pass out at a moment's notice. But sleep had eluded him, which was a first. Ronan had been the king of the catnap; his brothers could be causing a colossal ruckus, and he would sleep right through it. Nothing kept him from his sleep. At least, that is, until a certain sultry brunette had gotten under his skin and into his head.

"Woman has me spinning," he muttered. "And now I'm talking to myself."

Ronan took his suitcase out by the front door of his apartment, and the phone in the back pocket of his jeans buzzed. He set the bag down and yanked the phone out to see his captain's number glaring at him from the screen.

"Damn it," he whispered.

He hit the Answer button with his thumb and took the call, at the same time walking to the kitchenette and grabbing a beer out of his fridge. He hoped like hell that they weren't about to catch a case. Technically he wasn't off the clock until tomorrow; if they needed him for a search tonight, he'd have to go.

"Hello?" Ronan lifted his shoulder and held the phone to his ear while quickly opening the beer. "This is McGuire."

He tossed the cap in the dingy, white garbage pail and leaned one hip against the counter, staring at the frosty bottle. No sleep, and if he was catching a case right now, no beer.

Damn it.

"The son of a bitch dropped another one," Captain Jenkins said flatly. "No ID yet. The body was found this afternoon along the Bronx River Parkway, right by the zoo, about a half mile from where they found the Bowman woman. Female. Same MO."

"A serial killer," Ronan murmured.

"You said it." Jenkins voice was tight with tension. "Feds are already here. They set up shop down at the first precinct. Those boys don't waste any time."

Ronan's gut swirled to the point of nausea. He

hadn't heard from Maddy since yesterday. She usually answered his text messages quickly, but so far, she hadn't responded to the one he sent last night. He squeezed his eyes shut and forced himself to stay focused and keep breathing. A moment later, he felt Bowser's warm, furred body as the bloodhound leaned all his weight against Ronan's legs in a comforting gesture.

That damn dog knew him better than most people.

"The vic. Age?" he bit out. "Hair color?"

"It's not your lady friend, McGuire," Jenkins said calmly. "Besides, I wouldn't call you with something like that. Jeez, man. I'd deliver that in person."

"You're sure?" Ronan's words were clipped. "It's not Maddy? You've never met her or seen her. How can you be sure?"

"C'mon, I do my homework," Cap said. "When you started acting like a monk, I had to find out who this broad was who could get you off the market. I seen her picture on that fancy realty house website. Anyway, this definitely ain't her. Your lady is a curly brunette, and the vic was a redhead and older, late forties. You said you wanted to stay in the loop. So…consider yourself looped."

"Thanks," Ronan said with a short laugh. He let out a slow breath and sat on his couch, with Bowser dropping right in front of him. "Sorry. I'm exhausted, and I guess it's starting to show."

"Good thing you're going on vacation, then."

"You said it." Ronan stroked Bowser's head. "We both need a break."

"Your lady friend gonna be there too?"

"Yes, Cap. Maddy will be there." Ronan shook his

head and smiled. "She's the maid of honor and I'm the best man. Our presence is required. The wedding's two days before Christmas, and I think she's staying on through the holiday too."

"Good," Jenkins said with a gravelly laugh. "Then be sure to catch her under the mistletoe. You been lettin' her run away from you long enough."

"Cap…"

"Alright, I'll stop breakin' your balls. You and Bowser have a good vacation, and I'll let you know if there are any other developments with the case. But other than that, I don't wanna see or hear from you until January second. Got it?"

"Yes, Captain." Ronan saluted and made a face at Bowser who practically rolled his big, brown eyes. "We got it. McGuire and partner signing off until next year."

Jenkins's guttural belly laugh could still be heard when Ronan hit the end button and tossed the cell phone on the cushion next to him. He ruffled Bowser's ears while he finally took a long-awaited sip of his beer.

"I don't know about you, partner, but I'm glad as hell that Maddy is getting out of this city for a little while. With any luck, they'll find the SOB doing this before we get back."

Bowser barked his agreement and trotted off to the bedroom. Ronan grabbed his cell to text Maddy. He debated mentioning the latest victim to her but thought better of it. The last complication Maddy needed before going back to Old Brookfield was worrying about that ugliness. No, she had enough on her plate with the wedding and facing the flood of memories that would undoubtedly swarm her when she got

back home. Besides, they didn't know yet if the latest
victim was connected—although Ronan's gut told him
she was.

Nope, he would keep it simple.

> See you tomorrow.

His thumb hovered over the keyboard for a moment
before he added:

> Last one to town buys the first round of beers
> at Skinners.

~~~

Ronan lay in bed for what felt like forever. He tossed
and turned, but sleep refused to come. He couldn't stop
thinking about Maddy and the latest victim, and to make
matters worse, she *still* hadn't texted him back.

He grabbed the spare pillow and punched it before
turning on his side and pulling it against him. Yeah, it
was pathetic to be more familiar with spooning a pillow
than a woman. He didn't *sleep* with women. His college
girlfriend had been the exception to the rule, mind you,
and the only girl he might have really loved. But after
that, he'd never fallen asleep with anyone. Nope, Ronan
was really good at sticking around for a little while and
then bailing out.

Then why the hell could he think of nothing else but
sleeping with Maddy? He screwed his eyes shut and
recalled her perfume, a tantalizing mix of fresh-from-
the-shower clean and vanilla. Damn, what he wouldn't
give to have her here next to him, to pull her soft, curvy

body against his and revel in the warm expanse of that lovely skin.

It wasn't about sex. Nope, that was a lie. It wasn't *only* about sex.

He wanted to discover every possible way to bring her pleasure, but his desires went beyond the physical. In fact, right now, he'd give almost anything to have her here with him. To simply hold her and feel her body rise and fall against his with the slow, steady rhythm of sleep.

A grin curved Ronan's lips. That would be the best sleeping pill ever.

The phone on his nightstand buzzed, the dim glow lighting up the room with the announcement of an arriving text message. Ronan grabbed it and squinted as his eyes adjusted to the brightness of the screen. A second later, a full-blown smile cracked his face.

> Sorry I didn't get back to u sooner. Crazed at work. Got an asshat fired. Couldn't sleep. Decided to drive out tonight. Looks like the beers are on u. Safe travels. C u tmrw.

Ronan texted back quickly.

> Sounds good. C u soon.

He flopped back in bed and pressed one hand to his bare chest, a smile still lingering on his lips. With his eyelids growing heavy, one thought drifted through his mind… Tomorrow couldn't come soon enough.

Chapter 9

THE DINING ROOM OF KELLY'S OLD BROOKFIELD INN WAS blissfully quiet when Maddy came down for her coffee. Since it was in her hometown, she had never stayed at the quaint New England inn before, but over the years she had referred countless prospective buyers there. The massive eighteenth-century colonial was on the edge of town at the end of Main Street, which made it the perfect location for potential residents to check out the storybook hamlet of Old Brookfield.

The original structure, a grand white colonial with black shutters and lovely flower boxes in the summer, had been built by the Kelly family in 1745. It had been updated over the years and passed on through the generations, keeping it in the family, until Imogene and Bob had turned it into a B and B in 1986.

The lace-covered dining table was set for twelve, and a festive holly arrangement rested at the center of it all. The entire inn was decorated from top to bottom for the Christmas holiday, including three differently themed trees. Though the smallest of them all, the dining room tree sat in the corner by the bay window and was covered in blue and silver bows amid a blanket of twinkling white lights. The tree blended perfectly with the shades of periwinkle, cobalt blue, and white that adorned the lush dining room. A fire crackled in the marble fireplace, giving the entire space a warm and welcoming feel.

Maddy went to the large antique buffet table along the wall and poured herself some coffee. Based on the untouched cups and saucers, she was the first guest downstairs. No big surprise there. She'd woken with the sunrise and wanted to take a run before the holiday shoppers were out and about. Facing her old friends and seeing the familiar faces from town would be both wonderful and gut-wrenching at the same time.

"Is that my Maddy?"

Imogene's sweet voice drifted through the sunny dining room. Maddy turned to see the older woman emerge from the kitchen with open arms and a huge smile on her face. She was wearing a well-used apron over a pink sweater and blue jeans, and her long, white hair was tied up in a bun. Surrounded by all the garland and holly, she fleetingly reminded Maddy of Mrs. Claus. The swinging door shut behind her with a whisper as she rushed over and wrapped Maddy in a hug.

"Hey, Imogene." Maddy fought the sudden swell of emotion when the older woman's arms curled around her. "It's great to see you."

"Honey, let me look at you." Imogene pulled back and squeezed Maddy's shoulders, while her bright-green eyes studied Maddy from head to toe. "My, my, my. New York City looks good on you, but I am pleased as punch to have you back home. We have missed you around here! Jordan is doing a fine job with the flower shop, and that new real estate agent lady is perfectly nice, but she's not you."

"Thanks," Maddy said shakily. She sipped her coffee to try to steady herself. "I have to admit, I've missed being here. I guess it's like that old saying goes, there's no place like home."

"Yes, indeed." Imogene nodded and gestured to the table. "Now, how about you have a seat and I'll bring you some breakfast. We have the full-court press today. Eggs, bacon, pancakes, sausage. You name it and it's yours."

"Oh, no, Imogene—thank you," Maddy said quickly, then took another gulp from her cup. "I'm just having some coffee before my run, but I'll definitely take you up on it afterward. In fact, I may have to increase my time today just to account for all of that food."

"Alright then. Breakfast is served until eleven, and we offer a light dinner from four until seven in the evening." Imogene wiped her hands on her apron before going about the table and straightening what looked perfectly straight. "But you know that, I suppose. Have you seen anyone else yet?"

"No." Maddy drained the rest of the coffee and looked for somewhere to put the empty cup, but Imogene swept over and took it from her hand. "Thank you. I, uh, got in kind of late last night. I'm sorry I disturbed you and Bob."

Maddy tightened her ponytail, and her cheeks heated when she recalled how Bob had come running to the door in his pajamas, tightening his robe.

"Oh, now, honey, don't you give it a second thought." Imogene laughed out loud. "It's his own damn fault. We knew you were coming home late, and that man was supposed to leave you the keys in the old milk box on the porch. I just sent him over to the market to pick up some more bacon, or he'd be out here now saying hello to you too. I swear." She waved one pudgy hand in the air. "It's a good thing we never had children. I can barely keep track of *him*."

"Rick was forgetful too," Maddy said with a small

smile. She caught Imogene's eye and saw sympathy there. "But when you love someone…"

"Amen to that, darling." Imogene grabbed Maddy's hand and gave it a squeeze. "He was a good man."

"He was." Maddy's smile grew. For the first time in a good long while, she wasn't racked with grief when Rick's name came up. Instead, there was warmth and fondness, even gratitude. "I was lucky that I had so many years with him. Married or not, we had a lot of fun. I suppose that's more than most people get."

"Oh, now, honey," Imogene said with a short laugh. "You are a sweet young thing. You can still get married and have a family. Take Gavin McGuire, for example. His poor mama *never* thought he'd settle down, and look at him. Next weekend he gets an instant family with Jordan and her girls. Carolyn is over the moon."

"I'm sure she is," Maddy agreed. "If she's even *half* as happy as Jordan and Gavin are, then she's probably ready to bust."

"You know who should watch out?" Imogene lowered her voice to a conspiratorial whisper. "Gavin's brothers. Mmm-hmm. Now that Gavin is tying the knot, Carolyn has a bee in her bonnet about getting all her other boys married off."

"Oh really?" Maddy could barely hide her amusement. "She's looking for brides for her sons?"

"Oh well, come on now." Imogene's cheeks turned pink. "I wouldn't go that far. It's just that she sees how happy Gavin is and, well, I suspect she wants that for the rest of them. They're all as handsome as God could make them, so it can't be for lack of opportunities. Those boys have always been like catnip for the girls."

"That's true," Maddy said quietly. Images of Ronan flickered through her mind. "Not an unfortunate-looking one in the bunch. But I think those McGuire men are married to their jobs."

"Oh please." Imogene rolled her eyes. "*All* men are married to something—chasing women, work, play, what have you…at least, until they find *the one*. Then all bets are off. Nothing turns a man around like falling in love with the right woman. The same goes for us ladies, mind you. Life and love are both meant to be shared. What sense is there in working or living if you have no one to enjoy it with?"

Maddy nodded her agreement, and her thoughts went to Ronan. He had quickly become the first person on her mind every morning and the last one she thought of at night. It was time to admit to herself that her fears of falling for Ronan were a day late and a dollar short.

She'd already fallen for him. Big time.

"Thanks, Imogene," Maddy whispered. She pulled the older woman into another big hug. "You have a knack for saying exactly the right thing at exactly the right time."

"Sometimes." Imogene laughed and patted Maddy's cheek. "But if you ask Bob, he'll say that I'm too meddlesome."

"No way." Maddy shook her head. "You know, after my mom died, you were like my surrogate mom. Honestly, not only for me. Imogene, you're like the town den mother. So thanks…for the coffee, the lovely room upstairs, and the years of great hugs."

Tears filled Imogene's eyes and her lips quivered, but the sound of footsteps coming down the stairs had her swiping them away. A family of four, the parents and two sullen-looking teenagers, came around the corner and into the dining room.

"It smells wonderful in here," the dad said.

As the family settled in at the table, Imogene put on her best smile and grabbed the coffeepot.

"You go on your run now, honey," she whispered. "We have a full house for the holidays, but I'll be sure to save some for you. The food will be here when you get back…and so will I."

Maddy gave her a quick kiss on the cheek and headed out for her run. She pulled on her gloves and the wrap to cover her ears and fleetingly wondered if she should have added another layer.

The moment she stepped into the chilly December morning, she noted the stark difference between the air in Old Brookfield versus Manhattan. There were no choking fumes of car exhaust, and the dank odor of old garbage was missing. Instead, there was only the crisp, clean scent that was a combination of bread from the bakery down the road and a hint of salty ocean air. The streets were quiet, and while a few cars drove past, there were no blaring horns or screaming cabbies.

It was slower here.

Peaceful and welcoming.

She trotted down the front steps of the wraparound porch and walked toward the center of town. She had been greeted by the twinkling array of Christmas lights that were on almost every tree in town when she drove in last night. The massive towering pine in the little park by the town hall was decorated as it always had been, but for some reason, it looked even more spectacular than she remembered. Maybe it was because she had lived there for so many years; after a while, she had stopped appreciating the beauty that surrounded her.

Distance and time had given her a whole new perspective.

Her car had been the only one on the street last night; she'd pulled in close to midnight, and at that time, most of Old Brookfield was asleep. She must have sat in the car staring at that tree for close to twenty minutes, and the entire time she had questioned her decision to leave town.

A pang of regret had swelled when she thought about going back to the city.

Maddy started to do some stretches on the park bench but stilled when the firehouse caught her eye. Rick was gone. That part of her life was over. Ronan had been absolutely correct; she had been using Rick's death as an excuse. She'd left Old Brookfield last year to try to escape her grief, but of course, she couldn't run from it. She had done a damn fine job of compartmentalizing it and putting it away, but that couldn't make it disappear. Moving to the city merely allowed her to grieve alone, which was what she had wanted at the time. She hadn't wanted to burden anyone else or be the grieving girlfriend that people looked at with abject pity.

So what now, smarty-pants?

As Maddy took off on her run, she played that question over and over in her mind. Imogene was right. Life and love are both meant to be shared, and only one person in Maddy's world could possibly fit that bill.

Now all she had to figure out was how to go about it.

A smile played at her lips as she turned the corner

by the flower shop. It was a good thing she had Jordan to lean on for dating advice because while Maddy was great at business, she sucked at all the girlie stuff. She had a sinking suspicion that Jordan would be more than happy to oblige.

"Gavin, you have to have a bachelor party," Ronan said incredulously. He dropped his bags on the floor of the kitchen, and Bowser sat next to him. "Tristan, Finn, and Dillon are all coming home on Wednesday, and we've already got everything planned for that night. The wedding isn't until Saturday, and the bachelor party is totally on the up-and-up."

"Oh man," Gavin groaned. "No strippers or any of that crap. Please."

Ronan's big brother closed the refrigerator door in the spacious yellow-and-white kitchen of their childhood home before placing the carton of milk on the granite counter. He looked happier and more at ease than Ronan had ever seen him. A major part of that had to be because of Jordan.

"It's good to be home," Ronan said with a heavy sigh.

He'd missed moments like this more than he cared to admit. The plate of cookies, their mother's famous oatmeal chocolate chip, were still warm from the oven, and he'd smelled that delectable aroma before even stepping foot in the house. He had planned on bringing Bowser out to the cottage first, but that smell had made his stomach rumble, and he'd had to investigate.

Ronan sat on the stool while Bowser gave him that mournful, watery-brown gaze.

"You're not getting any of these cookies." Ronan peered down at his partner. "I mean it."

The dog snuffled as though totally annoyed and lay down on the tiled floor.

"Are you sure that's a dog? He's as big as a horse."

"Yeah? Well, he thinks he's a person."

"You better get him out of here before Mom gets back." Gavin took one of the cookies and pointed at the bloodhound. "She's gonna flip if she finds out he was in her kitchen. She and Dad will be back any minute. They had to go into town to pick up her dress or something."

"I know." Ronan let out a heavy sigh. "I don't think she's really allergic to him, but his shedding makes her nuts. That's why we're staying out in the cottage. Speaking of which, I was surprised to find you in here. You and Jordan bought that place on the beach last year. What gives?" He grinned. "She sick of you already?"

"No, wiseass, we decided that I'd stay here during the week leading up to the wedding." He shrugged. "You know, throw some tradition into our untraditional situation. I'm staying in my old room, though, so you and Bowser can have the cottage while you're here."

"Thanks."

Bowser barked loudly and wagged his tail, still staring at the cookie in Ronan's hand.

"You can't have chocolate." Ronan ate the rest. "Cut it out. No one likes a beggar."

"I mean it," Gavin warned. He poured two glasses of milk and slid one over to Ronan. "About Bowser *and* about the bachelor party."

"Relax, Bro. It's not gonna be some kind of nudie bar scene."

"We don't even have a nudie bar in Old Brookfield."

"I know that. No boobs or babes at your party. Bros only." He wrapped three more cookies in a paper towel for later. "The five of us, lots of laughs, a bit of razzing, and beers. Probably, lots of beers. Besides, isn't Maddy taking Jordan out for some kind of bachelorette thing?"

"She is…" Gavin said slowly.

"For all you know, Maddy could get her a stripper," Ronan teased. "You know, one of those *Magic Mike* guys."

Ronan had only said it to razz Gavin, but instead, he ended up with an unpleasant image of Maddy dancing with some half-naked, greased-up muscle head.

"She would never do that." Gavin glowered momentarily but then paled a bit. "Would she?"

"She better not," Ronan muttered.

"It would be easy enough to find out." Gavin shot a glance at Ronan before putting the milk away. "Her little party is tonight. They're going to dinner and then drinks at Skinners."

Ronan recalled his last text with Maddy.

"Skinners, huh?"

"Yeah," Gavin said with a grin. "How about it? Wanna grab a burger and a beer later?"

"Are you suggesting that we spy on your fiancée and crash her party?"

"Not exactly." Gavin raised his eyebrows and leaned both hands on the counter of the kitchen island. "Besides, it's not really a party with only the two of them. But if we just happen to bump into them…what could be the harm in that? The girls are staying with Jordan's mom tonight, and it would be a shame to let babysitting like that go to waste."

"I do owe Maddy a beer," Ronan murmured.

"That so?" Gavin arched one eyebrow. "You two drinking buddies now?"

"No," Ronan said too quickly. "I mean, we're friends, but I wouldn't exactly classify her as a *buddy*."

"How would you *classify* her?"

Ronan stared at his brother for a solid thirty seconds.

"I have no idea," he said wearily. He ran his hand through his hair and let out a growl of frustration. "I mean, don't get me wrong, Gav. I do have ideas. Lots, and *none of them* put her in the buddy category. She drives me nuts. She's stubborn, brilliant, funny, and laughs at my dumb jokes. Bowser even likes her."

The dog's ears pricked up at the mention of his name.

"That's great," Gavin drawled. "I'm thrilled that your partner likes her, but what about you?"

"Me?" Ronan grabbed the paper-towel-wrapped cookies and stuck them in the pocket of his coat. "What's not to like? She's not only all the stuff I said before, but she's the sexiest woman I've ever known. I didn't think it was possible for her to get more beautiful, but she does. Every damn day she's prettier than the day before. She's full of surprises and doesn't take crap from anyone, including me. Her independent streak turns me on *and* frustrates me."

"So that's a *yes* to liking her?"

"Aw hell, Gavin, of course I like her," Ronan shouted.

He rose from the stool, grabbed his bags, and headed to the door that led out to the backyard. Bowser was at his heels, as usual. Frustration bubbled up as he fought through the tangled web of emotions he'd been attempting to identify for the past few months.

Emotions that had gotten too strong and pervasive for him to ignore.

"You want to know the truth of it?" He wrapped his hand around the doorknob but couldn't bring himself to look at Gavin. "I think I *love her* like her."

"Well, I'll be damned," Gavin whispered. "Could it be possible? Has the ultimate ladies' man finally found *one* woman he can be satisfied with? Weren't you the guy who said he'd settle for one woman when hell froze over?"

"I did say that, didn't I?"

"Yeah, a bunch of times." Gavin's smile faded. "Are you sure about this?"

"She's it, Gavin." Ronan let out a curt laugh. "I can't think about anything or anyone else. I'm hooked, man."

Gavin closed the distance between them, his expression serious. Outside of their brothers, Rick had been Gavin's closest friend, and Gavin felt particularly protective of Maddy. In some ways, he felt an unspoken sense of duty to make sure that his fallen brother's loved one was taken care of.

"Have you told her how you feel?"

"Are you kidding?" Ronan said with a short laugh. "I just figured it out for myself."

"Ronan, you're my brother and I love you, man, but…" Gavin paused for a moment as though choosing his words carefully. "Maddy's been through hell, and I don't want to see her get hurt again."

"I'd never do anything to hurt her, Gavin." Ronan squared his shoulders and leveled a deadly serious gaze at his brother. "Don't you know me at all? I just told you that I'm in love with her."

"Yeah, I know you better than anyone, and that's what worries me." Gavin's mouth set in a grim line and his brow furrowed. "Bowser has a longer attention span than you do, at least when it comes to romance. You and I both know that commitment isn't your strong suit. You've never been in a truly committed relationship before."

"Look who's talking," Ronan drawled. "You were practically a monk until Jordan came back to town."

"Come on, Ronan." Gavin sighed. "All I'm asking is that you tread lightly with Maddy. She puts on a tough front but…"

"I know," Ronan said firmly. "I won't hurt her, Gavin. In fact, I'm going to try to talk her into staying for Christmas."

"Jordan's been working on that too. And for the record, if you do screw up with Maddy, it won't be me you have to worry about pissing off." Gavin pointed at him. "It will be your future sister-in-law."

"I got it." Ronan held up one hand. "I'm as worried about me messing it up as you are. I feel like I've had my head up my ass ever since she came back into my life. I don't know which end is up. One minute I want to kiss the life out of her, and the next she frustrates the hell out of me. I don't know if I should scratch my watch or wind my ass."

"Welcome to the club, Ronan." Gavin laughed and clapped his brother on the shoulder. "That sure sounds like love to me."

Chapter 10

MADDY PEEKED IN THE WINDOW OF THE FLOWER SHOP THAT had once been owned by her mother and now belonged to her oldest and dearest friend. Jordan was busily restocking pink roses in the refrigerated flower case on the far left wall, and it looked like she'd been doing it her entire life.

Still sweaty from her run, Maddy almost didn't stop, but she and Jordan had so much to catch up on. She suspected that Jordan would take a sweaty hug now rather than wait. Maddy was about to go inside when the swinging door at the back of the shop opened and Jordan's two adorable little girls came scurrying out, papers clasped in each of their hands.

Her heart clenched in her chest when Lily and her little sister, Gracie, went running to their mother to show her the pictures they had drawn. Maddy had always wanted children but Rick hadn't, and she'd never pushed it. Then again, she hadn't pushed about getting married either. They had both been happy with the status quo, but seeing Jordan with the girls again stirred up Maddy's maternal instincts. Maybe Imogene was right; maybe there was still time.

What if Ronan…

Maddy blinked and shook her head. What the hell was wrong with her? She had to shake off these ridiculous thoughts and focus on Gavin and Jordan's wedding.

That's why she was in town. She was here to support them—not to hook up with Ronan.

Liar, whispered a tiny voice.

She yanked open the door and jumped into the little shop with a flourish. Jordan and her girls spun around in shock, but their looks of surprise were swiftly replaced with outright joy.

"So, who's ready for a winter wedding?" Maddy shouted as she jutted both thumbs at her sweaty chest. "This girl is!"

"Maddy!" Jordan shrieked. She ran over and practically tackled Maddy with a giant, bouncy hug. Lily and Gracie joined in, one on either side of the two women. "I'm so glad you're here!"

"Me too." Maddy laughed. She released Jordan and bent at the knees, pulling both girls into her arms before letting go and looking them up and down. "Now, when did you two go and grow up? I've only been gone a year, and you practically look like teenagers."

"Nu-uh." Lily shook her head furiously. "I'm only eight and three-quarters, and Gracie is six and a half. Mama and Daddy Gavin told us we aren't allowed to grow up too fast."

"Six and a half," Gracie repeated, holding up six fingers.

"Those halves and quarters are super important, aren't they?" Maddy rose to her feet and smoothed Gracie's unruly blond hair. "But once you get to my age, you start to round down, not up."

"Girls, why don't you go clean up the crayons and hang your pictures on the corkboard? Meemaw will be here in a few minutes to take you to her house. I heard that she set up a playdate for you—her friend's grand-children are in town as well."

"Hooray!" The girls squealed before disappearing into the back room.

"They're gorgeous, Jordan. With you as their mother, that's no big shocker."

"Thanks. They're a couple of spitfires, alright. They keep us on our toes."

"Still no sign of your ex?" Maddy asked, referring to Jordan's asshole of an ex-husband. "Has he tried to see the girls at all?"

"No." Sadness edged Jordan's eyes for a moment. "We haven't heard a word from him in months. He called once or twice after he got out of rehab, but then… nothing. It's probably better that way. The child support shows up on time, but that's about it as far as contact goes. Honestly, Gavin's been more of a father to them in the past year than Ted *ever* was. The girls are happy. If they ever want to see him, I'll help them do that—but for now…we aren't rocking the boat."

"Some people shouldn't have kids." Maddy shrugged. "But you and Gavin aren't among them. Your girls are awesome, Jordan. Are they excited for the wedding?"

"Are you kidding? They try on their dresses every night before bed. Speaking of which, you and I have fitting appointments on Monday. Your dress came in, and Zipsie wants to make sure the fit is right," she said, referring to the bridal shop owner.

"Yes, ma'am." Maddy saluted her dramatically. "Maid of honor reporting for duty."

"You're a lifesaver, you know." Jordan settled her hands on her hips and smiled before going back to the refrigerated case. "I can really use the extra pair of hands."

"Where are Cookie and Veronica?" Maddy glanced behind the counter. "I don't hear their usual banter from the back room."

"They're dying to see you, but they're setting up two weddings today. Business was strong before, but now with the online orders? Forget it—it's totally nutsy."

"Online?" Maddy followed her and held the door to the case open while Jordan finished what she had been doing. "Get out of here! You started an online ordering service?"

"Yup." Jordan lifted one shoulder and her cheeks flushed. "It seemed like a natural next step. It has tripled our wedding business."

"That's amazing, Jordan." Maddy studied her friend closely, and her heart clenched. "You're really something else, you know that? Man, talk about a woman who has flourished."

"I owe a lot of it to you." Jordan closed the door tightly and grabbed Maddy's hand. "You were the one who encouraged me to come home after Ted and I split up. If I hadn't done that, then I wouldn't have this place and I definitely wouldn't be marrying Gavin."

"Get outta here." Maddy rolled her eyes and waved her friend off, trying to hide the sudden surge of emotion. She went over and fiddled with the little figurines on the stand at the center of the store. "All I did was give you a little push. After all, isn't that what friends are for?"

"True." Jordan went to the computer at the counter. Another new addition since she'd taken over. "Hopefully I can return the favor."

Maddy leveled a narrow-eyed gaze at her friend. "Like how?"

"I dunno," Jordan said all too innocently. She tapped on the keyboard quickly. "How was Thanksgiving?"

"I knew it!" Maddy pointed at her and let out a loud laugh. "Ronan blabbed to his brother."

"Only a little." Jordan held up two hands as if in surrender. "He *might* have mentioned that you two had dinner together, and he *may* have referred to it as a date."

"Mmm-hmm." Maddy folded her arms over her breasts and cocked her head. "Anything else?"

Had he blabbed about their little elevator liaison as well?

"No." Jordan shook her head slowly. "Guys don't talk about the juicy stuff the way we girls do." She glanced over her shoulder quickly, obviously making sure her kids weren't lurking, and lowered her voice to a whisper. "So, cough it up, Maddy. Did the man live up to his nickname?"

"You know what? He did." Maddy wagged a finger at her friend and backed toward the door of the shop. "The guy can talk. 'Motormouth' is wildly appropriate."

"You're no fun." Jordan stuck her tongue out.

"Ha!" Maddy yanked the door open, the little bell at the top announcing her departure. "You won't be saying that after our bachelorette night out. Which is tonight, by the way."

"I know. The girls are staying over at my mother's so that I can sleep in tomorrow. I'm looking forward to our evening, believe me! And then *you* can tell me all about your date with Make-Out McGuire."

"I'll pick you up at seven. And, Jordan?" Maddy had

her body out the door but her head sticking in the shop as she whispered, "He lives up to that nickname too."

The door closed on Jordan shrieking "I knew it!" and the grin on Maddy's face widened. She laughed loudly as the door shut behind her. With her heart full of joy and the long-forgotten feeling of hope, she headed back to the inn. For the first time in ages, she was looking toward the future instead of the past.

———~~~———

Ronan sucked in a deep breath and took a moment to revel in the clean, fresh air of his hometown while Bowser hopped out of the front seat of the truck and onto the pavement. As usual, all of Main Street was like one giant Christmas village. Old Brookfield definitely knew how to deck the halls.

He stuck a couple quarters in the meter as a family hurried past him, all bundled up against the cold. The father carried the little boy on his shoulders, and the mom held the girl's hand. A pang of longing flared in Ronan's chest, and he rubbed his fingers against it as though that might make it subside.

What the hell was that?

Ronan gathered Bowser's leash around his hand and walked toward the market behind the picture-perfect family. He'd never given much thought to children or marriage, but lately it seemed like no matter where he turned, that's what he saw. *What's the deal with that?*

He must have seen thousands of families in the city in his years on the job, and he'd never really paid them much attention. But for the past couple months, almost every laughing little kid and smiling parent caught his eye. It was exactly like when he'd bought his truck. All of a sudden, it seemed like everyone and their mother had that same make and model. Only now it wasn't trucks he was acutely aware of, it was families. For the first time in his adult life, Ronan imagined having one of his own.

He shook his head and let out a sigh. *Oh man. I've got it bad.*

The light turned when he and Bowser reached the corner. They stood patiently waiting, but the sound of a familiar laugh caught his attention.

Maddy.

She was walking along the sidewalk on the other side of the street, leaving the flower shop behind. Visiting Jordan, no doubt. She was decked out in her running gear, and her arms were swinging at her sides as she kept a brisk pace. Ronan almost called out, but he was enjoying the view too much to interrupt her. It had been a good long while since he'd seen her look as carefree as she did right that second, and he didn't want to do anything to disturb that.

Ronan squatted down and draped his arm over Bowser, who was also watching Maddy grow smaller in the distance.

"So, what do you think, partner?" Ronan ruffled the dog's ears and kept his voice low. "Any chance a fine woman like that would put up with two slobs like us?"

Bowser turned and licked Ronan's mouth.

"I'll take that as a yes."

He wiped his face with the back of his hand and rose slowly to his feet, watching Maddy disappear up the steps of the inn. Ronan reached in his back pocket and pulled out the page he'd pilfered from his mother's *Better Homes and Gardens Cook Book*—the same one that Maddy's mother had used for her apple-pie recipe. He unfolded it and checked the list of ingredients for the pie and crust.

"Let's go, man. We have groceries to stock up on and a tree to buy."

With his partner by his side, Ronan jogged across the street to the market and started putting his plan into action. It was time to make some new traditions, and with any luck at all, he would be making them with Maddy.

"To a great meal and an even better friend!" Maddy raised her wineglass and clinked it lightly against Jordan's. "And happily ever afters."

"Hear, hear." Jordan smiled and sipped her wine.

The brand-new Asian fusion restaurant in neighboring Southington, the one with the drag queen theme, provided the perfect spot for Jordan's little bachelorette outing. The atmosphere was fun and lively, and the food rocked. Their waitress, Charisma, was a stunning drag queen with the most epic blue Mohawk that Maddy had ever seen. As with all of the waitresses at Diva Changs, she sang when taking their order or delivering it. Since Jordan was a bride-to-be, Charisma had just finished belting out the chorus of "Chapel of Love."

"Girlfriend can sing," Maddy exclaimed.

Charisma winked, and her purple sparkly eyelashes glinted in the light before she strutted off with their empty plates.

"I love you, Maddy," Jordan said, laughing. "Thanks

for taking me out tonight and for coming into town early to help me out."

"Hey." Maddy lifted one shoulder. "Isn't that what a maid of honor is for?"

"This place is awesome!" Jordan giggled and waved at one of the performers. "I'd heard so much about it but never made it over here."

"Yeah, well, we would have been on time for our reservation if my stupid GPS hadn't glitched up like that." Maddy sighed. "I'm going to need a new one, which is annoying because I just bought that one."

"God bless technology," Jordan said with a small smile. She rested both elbows on the table and peered at Maddy over her folded hands. "Alright, I've been going on and on all night about the wedding, the shop, my girls, and Lord knows what else."

"And this is a problem because…?"

"Really?" Jordan tilted her head and gave Maddy that *Are you for real* look. "Spill it, sister. What is going on with you and Ronan? And don't try to tell me it's nothing, or you're only friends, because I know you well enough to know that isn't true. Besides—you already admitted that you kissed him, and last time I checked, you don't go around kissing random guys."

Maddy's smile faded, and an all-too-familiar knot of nerves coiled in her belly. Guilt and uncertainty swirled as she fought to put a name to what was happening with her and Ronan.

"I don't know what's going on with us," she said with an exasperated sigh. "I'm conflicted and feel like a big, fat, stupid mess."

"How so?"

Jordan sipped her wine again, and her expression remained curious. There was no judgment, not a whisper of accusation. Maddy let out the breath she had been holding, and the ball of tension in her chest slowly eased as her friend's warm brown eyes met hers.

"It's okay, Maddy," Jordan said quietly. "Tell me."

"I feel like I'm betraying him," Maddy murmured.

"Who?" Jordan's brow furrowed with confusion. "Ronan?"

"Rick," she whispered.

"Oh, Maddy." Jordan reached across the table and gathered Maddy's hand in hers, squeezing it tightly. "Honey, it's okay to move on and live your life. Rick would want you to be happy, wouldn't he?"

"Yes." Maddy nodded and swallowed the tears. "But he's only been gone a year... I keep thinking it's too soon. Well, my head tells me it's too soon, but every other part of my anatomy is primed and ready. I want Ronan more than I've ever wanted any man in my whole damn life. I feel like a teenager with overactive hormones or something."

"You do remember hearing me go on and on about Gavin, don't you?" A knowing smile curved Jordan's lips. "I get it. Trust me."

"We haven't even done it yet, but..." Maddy let out a growl of frustration. "To say that I'm confused would be an understatement. I feel guilty for being crazy attracted to him and for wanting to be with him so soon, but at the same time, I can't stay away from him or stop thinking about him. I'm basically at war with myself. I sound crazy, don't I?"

"No, you don't. It's understandable that you would

feel this way, Maddy. You and Rick were together for *years*. I mean, you guys were basically married, in spirit if not on paper."

"He didn't want to, you know," she whispered. "Rick didn't want to get married or have children."

Jordan's expression grew grim and she nodded.

"The job." Maddy smiled and lifted one shoulder. "He was married to it, and I even told people that I felt like his mistress. The job always came first, and I understood; I really did. We never even talked about getting hitched, you know? It was this unspoken agreement. His dad died fighting a fire when Rick was little, and he never wanted to do that to anyone else."

"I know."

"But he did die," Maddy said firmly. "He died and left me and everyone else who loved him behind, and I just don't know if I can go through something like that again."

"You mean with Ronan?"

"He may not be a fireman, but he is a cop. The guy puts himself in harm's way all the time." Maddy held up both hands. "I get it. It's part of the gig. But I don't know if I can be part of something like that again."

"Okay," Jordan said slowly. "Then why make it all so serious? Ronan isn't exactly known for his lengthy relationships. Why not just have some fun with him?"

"Believe it or not, I tried. *He* wouldn't go for it." Maddy folded her arms over her breasts, feeling a little embarrassed to admit the truth. "He told me that I'd been keeping him in the friend zone, and he wasn't settling for the friends-with-benefits category. He wants more."

"Come *on*." Jordan's eyes grew wide. "You're

seriously telling me that Ronan 'Make-Out' McGuire turned down no-strings-attached sex?"

"Yes." Maddy's cheeks flamed. "That's exactly what I'm telling you. But…it's not entirely on him. I was bluffing. I can't do no-strings sex either. I'm not wired that way. No matter how much I might want to be. But I can't stop thinking about him. It's like I'm obsessed! It's not only sexual. He's thoughtful, kind, funny, self-depreciating, *and* seeing him with that damn dog just about melts my heart. And even as I sit here telling you all of this, I feel like I'm stabbing Rick in the back. I know he's dead and he's never coming back, but still…"

"No wonder you're confused," Jordan murmured.

"Throw in a couple of murders and getting a psycho real estate agent fired, and you've got yourself a good old-fashioned clusterfuck."

Maddy sipped her wine, and silence fell between the two friends as Charisma delivered their dessert. She must have sensed the change of mood at the table because she didn't sing this time.

"I'm sorry. That sounded awful." Maddy ran both hands through her curly hair in an effort to soothe her swirling emotions. "But it's been an absolutely insane month."

"Gavin told me about the girl from your office and that other woman." Jordan pushed the strawberry around on her plate but hadn't touched her cheesecake yet. "I hope you're taking precautions. It sounds like some nut ball out there has it in for real estate agents in New York City."

"I am." Maddy nodded and glanced at her chocolate cake, which suddenly looked less appealing. "In addition to the handy-dandy Mace you and Gavin gave me,

Ronan read me the riot act about trusting my gut and everything. I'll be fine."

"We worry about you, you know."

"I know," Maddy said with a small smile. "But I've been doing this for years, and I can handle myself."

"True." Jordan's smile grew. "And you have your own personal NYPD K-9 officer as backup."

Maddy let out a cynical laugh and shook her head, leveling a serious gaze at her friend.

"What should I do about this thing with Ronan? Am I being silly or overly dramatic? Am I overthinking it? I've been out of the dating pool for so long that I have no idea what I'm doing. Part of me wants to jump in with both feet, and the other part is terrified to let go."

Jordan sat back in her chair and folded her hands in her lap. The expression on her face was serious, and Maddy could tell that she was searching for the right way to present a tough question.

"Let me ask you something first." Jordan opened her mouth and closed it again before finally saying, "If Rick *had* asked you to marry him, would you have said yes?"

Maddy stilled. Nobody had ever posed that question to her before. Her knee-jerk reaction and the publicly expectable response was *absolutely*. But she said nothing. Maddy sat quietly and looked away from Jordan, unwilling to admit the guilt-laden truth.

"No," she whispered. "I don't think I would. Maybe that's why we never spoke about it. I didn't bring it up, and neither did he, at least not directly."

"Why?" Jordan asked gently. "I know you loved him, and he adored you."

"I know." Maddy pressed her fingers to her lips, and

Rick's smiling face came to mind. "He was my best friend. We loved each other, you know? But maybe we weren't *in* love. It was comfortable and safe. Neither of us wanted to take the leap to marriage and kids, and we were both absorbed by our careers. I feel bad for even telling you this because I don't want to tarnish his memory or take away from what we had, but it's the truth."

"Every relationship is different, Maddy. What you had with Rick was special because it was between you and him. It's not worse or better than what you could have with Ronan—or anyone else, for that matter. It's simply *different*. Wouldn't it be weirder if you felt exactly the same feelings for Ronan that you had for Rick?"

"I guess... I mean... You're right. My feelings for Ronan are different. It doesn't take away or change what I had with Rick."

"Exactly," Jordan said gently. "Now, if you can wrap your head around that, let's tackle the next part. Why are you shutting out a possible future with Ronan? You seem set on not even entertaining the idea."

"Because the crazy, intense feelings for him, physical and otherwise, scare the shit out of me," Maddy said in a quivering voice. "Losing Rick hurt like hell, but I survived it. I'm terrified that if I let myself go there again, if I explore these out-of-control emotions, that there will be no turning back. It's like looking into a giant abyss. There's no end in sight. There's no bottom to the well, and if I allow myself to fall in..."

"He'll catch you," Jordan whispered. "But you have to trust him, and you have to trust in yourself. That's love, my friend—leaping into the mighty unknown because your heart overtakes your mind. That's what life is all about, but we can't and don't do it alone. Give Ronan a chance, Maddy."

Maddy nibbled on her lower lip. "You don't think it's too soon?"

"Last time I checked, there was no limit on how many people we can love in our lifetime, and there's no rule saying how long to wait between lovers." Jordan grabbed her purse and rose from her seat. "I'm going to the ladies' room, and when I get back, let's head over to Skinners. Word has it that my fiancé and his best man might be there."

"Sounds good." Maddy grabbed Jordan's hand before she walked away. "Thank you."

"Anytime." She bent down and kissed Maddy's cheek. "Can I add one more thing since you're so hot on my advice at the moment?"

"Sure." Maddy laughed.

"The only choice you'll regret is *not* giving him a chance." Jordan's voice lowered to just above a whisper. "If you don't, if you walk away from this possible future with Ronan, then you'll never know what could have happened. Wouldn't not knowing be worse than anything else?"

Maddy replayed that question over and again in her mind while she waited at the table for Jordan to return. The answer kept evading her. Would she let her fear override any chance at a future with Ronan, or would she choose to take the leap?

Chapter 11

Ronan and Gavin had polished off their burgers, fries, and a couple of beers at Skinners, but there was still no sign of Jordan and Maddy. It was well past nine o'clock, and Ronan was starting to wonder if maybe they *had* gone off to find a stripper. He considered texting her, but he didn't want to push his luck. Instead, he and Gavin sat at the bar watching the sports commentators blather on about the upcoming football game, and Ronan tried desperately not to look at his phone.

The front door of the pub opened and Ronan glanced up, but it wasn't them. A college-age couple came in and immediately went to the back of the bar. A huge group of kids, obviously home for the holidays, had taken over the two pool tables. The jukebox had been going all night, but now that they were past the big dinner rush, the volume was getting progressively louder.

"Can I get you boys another round?" John Skinner, the pub's owner, smiled and pointed at their almost empty glasses. "On the house."

"Not me," Gavin said. "I'm driving. I'd love a water."

"I'm not driving and I'm on vacation. I'll take you up on that beer." Ronan drained the rest of his glass and slid it to John. "Thanks, man."

"Where's that dog cop of yours?" John asked as he drew the beer from the tap. "Bozo? Bulldozer?"

"It's Bowser." Ronan shook his head and smiled.

"He's back at the cottage at my parents' place. We're both off duty, and he's probably snoozing on that huge sofa in the living room. I think he's enjoying this vacation as much as I am."

The sound of the front door opening captured Ronan's attention again, and this time when he looked up, he found himself staring across the room at a familiar pair of bright-blue eyes.

"They're here," he murmured.

Ronan waved and gave Maddy a big smile just as Jordan leaned in and whispered something to Maddy. Whatever it was, it made her cheeks redden, and she swatted at her friend before both of them broke into giggles. The two women wove their way through the bar crowd toward Ronan and Gavin. The closer Maddy came, the harder Ronan's heart started to pound, blood rushing in his ears. It was a wildest feeling in the world to be this excited to see another human being.

Maddy sidled up next to him, and Jordan went to sit beside Gavin, but Ronan hardly noticed. All he could see was *Maddy*. Ronan shifted on the bar stool to face her and found himself at a loss for words. Her fair skin was flushed and her blue eyes glittered brightly, reminding him of ice.

But that was Maddy all over, wasn't it?

Ice infused with fire.

"Hey," Maddy murmured. "Fancy meeting you here."

Ronan was about to respond but was interrupted by John.

"Look who it is!" John shouted. He gave Ronan his beer. "Maddy Morgan! When did you get back into town, little lady?"

The older man, as tall as Ronan but twice as wide, reached over the bar and pulled Maddy into a quick bear hug.

"The city girl has returned," he said with a gritty laugh. "For good, I hope?"

"Sorry, John." She shook her head and took off her coat and gloves. "I'm here for the wedding, and then it's back to the city."

"Not even staying through Christmas?"

"Uh…I'm not sure." Maddy ran one hand through her lovely curls. "I'm staying at the inn, and they're closed from the twenty-fourth through the first week of January. So, I may as well head back."

Ronan's smiled faded. Why would she go back to the city and be alone for Christmas? Hell, no.

"None of my business, I suppose." John waved one hand and smiled broadly. "What can I get for you ladies?"

"I'll have a glass of pinot grigio," Maddy said as she sat on the recently vacated seat next to Ronan. "Thanks, John."

"Nothing for me," Jordan said.

Ronan and Maddy both turned to look at the soon-to-be newlyweds. Jordan still had her coat on and was snuggled up against Gavin. He had his arm around her, and when he looked at Ronan, he shrugged.

"I think we're gonna head out." Gavin tossed money on the bar and smiled lovingly at his fiancée. "I'm beat."

"Me too." Jordan sighed. "Maddy, thank you for an amazing dinner, but I'm gonna call it a night. I'll see you tomorrow at my mom's place. Right?"

"Yeah, the seating chart and stuff." Maddy's brow furrowed and she flicked a glance at Ronan. "Um…I guess I'll see you tomorrow. You want me to drive you home, Jordan?"

"I'll take care of Jordan." Gavin winked. "But since I drove, that means you'll have to take Ronan home."

"How 'bout it, Mads?" Ronan took a sip of his beer and peered at Maddy over the rim of his glass. "Can you give me a lift?"

"I'm sure we'll figure something out," Maddy said quietly, her gaze not leaving his. "Besides, Ronan and I wouldn't want you two to waste the overnight baby-sitter situation."

"And that, ladies and gentleman, is why she's my best friend." Jordan kissed Maddy on the cheek and then Ronan. "Have fun, you two."

Gavin and Jordan made a quick exit, but Ronan kept his attention on Maddy.

"They planned this, didn't they?" she asked, a smile curving those beautiful lips.

"That's probably a fair assumption." Ronan rubbed the condensation off his glass with his thumb. "Is that so bad? Getting stuck here with me?"

"No."

Maddy crossed her legs and shifted toward him, which momentarily allowed their bodies to touch. Even that brief contact was enough to make him take notice. John brought Maddy her wine, and instead of making his usual chitchat, he made himself scarce. Ronan could have kissed the old man for that.

"Are you really going to leave before Christmas?" He sipped his beer again. "I thought you were thinking about staying."

"Jordan asked me to stay, but I don't want to crash

their first married Christmas." Maddy leaned one arm on the bar and sipped her wine. "Going back to the city was the plan."

"It's a dumb plan."

"Gee, thanks." She laughed.

"I have a better one." Ronan turned his gaze to hers. "Stay."

"I-I can't." She nibbled her lower lips. "Imogene and Bob close the inn for Christmas Eve and Christmas and go to their condo in Florida until the first week of January. They do it every year."

"Come have Christmas with me and my family."

The words were out of his mouth before he'd even fully thought it through. The idea was crazy, but at the same time, it felt absolutely right.

"All my brothers will be there. Plus Jordan, Gav, and the girls are coming for dinner, and Jordan's bringing her mom as well. It's not like it'll just be me and my fathead brothers."

Maddy stilled and her eyes widened. Ronan wasn't certain if he saw fear there or surprise, or maybe both—but he could practically see the wheels spinning. Oh shit. He was losing her.

"Hang on," he added quickly. "You don't have to stay with me out at the cottage. I mean, even with everyone home, my parents will have two open bedrooms. There are plenty of beds. If that's not cool, I'm sure you could crash with Jordan and Gavin."

"Oh, right." Maddy gave him a doubtful look. "And hijack the newlyweds? I don't think so. I know the girls will be there, but it's still kind of their unofficial honeymoon."

"See?" Ronan tipped his glass toward her. "You should do what I suggested and stay at my parents' place. It's only for two nights. Christmas Eve and Christmas. Besides, if my mother finds out that you're planning to go back to the city and spend the holiday *alone again*, she'll offer this to you herself. *Then* if she thought that I didn't offer…she would flip out on me. So, technically, if you come stay with us for Christmas, you're doing me a favor and saving my hide."

"Is that so?" Maddy laughed and shook her head. "McGuire, you are way too much."

"I'm serious." Ronan pressed one hand to his chest. "If you care about me at all, you do not want the wrath of Carolyn McGuire to be unleashed on me. It's not pretty."

"I find that hard to believe." Maddy tucked her curls behind her ear, and Ronan had to resist the urge to help her. "Your mother is as sweet as they come."

"Yeah?" he scoffed. "Well, she also raised five boys, and there's no more than eighteen months between each of us. It was organized chaos at our house for over twenty years. You don't survive that kind of environment with your sanity intact if you can't open up a can of whoop-ass every now and then."

Maddy studied him as though weighing her options, and for a minute, Ronan was sure he'd made a mistake. He clenched the glass, and his heart beat so hard he was sure she could hear it ramming against his rib cage.

"I'll think about it," she murmured.

"Good. That's all I ask." Ronan let out the breath he was holding. "Well, that's a lie. I'm gonna ask you something else."

"Okay," she said warily.

Ronan leaned close so that his face was only inches from hers and their knees bumped. Her eyes widened and her nostrils flared with an unmistakable whisper of desire. The pulse in her throat quickened beneath her creamy skin, and he had the overwhelming urge to kiss it, to lick and nibble at the tender spot until she begged him not to stop. His gaze skittered over her face, lingering for a moment on that beautiful mouth. Even though all that Ronan could think about was getting another taste of her, this was neither the time nor the place.

Then with all the seriousness he could muster, Ronan asked, "When was the last time somebody kicked your ass at darts?"

"Yes… Wait…" Maddy blinked. "What?"

A grin slowly curved his lips. God, he loved surprising her.

"Darts." Ronan stood up and caught John's eye. "Just the check, man. Thanks."

"Got it right here." John slid the paper over, and Ronan made quick work of settling up. "That last round was on me."

"Unnecessary but much appreciated." He grabbed his coat, which he'd been sitting on. "Come on. It's time for me to school you. But I promise I won't be a sore winner."

A sly smile covered her face. Maddy slid from the seat and draped her coat over her arm. She inched closer, so that her body brushed his. The soft, pink sweater she wore hugged her breasts, and when it swept against his bare forearm, Ronan stilled.

"You seem pretty confident about this, McGuire," Maddy whispered. She drew in a deep breath, the movement pressing her breasts against him harder for one delicious second. "Are you willing to put a wager on it?"

"I really wouldn't want to take advantage of you, Mads," he said playfully.

"See?" Maddy shook her head and made a soft *tsk*ing sound. "Now that's a damn shame."

"What is?" Ronan laughed.

"Maybe I want you to take advantage of me," she whispered before slipping past him toward the dartboard.

Ronan was rendered speechless as all of the blood rushed from his head to other parts of his body. Maddy tossed her coat over a chair by the dartboard and reached in the pocket for something. When she bent forward, he got an excellent view of her backside. And what a fine view it was—round, firm, and covered by a pair of black jeans that barely contained her beautiful bottom.

A second later, she'd pulled out a hair tie and slung her mass of curls up into a messy bun. She grabbed the darts from the board and pushed her sleeves up before taking her place on the white line. She lined up her shot, and in less than one minute, the woman threw three perfect bull's-eyes, one right after the other.

Maddy settled her hands on her hips, tossed her head, and winked at him over her shoulder, then headed off to retrieve her magic darts.

"Holy shit," Ronan whispered.

"She's something, isn't she?" John's voice drifted over his shoulder. "The Skinners dart team held the champion title in the league every year Maddy was on it. I guess you didn't know that."

"No." Ronan's mouth set in a firm line.

Gavin's warning fired through Ronan's mind. *Take it slow.*

He and Maddy might have known each other since high school, but apparently, he still had plenty to learn about the woman he'd fallen hopelessly in love with.

Ronan spent the next two hours getting his ass kicked at darts and loving every minute of it. Maddy matched every surprise he had up his sleeve, and then some. He might not know what was coming around the corner or what the future held, but whatever it was, he wanted Maddy to be a part of it.

Chapter 12

RIGHT BEFORE LAST CALL, THEY STEPPED OUT INTO THE frigid evening air, and the shock of it stole Maddy's breath. She hugged herself and fought the shiver that had already begun. That didn't help—her trembling wasn't only from the cold. She was a bundle of nerves, turned on as all get-out. She had been brazenly flirtatious all night, probably thanks to the dangerous mix of liquid courage and the safety of the crowd. Maddy could bluff with the best of them, and she had acted like she had everything under control, flirting her butt off with Ronan. But she didn't have anything under control at all.

Though it had been devilishly fun to kick his handsome ass at darts.

"I'm supposed to drive you home, aren't I?"

"I don't think so, Mads."

Maddy rolled her eyes and dug through her enormous purse for the car keys. She wavered on her feet and stumbled forward, but Ronan caught her before she could fall. His strong hands curled around her biceps and helped her regain her footing. Maddy pressed one hand against his chest, while the other stayed stuck in her huge bag. The wool of his coat rasped against her cheek, and his woodsy, soapy scent floated around her.

"You smell good," Maddy murmured. She lifted her head and smiled back at the amused look in his eyes.

"I'm so glad people can't smoke inside anymore. Back in the day, we'd leave Skinners and everyone reeked of it. Not anymore. Ronan McGuire, you smell like the woods at night."

"That so?" His eyes crinkled at the corners, and he let out a gruff laugh. "I have no idea what that smells like, but I guess I'll say thanks."

"You should," she whispered. "It's a compliment."

Maddy tugged her hand from her purse and curled her fingers around the lapels of his coat. Her toes bumped his and she pulled him closer, then rolled up on the balls of her feet and nuzzled her face against his throat.

"Earth and snow," she murmured. Her lips brushed against the warm flesh of his throat, and his fingers tightened around her arms. "I think that's it...or maybe it's the air. Whatever it is, I like it."

Maddy giggled and pulled back so she could look him in the face. His gaze was as sharp as ever, more gray than green in this light, and Maddy felt the impact deep in her belly. She sucked in a shuddering breath and glanced at his lips, stifling a groan. All she wanted was to have that talented mouth all over her body.

But nothing broke a sexy moment like a case of the hiccups.

A second shrieking sound popped from her lips. Mortification of the highest order flooded her, and her hand flew to her mouth.

"Ohmigod." Maddy giggled through her fingers. "I have the hiccups."

"So I hear. Gimme the keys." Ronan held his glove-covered hand out and waggled his fingers at her. "You aren't driving, Mads."

She dropped her hands and straightened her coat, tilting her chin in the air defiantly. "I'm not drunk. I'm a little tipsy and…I'll admit that I probably shouldn't drive."

"Probably?" Ronan arched one dark eyebrow as he grabbed the purse strap slung over her shoulder and pulled her close. "Try *definitely*."

"What about you?" she murmured. "Why aren't you a little *tipsy*?"

"Me? I wish I were. Then I'd have an excuse for why I sucked so bad at darts." A smile bloomed. "I stopped drinking a few hours ago, right after you tossed those first three bull's-eyes."

Maddy hiccupped loudly. Her body pressed against his and he leaned down, his face precariously close to hers. Maddy's eyes fluttered closed as she waited for a kiss, but none came. Instead, something tugged and shuffled in her huge shoulder bag.

She flicked her eyes open to find Ronan dangling her keys in front of her face.

"Got 'em," he said with a self-satisfied grin. "Come on, Mads. It's late. I'll get you back to the inn, and then I'll grab a cab home. I saw the schedule of stuff Jordan has planned this week, and you girls are gonna be busy."

Ronan hit the unlock button on her remote. The car's alarm chirped briefly, and the lights on her BMW convertible flashed across the parking lot. Disappointment fired through her as they walked to the car. She'd thought, she'd *hoped* that they'd take this *thing* between them to the next level. Tonight had evolved into the perfect opportunity. They'd had a great time and now they were alone—but still he didn't try anything.

Like the gentleman he was turning out to be, Ronan opened the passenger door for her before jogging around to the driver's side. She stole a look or two at him during the brief ride back to the inn, but he kept his eyes on the road and both hands on the wheel. To call her feelings "confused" would have been a massive understatement.

They parked the car and Ronan walked her to the front steps of the inn, but Maddy moved slowly. She didn't want the night to end yet, despite how imminent that ending seemed.

"It's beautiful, isn't it?" she asked wistfully.

The town usually looked like it had been plucked out of a Norman Rockwell painting this time of year, but the inn in particular was storybook perfect. Little white lights were wrapped around the porch rails and twinkled brightly in the crisp evening. Both the huge Christmas tree in the living room and the smaller one in the dining room could be seen through the front windows on either side of the graceful front door. To cap it all off, smoke curled up from the chimney, and the scent of a wood fire permeated the air.

They stood together at the foot of the steps for a moment, neither one saying a word. This. This situation right here was exactly the kind of awkward, weird dating stuff Maddy didn't know how to handle. He'd had plenty of opportunities to kiss her in parking lot or in the car, especially once her hiccups had stopped.

Except he hadn't.

"You're home safe and sound." Ronan gave her back the keys and stuck his hands in the front pockets of his jeans. "Thanks for tonight, Mads. I've never had so much fun getting beat by a girl."

"I should be thanking *you* for driving." She folded her arms over her breasts and tried to squelch the over-whelming sense of embarrassment. She was sobering up by the second. "I don't usually overindulge—to be honest, I kind of forgot that I had to drive."

"See that?" Ronan winked. "City life is rubbing off on you already."

"Maybe," she murmured. Maddy bit her lower lip and nodded toward the door. "Do you, uh, want to come in for a nightcap?"

"No," he said quickly. Too quickly. Ronan jutted a thumb over his shoulder. "I'm gonna call a cab and head home. Bowser's been in that cottage alone for about five hours, and I'm sure he needs to go out."

"Of course." Maddy nodded and grabbed the railing. "Right, sorry. Good night."

Before he could say anything else, she ran up the stairs and quickly went inside. Maddy didn't look back. She didn't even stop to see if Imogene or Bob were down-stairs. She was embarrassed and confused, and all she wanted to do was dive into that four-poster bed upstairs and go to sleep. Maybe tomorrow, after her head was clear, she'd feel better about how the night ended.

Then again…maybe not.

⁓

The week had flown by with almost preternatural speed, and Ronan had barely seen Maddy since Saturday night. Their paths had crossed a few times, sure, but with all the wedding preparations and dress fittings or whatever, he'd hardly had a glimpse of her. He kept telling himself it was better that way. It sure didn't feel better.

In fact, Ronan missed her more than he'd ever expected.

That, and he felt shitty about the way their night had ended. His body had screamed *hell yes* when she'd asked him up to her room for a drink, but his brain and an unfortunate dose of common sense had taken over. Gavin's warning kept nagging at him. Maddy was in a fragile place, and she'd had one too many drinks. He wouldn't have been able to stop with a few kisses. So instead, he'd opted for nothing. He hadn't even bothered to get a cab home, the long, freezing walk serving as the proverbial cold shower.

Ronan had a pretty solid feeling that Maddy was pissed at him. There had been no more flirty text messages, and the few times they bumped into each other, she'd kept the conversations short. The fire had been doused and only ice remained.

Damn it all.

He was screwing everything up, and he didn't know how to fix it. He had obviously sent her the wrong message the other night, and he had to straighten things out. Fast.

Ronan glanced at the clock in the kitchen of the cottage. He still had half an hour before he had to leave for the rehearsal at the church. At least Maddy wouldn't be able to avoid him there, and he could make sure she knew where he had been coming from.

Maddy being pissed at him wasn't the only thing on his mind—her safety was as well. If he couldn't get her to stay in Old Brookfield for Christmas, she would be going back to the city alone. His thoughts immediately went to the case, and within seconds, he had dialed the captain's number.

Ronan hit the speaker button and placed the phone on the kitchen counter while he tied his tie. Jenkins picked up on the second ring.

"You son of a bitch," Jenkins barked. "You're supposed to be on vacation."

"I miss you too," Ronan said sarcastically. "Any new leads?"

"You know how those fed boys are." His captain let out a snort of derision. "They don't like to share."

"Shit."

Ronan checked the tie in his reflection on the stainless-steel fridge. Still crooked. He undid it and attempted a better knot.

"But you know that don't mean much to me," Jenkins scoffed. "I got connections. Remember Robinson? He used to be on K-9, but he's over in the first precinct now, and he's been keepin' me in the loop."

"Right," Ronan said, recalling the older man's name. "You two were pretty tight."

"Still are."

"So no new vics?" Ronan tightened the knot of his tie. "Still just the three?"

"No more yet but..."

"There will be," Ronan finished for him. "Listen, Cap. Maddy might be heading back to the city and—"

"I told you that I'd tell you if there was any news, McGuire, and I meant it."

"Thanks, Cap."

He was about to hit End when Jenkins said, "You seal the deal with your lady friend yet?"

"*Good-bye*, Cap."

Jenkins's gritty laugh was cut off when Ronan ended

the call. He couldn't squelch the grin that bubbled up because if everything went as he hoped, the deal would be sealed by Christmas.

"How do I look?" Ronan held out his arms and looked at his partner.

Bowser snorted and trotted out of the kitchen.

"Way to give a guy a confidence boost," Ronan called after the bloodhound. "Some partner you are. Just for that, no doggy bag from the rehearsal dinner."

Ronan grabbed his overcoat and headed for the door. If he could get to the church a little early, maybe he could clear the air with Maddy before the night got rolling.

Ronan scanned the parking lot for her car and blew between his hands, rubbing them together to warm them up.

"Ronan!" Gavin's voice pulled him from his private pity party. "Come on, man. We gotta get inside. We're starting in ten minutes."

Gavin stood at the bottom of the steps of the small, white church with an impatient look on his face. Tristan, Finn, and Dillon rounded the corner from the parking lot, their mom and dad right behind them. His mother made a face at Ronan—the same one she used to give him as a kid when he was about to get in trouble—and waved him over to join them.

"Shit," he said under his breath. Then "Coming!"

He took one last look around before following his family into the church.

His mother held the door and waited for him. She took his arm and smiled when he kissed her soft, round cheek.

"Thank you," she chirped, then gave him the classic *Mom look* as they stepped into the vestibule. "What's going on with you? You're not still sulking about Bowser not being allowed in the house, are you?"

"No, Mom." Ronan let out a sigh and clasped his hands in front of him. "I'm not sulking about Bowser. I'm fine."

"No, you're not." She patted his arm and laughed lightly. "You have that way about you."

"What way is that?" He helped his mother out of her coat and hung it on the rack along the right side of the vestibule.

"When you were a little boy, you would get so frustrated and sullen when you couldn't figure out the answer to a riddle or problem. I suppose that's why you became a police officer. You've had that same sullen, moody thing going for the past few days. Even your brothers have noticed."

"It's true," Tristan piped up. He reached behind Ronan and hung up his leather jacket. "You've been no damn fun at all this week, even at Gavin's bachelor party. Not cool, Bro. Not cool."

"Yeah," Dillon added. "And no strippers. What kind of bachelor party doesn't have at least *one* stripper?"

"Lots of beers but no boobs," Finn interjected.

"I should hope not!" Their mother swatted Dillon's arm and lowered her voice to a harsh whisper. "Boys, we're in church, for heaven's sake. Try to control yourselves."

"Carolyn!" Ronan's father called from the doorway that led from the vestibule into the church itself. "It's time to get this show on the road, darlin'! Jordan and the girls are here."

Ronan flicked his gaze to the doorway and briefly caught Maddy's eye. Her black wool coat lay open, the bright-red dress she wore beneath it peeking out. The color was perfect against her alabaster skin, and her dark curls were loose and free, just the way he liked them. She looked away and immediately went to help one of Jordan's daughters with her coat.

She was definitely avoiding him.

"Ronan?"

His mother's hand curled around his and broke the spell.

"Yeah." Ronan let out a short laugh and shook his head. "Sorry, Mom. What were you saying?"

"Just that I'm confident you'll figure it out." She followed his gaze to look at Maddy, and then a knowing smile covered her face before she turned back to him. "Sometimes the answers are simpler than we imagine, and are right in front of us the whole time."

"What do you mean?"

"I *mean*, don't make it more complicated than it needs to be. Life is hard enough." She patted his cheek quickly. "Be honest and open with your feelings, Ronan. The truth is the fastest way to get a solution."

Looking into his mother's earnest green eyes, the knot of concern and stress in his chest started to loosen. She always had a knack for making him feel better and putting life in perspective.

"Can all moms do that?" he asked, his eyes narrowing. "Make it okay with a few words?"

"Yup," she said brightly. "You get that superpower when you have your first baby."

"Mother of mine?" Finn asked as he and his twin

brother, Dillon, flanked her and offered their arms. "Dillon and I have been told that we'll be walking you down the aisle."

"Then let's get a move on." She gave Ronan a knowing look. "No point in wasting time."

While everyone was getting their instructions about where to go and what to do, Ronan kept his eyes on Maddy. Minister Wallin went over the order of the ceremony step by step, but Ronan barely heard a word. He stood by Gavin's side at the altar and waited until it was time to walk down the aisle with Maddy. At that point he'd have a captive audience.

After what felt like forever, he finally had his chance.

"Ms. Morgan?" He stepped into the aisle and offered her his arm. "It seems I'm your escort for the next twenty-four hours. You know. The whole 'best man and maid of honor thing.'"

"Really?" Maddy's eyebrows rose, and she kept her voice to a whisper. "Well, I hope that won't be too torturous for you. I hear that a few available young women are attending the wedding. As best man, you should have your pick."

"Is that so?" Ronan placed his hand over hers as it rested on his arm. He leaned closer and purposely slowed his pace. "Can I stake my claim now, or is it customary to wait until the reception?"

A look of confusion flickered over her beautiful face, and she gave him an icy glare. Maddy squared her shoulders, and that determined chin tilted upward in a gesture of defiance. Holy cow. He had been kidding, but she was serious. Maddy thought that he was interested in chasing other women?

"Don't ask me." She lifted one shoulder. "You can do whatever you like. I'm sure you'll have plenty of opportunities to try your charms on the ladies. And don't worry—I won't get in the way or give anyone the wrong impression about our *relationship*."

She tried to pull her arm away when they reached the end of the aisle, but he held her hand in place. Her body tensed and she shot him a look, but Ronan escorted her to the back of the vestibule by the coats. Nobody seemed to notice, since everyone was still listening to the minister as he gave the final recap.

Ronan inched his way backward into the corner and pulled Maddy with him.

"Let go," she said in a harsh whisper.

"No."

"Ronan," Maddy warned, "we're supposed to be listening to the minister's instructions."

"We walk down the aisle together. Smile for the camera, and get in the limo. *We* aren't the show tomorrow. Jordan and Gavin are." Ronan kept his voice quiet so only she would hear. "I think I can handle the gig. It's clear."

The minister glanced at the two of them briefly but continued speaking to the group gathered at the back of the church. She was right. They probably should go stand with everyone else and listen, but this was more important at the moment.

"But something else *isn't* clear, Mads."

Her body stilled against his, and he leaned close so that he could whisper in her ear. Ronan curled his fingers around hers, still resting on his arm, and he tightened his grip, afraid she'd run away.

"When I dropped you off at the inn the other night, I wanted to kiss you."

Maddy turned her face toward him slightly, and her warm breath, minty and sweet, puffed across his chest. He could feel her body tense and pull almost imperceptibly closer to his. He had a sinking suspicion she was holding her breath. Ronan licked his lower lip and fought to keep his voice quiet and calm, in spite of the way he was spinning inside.

"Then why didn't you?" Her voice wavered.

"Because I wouldn't have stopped with a kiss."

A soft sigh, a tantalizing sound laced with pleasure, escaped her lips. Her lashes lifted and those blue eyes danced before meeting his. Ronan cupped her cheek with his free hand and brushed his thumb over her lower lip, his gaze flicking there briefly.

"You'd had a few drinks," he whispered.

"Ronan, I wasn't drunk," she said quietly. "I was totally—"

"When I take you to bed, Mads, and please understand, I have every *single* intention of doing that, I don't want there to be any excuses about why it shouldn't have happened. No morning-after loopholes or simple ways to explain it away."

Maddy's cheeks flushed, and her eyes widened with every passing word.

"So you can forget about me chasing any other women at the wedding—or any place else, for that matter. Unless you tell me to get lost and get the hell out of your life, you're stuck with me." He pressed his lips to the warm skin of her forehead and murmured, "I was trying to be a good guy, to dispel my hound dog image, but I still ended up making you think I'm a jerk."

"Well, you *are* kind of a jerk," Tristan said flatly.

Ronan, who had been completely absorbed in his own little world with Maddy, looked up to find the vestibule almost totally empty. The group was gone, and only Tristan remained. Maddy laughed, the light and playful sound floating around him and tugging at his heart. Ronan pulled her into his arms and kissed the top of her head.

"Oh man." She elbowed Ronan and turned to the coatrack. "Some maid of honor I am…too busy canoodling with the best man to help the bride."

"Canoodling?" Tristan was the middle kid and loved to stir the pot. He flashed a sly grin at Maddy. "That's what that was?"

"Tristan," Ronan said in a warning tone. He gave him a playful shove toward the door. "Thanks for the heads-up. We'll be right behind you."

"I have my motorcycle outside and an extra helmet." Tristan pulled on his well-worn leather bomber jacket. "You need a ride to the restaurant, Maddy?"

"Sorry, Tristan." She gave him the side eye. "It's a little too cold out for my taste."

"Don't knock it until you try it." He winked and zipped up his coat. "See you kids at Luca's."

"*Bye*, Tristan."

Ronan shot his brother a look, but the man just laughed as he went outside.

"While my truck isn't as cool as Tristan's Harley, I can offer you a warmer ride."

Ronan extended his hand, which she accepted with a smile.

"Great, because Jordan drove me here in her car. So it's either you or that Harley."

Ronan pushed the heavy wooden door open with his shoulder and held it for her. "No more excuses, right?" she said as she brushed past him.

"Right." Ronan nodded and trotted down the steps with her hand in his. "None."

"Good." Maddy's grin grew, and she let out a slow, sexy sigh. "Because tonight, we aren't stopping with a kiss."

Ronan groaned and his heart thundered in his chest as the heat of her palm seeped into his. It was going to be a long dinner.

Chapter 13

MADDY MADE IT THROUGH HER TOAST AT THE REHEARSAL dinner without crying and considered that a small victory. Even so, she still couldn't completely escape the tears. Seeing Jordan and Gavin together—finally, after all these years—was exquisite. They barely took their eyes off each other, and if they did, it was to tend to Lily and Gracie. Though Maddy had to admit that sitting next to Ronan at the table was more distracting than she'd expected it to be.

His leg would brush hers from time to time, and at various points, he draped his arm over the back of her chair in an easy, familiar gesture. Once in a while, he shot her a sly glance or a cheeky wink full of seductive promise. It felt like they had a dirty, naughty secret just between the two of them, which got her pulse racing.

Ronan's three brothers were at their table, along with Bill, a firefighter in Gavin's squad, and they certainly kept the conversation lively. Maddy hardly noticed she was the only woman at the table because they treated her like one of the boys. Except for Ronan, whose hand had drifted under the tablecloth and was currently curled over her knee.

Maddy stilled while she sipped her wine, though she was careful not give anything away to the others at the table. Not even when he slowly but surely pushed the hem of her skirt up and wrapped his hand around her inner thigh. His thumb brushed over her skin with slow, tantalizing strokes, giving her a taste of what was surely to come.

Ronan tightened his grip before leaning over and whispering, "Do you have any idea how much I want you?"

His long, strong fingers bore down a bit harder into the soft part of her thigh, and his breath tickled hot over her neck, heightening her arousal. Maddy settled her wineglass on the table before gathering up her small evening bag and scooting her chair back.

All of the men at the table stood when she did, and the sight was almost comical.

"If you'll excuse me, gentlemen." Maddy gave them all a small smile. "I'm going to check in with our bride and groom before calling it a night."

Maddy went over to see Jordan, hoping that Ronan would get the hint and follow her. Jordan was snuggled up next to Gavin, who had Gracie on his lap. Lily was chattering away with Carolyn and Charles, as usual.

"Hey, girl." Maddy kissed her friend's cheek. "You ready for tomorrow?"

"Are you kidding?" Jordan asked with a huge smile. "I've been ready since the day I met him."

"I have a Christmas special present for Mama and Daddy Gavin," Gracie chimed in. "It's a surprise. I asked Santa to bring it."

"Is that so? Your Uncle Ronan is a big fan of surprises too," Maddy said, her eyebrows lifting in response. "But he doesn't give hints. How about you? Any hints?"

"Nope." Gracie giggled. "I didn't even tell Lily or nuffin'!"

"Or anything," Jordan corrected her daughter.

"Or anyfing," the little girl exclaimed.

"I bet they'll love it no matter what it is, Gracie."

"Are you gonna have Christmas wif us, Aunt Maddy? Uncle Ronan said you might." Gracie's gap-toothed grin widened. "Don't worry. Santa will know how to find you 'cause he knows everyfing."

"Yeah, Maddy?" Gavin asked, a knowing smile on his face. "Will you be having Christmas with us?"

Maddy let out a small laugh and shrugged at the same moment she caught Carolyn McGuire's knowing gaze. It was plain to see which of his parents Ronan took after. He had his mother's eyes and, it would seem, her inquisitive nature.

"Oh, yes," Carolyn exclaimed. "I do hope you'll be joining us for the holiday. Ronan tells us that you were planning on going back to the city, but I simply won't hear of it. You must stay! The guest room on the third floor is quite private and even has its own bathroom."

"Thank you so much, Mrs. McGuire, but—"

"Ah-ah," she scolded playfully. "It's Carolyn, and I really won't take no for an answer."

"She's not lying," Charles McGuire chimed in. "My wife is persistent, like a dog with a bone."

"Hush, now," Carolyn said, elbowing her husband.

"Tunnel vision," Maddy murmured.

"I see you've heard of it." Carolyn brightened and pointed over to the table with her sons. "They all suffer from it, but Ronan most of all."

Maddy looked over her shoulder and was met by Ronan's handsome smile. He had obviously been watching the whole exchange and probably had heard it all too. She narrowed her gaze and shot him a playful look.

"He has a good dose of it," she said quietly. "That's for sure."

All of them were grinning at her in one way or another by the time she turned back to the table, and she obviously wasn't going to be allowed to go without giving them her answer. What *did* she have to go back to? An empty apartment and a closed office weren't exactly the most festive of locations.

That old real estate adage flickered through her mind—*location, location, location*.

"So whaddya say, Mads?" Ronan's deep voice rolled over her as he sidled in and slipped his arm around her waist. "Christmas with the McGuires?"

"And," Jordan interjected, "it's supposed to be a white Christmas this year. They're calling for snow, but hopefully not until *after* the wedding."

"A white wedding and a white Christmas? How can a girl say no to that?" Maddy sucked in a deep breath and took the leap. "Absolutely. I'd love to but only if Carolyn lets me contribute to dinner. I make a mean apple pie."

"Perfect!" Carolyn clapped her hands together before casting a loving look at her husband. "This might be the best holiday yet. All of my boys are home; we have a new daughter and two instant grandchildren! Now if I could only figure out how to get the rest of you to move back to town, I'd be all set."

"They could always use an experienced cop like Ronan in the Old Brookfield police department," Gavin said with a sly smile.

"Bowser is an NYPD K-9." Ronan held Maddy a bit closer. "But who knows? Maybe after he retires, I'll relocate."

"Now, don't you tease your old mother with an idea like that unless you mean it," Carolyn interjected.

"Maybe, Mom." Ronan peered at Maddy and winked. "The future is the big unknown."

"Well, I can't have Christmas dinner be the big unknown," Carolyn said with a laugh. "While I have you all here, let me make sure I know who's bringing what."

As everyone started chatting about what they would contribute, Ronan whispered into Maddy's ear again. "What's it gonna take to get you out of here and have you all to myself?"

"I thought you'd never ask," she murmured.

After saying a quick good night and giving them all kisses, Maddy assured Jordan that she'd be at the cottage on time first thing tomorrow to help everyone get ready. Best of all, no one made suggestive comments or implied anything when she and Ronan left together. Part of her had expected comments, but to her relief, if anyone suspected what the two of them were up to, they didn't say it out loud. Thank goodness for that. Despite her bravado earlier, Maddy had devolved into one big bundle of nerves.

Even as they left together, she was still trying to figure out this thing between her and Ronan. And all of her feelings about it. Everyone at that table had known and loved Rick, and she'd been part of *MaddyandRick* to all of them for the better part of a decade. She knew it was silly to feel like she was betraying him somehow, but that didn't make the thought any less real.

There was no doubt about it. Maddy was ready to take it to the next level with Ronan, physically and otherwise. But she hadn't *been* with anyone other than Rick for more than a decade. All of a sudden, that bravado she'd felt back at the table was gone, and all she had left were apprehension and anticipation. What if she wasn't what Ronan was expecting? Or what if she freaked out in the middle of it?

They got in the car and Ronan pulled out of the parking lot, but he turned left, instead of right toward the inn.

"Where are we going? If you're planning an adventure, don't try using GPS. I tried using mine the other day and it got me totally lost. The damn thing is all screwy. Technology and I aren't friends lately."

"No GPS needed for what I have in mind," he said quietly. "I know the way."

"Ronan?" Maddy set her small purse next to her on the edge of the seat. "You look like the cat that ate the canary… What's going on?"

"I'm taking you back to the inn, as promised." Ronan laid his hand on her knee again. "But we're gonna go the long way."

A shuddering sigh escaped her lips as he inched his hand higher up her inner thigh. Opting for no stockings had been a good choice; maybe she'd even done it in the subconscious hope that he would do exactly what he was doing.

"Open your legs for me," he rasped.

Maddy licked her lower lip and did as he requested, laying her head on the headrest. It was wanton and erotic to have him touch her this way while driving through the dark streets of their hometown. While the likelihood of anyone seeing what was going on was small, the risk remained—and that was part of the turn-on.

"Wider, baby. Don't hide from me."

She obliged and parted her legs as far as the car would allow. The skirt of her dress drifted higher as Ronan's hand disappeared beneath. Her breathing quickened as his talented fingers brushed the edge of her panties before rushing over the heat of her sex. She let out a gasp when he applied pressure to her most sensitive spot. Her hands flew to the edge of her seat as her body arched and zings of pleasure shimmied beneath her skin.

"That's it, Mads," Ronan said. His deep voice, quiet and powerful, filled the car and surrounded her completely. "I want you to let go. Just close your eyes and feel me. Don't think. Don't try to control it. All you have to do…is feel."

She'd closed herself off for so long, too afraid to feel anything because grief had been her most recent bedfellow. Grief, pain, and emptiness, an ache so great she believed it could have swallowed her whole. Until Ronan McGuire had come back into her life. He would never let anything hurt her. The man was born to protect those he cared for. With Ronan's hands on her body and his seductive words in her heart, she finally felt safe enough to let go.

Maddy shuddered and her eyes fluttered closed as Ronan found the top edge of her thong and slid his hand beneath. He cupped her sex but didn't move further. Was he teasing her? No way. She'd waited long enough and needed more.

She tilted her hips, urging him to do what he *knew* she wanted.

As though reading her mind, Ronan slid one finger between her slick folds, rubbing slow, tantalizing strokes over her. She moaned and allowed herself to fall into the sweet waves of pleasure that built higher with every stroke. The orgasm coiled deep and began to crest, but when he pressed two fingers deep inside her, adding pressure to exactly the right spot, she came apart. The bright climax racked her body in spasm after spasm, and Maddy shouted his name before the final wave of ecstasy washed over her.

Limp and bone-meltingly satisfied, Maddy fought to catch her breath. Ronan withdrew his hand and carefully pulled her skirt back to the tops of her knees. Maddy let out a shaky laugh and finally opened her eyes. Ronan had a satisfied, almost smug smile on his face and both hands on the wheel as he hit the blinker and turned the corner.

"That," she said through huffing breaths, "was unexpected."

"Like I said," Ronan murmured, "I enjoy surprising you."

Her face heated with embarrassment as the glow of pleasure faded and the lights of the Old Brookfield Inn came into view. She made quick work of closing her coat and went to check her makeup in the mirror on the visor. She flipped the plastic cover open but stilled when she saw her reflection. The woman there was vaguely familiar, and someone she hadn't seen in far too long. Color filled her cheeks, and her eyes glittered with the undeniable glow of satisfied lust.

She looked *alive* for the first time in months.

Ronan got out of the car and opened her door for her. Maddy took his hand and rose to her feet on unsteady legs. Her entire body was still humming from the carnal dalliance in the car, and based on the cheeky twinkle in Ronan's eye, he was fully aware of the effect he'd had on her.

"M'lady." He offered her his arm as he closed the car door before walking her to the steps. "This is where I leave you. For tonight, anyway."

"You're kidding." She wasn't angry, but she was taken aback. "You're not coming up?"

"Not tonight." Ronan cradled her face with both hands and rasped his thumb over her cheek. "Like I said, I want to take this slow. You and me. One step at a time. Besides, there's no need to rush it. Not only do we have the wedding, but we'll have Christmas too."

Maddy opened her mouth to respond, but he silenced her with a deep, slow kiss. She sighed into his mouth and linked her arms around his neck as his tongue swept along hers possessively. Ronan's embrace tightened, and the intensity of the kiss grew as her blood burned hot.

Take it slow? Every time he touched her, all she could think about was going faster, moving forward, running headlong into whatever came next. The consequences be damned!

He tilted her head and slowed the pace of the kiss until finally breaking it off.

"I'll see you at the church tomorrow." Ronan gently pressed his lips to the corner of her mouth. "And be sure you save me a dance—or ten. I am your date."

Breathless and with her heart spinning, Maddy shivered as Ronan drove away. She didn't know how long she stood there, but it was at least until the red taillights of his truck vanished in the distance. She was so caught up in the moment that until she snapped out of it, she didn't even notice that snow had begun to fall.

A smile tugged at her lips as she climbed the steps of the inn, and little icy flakes landed on her cheeks. It looked like there would be a white wedding after all.

Ronan had never been a big fan of weddings. Then again, he'd never been best man before. The ceremony went off without a hitch, and the cheers when Jordan and Gavin kissed as man and wife practically shook the roof off the church. They looked as happy as any two people could be. Jordan's daughters, adorable in their little red-and-green-plaid dresses, completed the family picture perfectly.

Ronan's mom had hit the nail on the head—it was an instant family.

He found himself wondering what it would be like to do that with Maddy.

He pictured himself coming home to her every night…but which home? His shithole apartment or her fancy penthouse? Neither seemed fitting. Frustration simmered, and he shoved the conflict aside. At the end of the day, none of that mattered. He really wouldn't care where they lived, as long as she was with him.

In fact, if he had his way, he would move back to Old Brookfield and raise a family with Maddy.

Ronan could barely take his eyes off her throughout the ceremony and the reception that followed. Maddy looked elegant in a long, strapless, green velvet gown that hugged her curves with wicked perfection. Her dark, curly hair was tied up in a fancy hairdo, earrings dangling from her ears, but all Ronan could think about was taking the pins out, burying his nose in the nape of her neck, and breathing her in. Whatever shampoo she used smelled like vanilla and cinnamon and conjured up images from their little car ride last night.

Finding his pleasure was easy enough, like it was for most guys. Ronan was well aware that wasn't always the case for women. Last night's adventure was meant to put Maddy at ease, to assure her that he had *her* pleasure in mind.

However, that wasn't his only motivation.

Ronan wanted to learn as much about Maddy as he could, and that included how she liked to be touched. He'd committed it all to memory: the sounds she made and the delicious way she arched her back as her orgasm built. When he got out of that car and walked her to the steps, he'd wanted nothing more than to continue exploring all the possibilities up in her room.

But that would have been about *him*. He'd wanted last night to be about *her*.

He stood at the bar and waited patiently for his order. Maddy had been twirling around the dance floor most of the night but was now sitting at one of the tables with Jordan's mom and the two little girls. Her laughter, robust and full of life, could be heard over the taped music being played during the band's break. Ronan's gut clenched at the sound of it, and at the same time, something loosened in his chest when she tossed her head back and let out another raucous laugh.

There she is.

The bright, lively woman who had been in hiding for so many months had finally reemerged. Ronan fought the sudden surge of longing. She was incredible. He wanted to spend the rest of his life finding out how many different ways he could make her laugh like that.

It might have been the most beautiful sound he had ever heard.

The phone in his tuxedo pants pocket rang with the ringtone assigned to Captain Jenkins. It had been so long since Ronan had heard it that he needed a minute to register who was calling.

"Shit," he whispered, quickly reaching in his pocket.

Sure enough, Jenkins's name blinked on the screen and Ronan's stomach churned. If the captain was calling him again after the conversation they had yesterday, then it was nothing but bad news. Ronan pressed the phone to his ear and quickly excused himself out of the country club's ballroom.

He hoped like hell that nobody noticed him leave, but as he turned to go, he caught Maddy's eye. She looked concerned, her brow furrowing, but he waved and smiled before holding up one finger and slipping out of the party.

"Please tell me you're just calling to wish me a Merry Christmas," Ronan said tightly.

He strode to the bank of windows at the end of the hallway. The snow had been coming down slowly and steadily all day, but now it looked like it was picking up. They were calling for a big storm for Christmas Eve, but apparently the weatherman had been wrong again and it was hitting tonight instead.

Shocker.

"Sorry, McGuire." Jenkins's voice was gruff. "We

ID'd the vic they found last week, and we had another one turn up today."

"Damn it," Ronan whispered. "That makes four."

"One was a real estate agent, and the other was an executive assistant. I thought you'd wanna know."

"Oh man." Ronan ran one hand over his face and pressed his fingers to his eyes. "Please tell me neither of them worked at Cosmopolitan Realty."

Silence hung heavily but Jenkins finally said, "No."

Ronan's breath hissed out, relief bubbling up from inside.

"Both of 'em worked at some other fancy brokerage house." Jenkins cleared his throat. "They got DNA off the woman from last week. Doer's a white male with no hits in the system—but he's gettin' sloppy, which means we're closer to findin' this guy. It's gonna be on the news, though; the press is all over it. They're callin' him the West Side Ringer, since all the vics were strangled and came from pricey real estate houses on the West Side. And get this—tox screen found a tranquilizer in all the women and puncture wounds. He doped 'em up."

"That would explain why they didn't fight back. And if he's not in the system, that may be why he wasn't worried about leaving DNA behind. He knew we couldn't nail him that way."

"The ME said that the women may not have been conscious during the actual assaults." Jenkins made a grunt of disgust. "Based on the timeline, it's looking now like he holds on to 'em for up to two days."

"Any leads?"

"Yeah, the same bogus email account was used to

contact all of the victims. Networking's having a hell of a time tracking the origin. Something about using fake IP addresses or routing the emails or some shit like that. I don't know about tech stuff, but they're gettin' close. Robinson said they're trying to hunt down the source for the drugs and come at it that way."

"Can you give me the names of the last two victims?" Ronan pressed his fingers against his eyes, feeling a massive headache coming on. "I'm gonna have to tell Maddy what's going on, and it's a good bet she knows who these women are. But I'd rather wait until after the holiday, to say nothing of my brother's wedding."

"Ah, crap," Jenkins blurted out. "Did I call you in the middle of the wedding?"

"It's okay, Cap." Ronan let out a slow breath. "The reception is almost over. Now how about those names?"

Ronan finished his call and headed back into the ballroom. The band had started playing again and was in the middle of a rowdy eighties cover. Everyone was dancing away, including Maddy, jumping up and down with her hands in the air and singing at the top of her lungs like she didn't have a care in the world. Jordan, Gavin, and all of his brothers, the whole room of people, reveled in the joyous celebration.

Everyone except him.

Ronan slipped his phone back in his pocket and shoved the conversation aside in his mind. This was not the time or place to share this kind of news; there would be plenty of time later.

And what about tomorrow or Christmas Day? Will it be any easier then to dampen the vibrant spirit she'd worked so hard to find again?

Maddy caught his eye and waved him over wildly, her smile practically blinding him with its beauty.

It would crush her to learn that two more people in her professional world had been robbed of their lives and their futures. But did he really *have* to tell her? The women didn't work in her office, after all. She might not even have known them. No, he had gotten this far with her and brought her out of her self-imposed isolation. The last thing he wanted to do was squelch that reemerging wild spirit. Besides, dropping this bit of information in the middle of Gavin and Jordan's wedding was hardly the kind of gift anyone was looking for.

"Everything okay?" Maddy shouted above the music.

How could he possibly share this news with her now when she had finally found that smile again? The answer was simple. He couldn't and he wouldn't.

"It's fine." Ronan kissed her cheek and pulled her into his arms. "I believe you owe me a dance, woman."

With Maddy in his arms and the sound of her laughter filling the air as he twirled her around the dance floor, Ronan kept telling himself he was doing the right thing.

A generous lie was less painful than the truth.

Chapter 14

"HOW WAS THE WEDDING?"

Imogene's boisterous voice bounded through the foyer from the living room. She scurried in to greet them before Maddy and Ronan had even closed the front door. The two of them shook the snow off their coats in an attempt not to drag it through the house.

"Hey there, Imogene," Ronan said.

He smiled but Maddy could tell something wasn't right. He'd been acting weird for the past couple of hours. His playfulness had faded, and the gleeful, naughty-boy glint in his eyes had dimmed. He was weighed down or burdened somehow, but Maddy didn't have the faintest idea what could be responsible. She'd asked him a couple times if he was alright, but each time he waved her off and said he was fine.

It must have had something to do with the call he'd gotten at the wedding.

To make matters worse, he'd been avoiding looking her in the eye. Not completely, but enough for her to notice. Normally, Ronan wouldn't merely look at her. Oh no. The guy practically attempted to bore into her soul every time their eyes met, like he was searching for something.

Not tonight. For the past few hours he had been distant and disconnected.

"It was wonderful," Maddy said, forcing a smile. "I wish you guys could have been there."

"Me too, hon. But with the storm coming in, we knew folks would be checking out early and getting on the road before it got too bad out there." Imogene took their coats and hung them on the brass coatrack in the corner by the front door. "Now, you two go on in and get warm by the fire. How about a nice brandy to heat you up a bit?"

"No, thank you," Ronan said quickly. "The roads are getting bad, and it's already gonna be a tough ride back to the house."

Maddy blinked. He was *leaving*? Her jaw clenched, and she fought the urge to punch him in the gut. What kind of game was he playing with her?

"That it is. You're the last guest standing, Maddy. The rest of the folks have checked out already."

"Really?" Maddy said tightly. "Well, I guess people wanted to get home for Christmas. Speaking of which, what about you and Bob? Aren't you supposed to be leaving for your place in Florida tomorrow? Don't you two always spend the holidays down there?"

"We do but we're going to fly out on Christmas Day instead. Provided the weather has cleared by then." Imogene arched her back as though working out the kinks. "One of these days, I may have to retire. Honestly, I'm starting to dream about spending all winter down south."

"Would you do that?" Maddy asked with genuine surprise. "Sell the inn and turn into snowbirds?"

"Maybe." A mischievous twinkle glinted in her eyes that crinkled at the corners when she smiled. "If Bob and I could find the right person to run this place, then, yes, I think we would."

"I can't imagine Old Brookfield without the two of you running this inn," Maddy said wistfully. "It's like the heart of the town."

"All the more reason we would *only* sell it to someone who would love it the way we have." Her smile instantly shifted to an expression of concern, and she quickly added, "Oh my. I just realized something! I know you were supposed to check out tomorrow morning and go back to the city for Christmas, but please feel free to stay on. This weather is awful, and I can't imagine you driving back to the city in it."

"Actually"—Ronan slipped his arm around Maddy's waist—"Maddy is staying with my family for the holiday. Speaking of which, you better shake a tail feather and go pack your stuff, or we run the risk of the truck getting stuck on the side of the road."

So that's what he was up to? The knot in Maddy's belly loosened as his behavior started to make a bit more sense.

"Wouldn't want to get stranded." His lips tilted and mischief swam in his eyes briefly. "What on earth would we do then?"

"I can't imagine," she said with a sidelong glance at him. Her face heated at the memory of their last automotive escapade, and she quickly slipped out of his embrace. "I'll go gather my things."

"I can help," he said, waggling his eyebrows. "I'm an awesome helper."

Before Maddy could protest and assure him that she would get far less packing done with him around, Imogene grabbed his hand and pulled him into the living room toward the roaring fire.

"While she packs, why don't you tell me all about the wedding."

The disappointed look on Ronan's face was both adorable and comical. Maddy stifled a giggle and gathered the long skirt of her dress as she trotted up the stairs. Maybe she had been oversensitive before. Ronan seemed fine now, and back to his playful ways. If she had anything to say about it, there would be much more of that later tonight.

Maddy hoped that guest bedroom on the third floor of the McGuire's house was as private as Carolyn had said.

———

Ronan's truck slid sideways as it pulled up the long, curved driveway of the McGuires' place on the bluff. Maddy clung to the sides of her seat with both hands. She only let out a sigh of relief once the sliding finally stopped and they reached the safety of the top of the driveway. The snowy winds howled and whistled past the truck, but the lights of the massive house shone like a beacon of safety. The huge pine tree to the right glinted with little white lights, and electric candles flickered in the windows as though to welcome them home. But other than the lights of the Christmas tree and one or two rooms lit upstairs, the rest of the house was dark.

The digital clock on the truck's dashboard said it was after one in the morning.

"Oh man," Maddy murmured. "I hope we don't wake your parents. They're probably exhausted from the wedding. I didn't realize how late it was."

"It's okay." Ronan smirked and gently hit the gas before turning to the left. "You're staying out in the cottage with me and Bowser. So you don't have to worry about waking anyone up."

"I am, am I?"

"Yes, ma'am. There's been a last-minute change of plans." He held the steering wheel steady and drove slowly along a shoveled-out pathway that led around the property. "Gavin, Jordan, the girls, *and* her mom are all staying here tonight. Nobody wanted to risk getting snowed in on Christmas. Since space is at a premium, I told them you could stay with me."

More snow had fallen since the path had been cleared, but Ronan's four-wheel-drive vehicle handled it easily. The road led directly to the small cottage at the back of the McGuires' extensive property—the one that overlooked the ocean and, until recently, the place Gavin had called home. Maddy stole a glance at Ronan and her stomach fluttered. He was strikingly handsome, and in the moment, he looked like he'd been carved from stone: hard, masculine, and seemingly indestructible.

"Who says that I want to stay out there with you all alone?"

"We won't be alone." He smirked and pulled the truck to a stop before putting it in Park. "Bowser is here."

"You think you're really slick, don't you?"

"Sometimes." He undid his seat belt and shut off the headlights, immediately plunging them into darkness. "But I like—"

"Surprising me," Maddy finished for him.

Her eyes adjusted to the dim light in the truck, and she could see that he was staring at her. That playfulness had faded, and a concerned look edged his handsome face. Even in the darkness she could detect the change in him.

"Ronan?" Out of instinct, she reached over and covered his knee with her hand. "What's wrong? You've been acting funny tonight. And not your usual ha-ha funny. More like strange funny."

"It's all good, Mads." Ronan cut the engine and covered her hand with his, then brought it to his mouth and pressed a kiss against her palm. "Let's get you inside and warmed up. Your hands are like ice."

Ronan got out of the car and grabbed her bags from the backseat—her suitcase, as well as the bag of presents she'd brought for various McGuires...including Ronan. Even though she hadn't originally planned on staying, she'd picked up a few things in town. Oh hell; maybe deep down, she'd always wanted to spend the holiday with Ronan's family.

Her belly swirled with nerves and anticipation. This was it.

The car was already starting to get unbearably cold, and Maddy had little choice but to follow Ronan inside. She climbed out of the truck and braced for the bitter air. Squeezing her eyes shut, she sucked in a sharp breath. She had almost forgotten how frigid it could be by the ocean. The snow stung her cheeks, but light spilled out from the open door of the cottage.

She stopped for a moment. The silhouette of Ronan's broad-shouldered frame filled the space as he did most others, completely and confidently.

"Come on, Mads," Ronan shouted. "You're gonna freeze that beautiful bottom off if you don't get in here soon."

Maddy nodded but was too cold to respond. She was just grateful that she'd taken the time to change back at the inn. The sweater, jeans, and snow boots were a much better choice for weather like this than her velvet gown, but she was still freezing. Bowser ran out of the house as she ran in, presumably to do his business.

She let out a sound of relief when she stepped into the open living room and Ronan closed the door behind her. Maddy shook her head and snow flew off her hair. Laughing and still trying to warm up, she took off her coat and hung it on one of the hooks, then pulled off her snowy boots and socks and placed them by the door. Having her back to him and the wintry ocean air seeping into her bones almost kept her from thinking about what was undoubtedly going to happen between them tonight.

Almost.

She had considered cutting to the chase and jumping him, but when she turned around, the sight in the cozy living room stunned her into silence.

A fire blazed in the small fireplace, and in the corner, between that and the sliding doors to the deck, sat a little Christmas tree. It was only about three feet tall, decorated simply with colorful lights and a silver star perched precariously on top. Ronan stood beside the tree, behind a large overstuffed chair that was just past the sofa. Moonlit snowfall swirled behind him outside on the deck, enclosing them in their own little world. He was still wearing his classic black tuxedo but had ditched his snow-covered shoes and was now barefoot. The tie was long gone, and he'd unbuttoned the top few buttons of his shirt, giving her a glimpse of dark chest hair.

He looked like one of Santa's sexiest elves.

"When did you do all this?" she asked with genuine awe. "The fire alone..."

"It's a gas fireplace." He held up a black remote control. "Gavin had it installed a few years ago."

"But...the tree?"

Bowser barked loudly outside, and Ronan quickly ran to let his partner in. Maddy crossed the room to get closer to the warmth of the orange flames. She'd made it as far as the couch and coffee table when Bowser shook the snow off his huge, furry body. Maddy laughed as Ronan flinched and held up one hand to shield his face.

"Alright, that's enough." He laughed and rubbed Bowser's flanks briefly before pointing toward the hallway to the right. "Go to bed, pal."

The bloodhound snuffled loudly before loping away past the kitchen and down the hall that must have led to the bedroom. Maddy stilled. Oh boy. They were alone again, the air thrumming with the pulse of unfulfilled desire and a hint of uncertainty.

She was suddenly nervous and unsure of herself, like some kind of high school girl. Self-conscious, Maddy hugged her shivering body and looked at the lovely little tree. A few wrapped gifts were even nestled beneath it.

"It's adorable," Maddy said quietly. "When did you put this together?"

Ronan hit the light switch on the wall, and the room was doused in darkness, softly infused with the flickering glow of the fire and the gentle lighting from the tree. It was magical and sweet and heartbreakingly beautiful...and he had done it all for her.

"A couple days ago." He shrugged amicably and slipped his hands into his pants pockets. "I wanted you to a have a tree for Christmas in case you decided to stay. My mom has a great big one in the family room at the main house, but I had a hunch you'd be out here with me."

"Is that so?" She wagged one finger at him and narrowed her eyes. "I thought I was supposed to stay up with your parents."

"I'm a cop, Maddy." Ronan smirked. "I don't leave any stone unturned. So, on the *chance* that I got you to stay out here with me...I wanted it to be *Christmasy*."

"You're pretty sure of yourself, aren't you?"

"Like it?"

Ronan moved closer and took off his tux jacket, draping it on the back of the sofa that faced the fire. He rested a hand on either side of it and leveled that intense gaze at her. It was now or never. Maddy had to find out exactly what Ronan's feelings were and where this was going because the uncertainty was driving her mad. He had been running hot and cold, and she didn't know what to expect next. For all she knew, he was going to sleep on the couch and let her have the bedroom.

"Tell me, Ronan." Maddy swallowed hard. "Why would you go to all this trouble for me?"

"To see you smile," he murmured.

"You've seen me smile several times." Her brow furrowed with confusion. "Like you said, I always laugh at your goofy jokes."

"Not exactly." Ronan pushed himself off the back of the couch and slowly walked around it, heading in her direction. "I've seen that *halfway* smile a bunch."

He stalked toward her with stealthy, steady precision. His arms remained at his sides, and his fierce gaze was pinned on hers. Maddy couldn't move. She was enthralled by his presence, his words, and his voice.

And, most of all, struck dumb by his observations.

"It's been a damn long time since I've seen *you*, Mads. Not the *I'm-fine-I'm-tough-nobody-has-to-worry-about-me* smile—that's the one you give your fancy clients in the city or your coworkers or the big-money bankers who sign off on those sky-high mortgages. No, Mads. That's not the smile I'm talking about. I hadn't seen a real one on you until tonight at the wedding, when you were dancing like you didn't have a care in the world."

Maddy's vision blurred as tears stung her eyes and a wave of vulnerability swamped her. Even if she wanted to say something now, she wouldn't have been able to.

"No, baby. The real you? That was in the smile you flashed when you saw this little tree. It was open and full of life. In that moment, you were the wild, free, spirited woman that you have always been."

Ronan stopped about a foot away from her. Her head and heart were swimming with gratitude and affection. No one had ever seen her so clearly. It was more than that though. Ronan was able to see what she truly needed. He understood her wants and desires, ones she hadn't admitted to herself or even dared to consciously entertain.

He cupped her face with both hands and brushed away a tear with his thumb. Maddy's eyes fluttered closed, and she reveled in the rough, manly feel of his palms while his words settled over her like a warm blanket.

"I can't get you out of my head. You're the first person I think about every morning, and when I lay in bed at night *alone*, it's your face I see when I close my eyes." Ronan's voice wavered, and he drew in a shuddering breath. "I am in love with you, Madolyn Morgan, and I want to spend the rest of my life finding out how many different ways I can put that smile on your face."

Her heart beat wildly against her chest, and she curled her hands over his. Maddy worked to steady her breathing because it seemed to be racing out of control—but then again, that's how she felt almost all the time lately with Ronan. The tight grip she'd been using to hold on to her life was slipping away, all due to him.

Her heart and soul were in free fall, and the chasm was so deep that there was no end in sight. The vast unknown loomed, terrifying and exhilarating. Anticipation buzzed in her blood, and heart spinning, Maddy opened her eyes to be met by Ronan's glittering stare.

She finally understood why it was called *falling* in love.

"Please say something," Ronan murmured. His greenish-blue eyes glimmered in the firelight. "You're killin' me."

She searched his eyes, and even though she ached to tell him how desperately she loved him, the glimmer of fear clung to her like an anchor. Maddy knew, better than anyone, what the risks could be when you offered your heart completely to another human being—when you gave away a piece of your soul. She opened her mouth, but the words wouldn't come.

All right, then. If she couldn't tell him what he meant to her tonight, she would damn well show him.

"No more talking." Maddy rose up on her toes and captured his lips with hers. Her fingers immediately went for the buttons of his shirt. A groan of pleasure rumbled in Ronan's throat as they kissed, his tongue pressing deeply into her mouth. He grabbed the hem of her sweater, and they broke the kiss long enough for him to whip the garment over her head, then toss it casually aside. Maddy laughed and shook her curly hair from her face before pushing his shirt off his shoulders. Her suspicions about how well built Ronan had to be were all on point. His perfectly sculpted chest, with a dark dusting of hair, was a feast for the eyes.

She let out a soft sound of appreciation and trailed the fingertips of both hands over the dips and valleys of his ripped belly. A thin trail of dark hair disappeared below the waistband of his trousers, the dark fabric doing little to hide his arousal. Maddy ran one hand over the bulge hidden there, and the heat of it in her palm almost made her lose it completely.

"Careful, babe," Ronan ground the words out between his teeth. He grabbed her wrists and tugged them against his bare chest. "You're getting ahead of yourself. If you keep that up, this is gonna be a short night."

"We can always do it more than once," Maddy murmured. "In fact, I was counting on it."

"I knew you were the perfect woman."

Ronan covered her mouth with a savage possessive kiss, and Maddy sank into the strength of his embrace. He unhooked her lacy black bra and peeled it from her body with all the ease of experience, never once breaking his thorough kiss.

She shivered and let out a satisfied sigh when he tugged her against him, their heated flesh meeting in a satisfying slap. Maddy linked her arms around his neck and threaded her fingers through his short hair. Without warning, Ronan dropped to his knees and trailed kisses over her breasts, then took one nipple into his mouth and suckled hard. Maddy groaned and tossed her head back, holding him against her. Tiny zings of pleasure fired to her core as he licked and suckled first one breast and then the other.

"You're so beautiful." Kneeling in front of her, Ronan lifted his head and peered up at her. His fingers dug into the soft flesh of her waist and he growled, "I want to see all of you, Maddy. I want to see every single inch of your gorgeous body. No more barriers."

Maddy bit her lip and nodded. She went to unbutton her jeans but Ronan grabbed her hands and shook his head slowly, then gently pushed her hands away. A wicked grin curved his lips as he undid the top button and slowly pulled the zipper down.

"Put your arms over your head," he whispered.

The sharp angles of his face were highlighted by the flickering light of the fire, turning him into something almost dangerous. The heated look in his eyes, combined with the possessive and almost rough way he touched her, made her weak with desire. Maddy complied and stretched her arms above her head, reveling in the heady combination of carnal lust and vulnerability.

Ronan tugged her jeans over her hips and down her legs, taking the flimsy thong right along with them. He held her waist with one hand and helped her step out of her clothes. Maddy dropped her arms and pressed one hand to Ronan's cheek. With lust in his eyes, he stared at her from her head to her toes and back again. His scruff-covered jaw was rough against her palm, a beard already beginning to peek through, and she simmered beneath the heat and intensity of his gaze.

"Tell me what you want, Mads." Ronan ran one hand up her belly and then between her breasts, before trailing his fingers lightly over one of her sensitive nipples. "Making you smile isn't all that I want to do. Bringing you pleasure, in every single way possible, is my new mission in life."

"You," she said in a shaky whisper. "I want *you*, Ronan."

His reflexes lightning fast, Ronan rose to his feet and swept her up in another knee-buckling kiss. He wasn't the only who needed more. She reached between their eager, heated bodies and made quick work of freeing him from the confines of the unyielding fabric. When his hot length settled in her palm, Ronan groaned and deepened their kiss, swiftly stepping out of the tux pants and kicking them aside.

As amber firelight flickered over the broad expanse of his back, Maddy trailed her fingers over his heated flesh, his muscles moving and flexing beneath her touch. She went to reach for him again, but he bent down, quickly unhooking the leather gun holster around his ankle. The reality of his job and who he was came roaring back, but Maddy shoved it aside.

Tonight he wasn't a cop. For tonight, at least, he was hers.

He gave her a sheepish grin before placing the gun and holster on the coffee table.

"Sorry, Mads." He gathered her naked body against his and slid his hands over her ass, tugging her against his solid heat. "Now where were we?"

"Right about here," she murmured against his lips, then reached between them and curled her fingers around him. "Or here?"

She moved her hand up and down the silky, steely flesh and he groaned. Maddy felt a surge of bravery. What had she been worried about? This man not only loved her, but also wanted her with a ferocity she had never encountered. Lovemaking before had been satisfying but had never burned with this new intensity. The stuff she had always seen in the movies or read about in books was now a reality.

Maddy pressed kisses to his collarbone as she worked him in her hand, heady with the scent of musk and sex. She let out a satisfied sigh. Part of the turn-on was finding out what Ronan enjoyed and what she could do to get him to make that guttural groan again. Each time it rumbled in his chest, matching heat ran through her. She popped onto her toes and captured his lips with hers. One hand threaded through his hair, and the other continued to learn the feel and shape of him. With each stroke, he held her tighter, and his kiss devoured her.

Breathing heavily and with his shoulders heaving, Ronan broke away and picked Maddy up, forcing her to release him. She yelped with surprise that quickly dissolved into a laugh as she wrapped her legs around his waist and clung to his neck, burying her face there. She licked and suckled at his throat while he settled his hands around her ass and carried her to the chair.

Ronan set her down on the enormous soft cushions, and Maddy let out a sound of disappointment as he pulled away. But he didn't stay gone for long. He dropped to his knees again and hooked his arms under her thighs before tugging her so that her bottom was the edge of the cushion. Maddy gripped the arms of the chair, eyes wide and tight with anticipation, and struggled to catch her breath.

With that cheeky grin on his face and mischief dancing in his eyes, Ronan dove deep. Maddy cried out when his mouth covered her sex. He held her open, licking and suckling her clit with swift, sure strokes of his tongue. Maddy writhed as the pleasure, almost unbearable in its intensity, fired through her body. Ronan held her tightly in place. She closed her eyes and let her body sink into wave after sensuous wave. Maddy arched her back and fought the orgasm as it curled tight and deep in her belly. She didn't want it to end. No yet.

She wanted him to fall over the cliff with her.

Then, as though reading her mind, Ronan released her from his grasp. Amid their heavy breathing and the winds howling outside, she heard rustling and a quiet curse word as he presumably searched for a condom. The sound of a wrapper crinkling confirmed her suspicions.

With her eyes closed and her body humming, Maddy was practically drowning in her eagerness and need. A moment later, Ronan's hand curled around hers and he pulled her to her feet, kissing her deeply. His erection pressed against her stomach, but only for a moment— then Ronan sat in the chair and pulled her to him.

Knowing what he desired and wanting to give it to him more than anything, Maddy settled both hands on his shoulders. She straddled him, her knees sliding between him and the soft leather of the chair. She briefly registered that contrast. The heat of flesh on one side and cool smooth leather on the other heightened the eroticism of the moment.

Ronan gripped her hips as Maddy bent, touching her lips to his. She hovered over the tip of his erection but she didn't take him inside. Not yet. Maddy flicked her tongue over his mouth and rocked her hips, teasing him with what was to come. She bit his lower lip playfully and dug her fingertips into the muscles of his shoulders.

"This is what I want, Ronan," Maddy whispered against his mouth. Then, painstakingly slowly, she lowered herself onto his shaft. "Every. Single. Inch. Of. You."

Ronan pulled her down hard, groaning and burying himself to the hilt. She moaned along with him as he filled her completely.

He moved and Maddy moved with him in unhurried, languid passes. Each roll of her hips put pressure in the sweetest of spots. Ronan's fingers gripped her ass tightly, and lust was stamped into his face as their pace increased.

Maddy shuddered and raised her arms over her head, riding him harder and faster. This was what she wanted. To lose herself in pure, unadulterated lust. She moved faster, needing and wanting to bring them both the climax they'd been chasing for months.

As Ronan's body tensed and shuddered beneath her with his climax, he shouted her name and Maddy collapsed on top of him as her own pleasure peaked.

She didn't know how long they stayed like that, bodies intertwined, skin sweat-slicked, his chest pressing and contracting with hers as their breathing slowed. But as the glow of the orgasm faded, reality came roaring back in.

Ronan's gun lay on the coffee table. The firelight cast shadows over it one moment and revealed all the ugly details the next.

That's what she had been doing with him.

One second she wanted to hide, and the next she

felt compelled to reveal everything. Yet through it all, Ronan had remained steady. Solid. There was no waffling on his part, and perhaps that was part of what was scaring her. She squeezed her eyes shut and tried not to think about what might come next.

Was she really capable of giving Ronan what he wanted, or was the risk more than she could wager?

Chapter 15

Ronan had never told a woman he loved her before. Not even his college girlfriend. He would say *Same here* or *Me too* but never, in all his years, had he told a woman he was in love with her—because it would have been a lie. He had even begun to believe that he wasn't capable of it. But Maddy had changed all of that.

He was trying not to think about the fact that she hadn't said it back.

She cared for him. That much he knew. Hell, she'd showed him over and over again last night, making love three times, and then once again this morning.

But she hadn't *said* it.

The sting of not hearing those words from her was a hell of a lot stronger than he had expected. He scolded himself for being such an idiot. The Christmas Eve festivities were underway, and all of the traditions he counted on and valued were in full swing. The Chinese food still got delivered even through the steady snowfall, and Ronan was currently standing in the doorway to the kitchen, shoveling the rest of the pork lo mein into his mouth right out of the white container.

Maddy sat by the tree with Jordan and her girls, and his brothers were sprawled on the massive leather sectional watching *It's a Wonderful Life*. The fire was roaring in the stone hearth, with the stockings his mother had knitted hanging off to the side. Jordan's mother, Claire, was chatting with his mom, and his dad was snoring away in the recliner.

It was a perfect scene. The woman he loved had blended into his big, loud family like she had always been a part of it. They were all together. They were safe.

Then why did he have an ache in his chest that wouldn't quit?

"Hey, man." Gavin's voice pulled him from his private pity party. "What's going on? Are you sulking because Mom won't let Bowser in the main house?"

"I'm allergic to dogs," his mother piped up from the other side of the big family room. "All that hair."

"It's okay, Mom." Ronan waved his chopsticks at her. "He's fine out at the cottage."

"She's not allergic," Gavin whispered. "When is she gonna admit that she just doesn't want dog hair on her furniture?"

"It's not a big deal." Ronan went back into the kitchen and tossed the chopsticks and empty container in the garbage. "Maddy and I will head back out there after Mom does the Christmas pajama thing."

"Okay," Gavin leaned back against the granite counter and eyed Ronan warily. "Then why are you moping?"

"I'm not moping," Ronan insisted.

"Yes, you are."

"Forget it, okay?"

He snagged a beer from the fridge and popped it open before taking a long sip. Gavin kept staring at him, which was starting to piss Ronan off.

"Didn't Maddy stay with you out at the cottage last night?"

"Yeah." Ronan grabbed the green ceramic cookie jar and pulled out two cookies, handing one to Gavin.

"What?" His brother took a bite and smirked. "Did you sleep on the sofa or something?"

"No. I didn't sleep on the sofa." Ronan's tone was mocking but he couldn't hide his frustration. "Just forget it, man. It's embarrassing."

"What? Did you forget how to do it?"

"Gavin!"

"Come on, man." Gavin crossed to his brother and elbowed him, urging him on. "Obviously, you and Maddy have taken it to the next level, so—"

"I told her I'm in love with her," Ronan blurted out.

"Whoa." Gavin's playful expression settled into one of understanding. "That's big. Especially for *you*. What did she say?"

"Nothing." Ronan let out a sharp laugh but kept his voice down and checked the door to reassure himself that they were still alone. "In fact, she told me to stop talking. Can you believe it? I finally fall in love *and* have the balls to say it out loud and—"

Gavin tried to conceal his amusement but failed miserably. His shoulders shook with the laughter he was trying to keep in. He held up two hands to apologize, but Ronan punched him in the arm anyway.

"Nice. Real sensitive, Gav."

"I'm sorry," Gavin said in a loud whisper. He backed up and glanced toward the still-empty doorway. "It's just…well… You *do* see the irony in all of this, don't you?"

"Yes, and it sucks."

"Give her some time, Ronan. Think about it for

a minute. You waited about thirty years to say those words, right? To take the big, bad leap into love."

"Yeah, so?"

"Ronan." Gavin let out a sigh and gave his brother a look that bordered on pity. "Maddy already made that leap once. She took it with Rick, and in the end…she lost him. Can you blame her if she's a little wary to take a chance again? And with a cop?"

"Oh man, some cop I am." Ronan leaned back against the refrigerator and let out a curt laugh. He tipped his beer to Gavin. "Does it get any easier? This love stuff? Because, so far, I suck at it."

"Some days yes, some days no." Gavin slapped Ronan on the shoulder, then dragged his arm around Ronan's neck and pulled him into a solid hug. "Keep doin' what you're doin' and love her," he said quietly. "It'll all work out."

"Are you gonna kiss me now?" Ronan teased, breaking the unusually emotional moment between the two men. "Because your breath stinks."

Gavin shoved him away with a curse and a smile.

"What are you two saps doing in here?" Tristan strode into the kitchen. He gave his brothers a look of disbelief before shaking his head solemnly. "Another one bites the dust, eh, Ronan?"

"Is it that obvious?"

"You mean, you and Maddy? You chased her like a puppy dog all through high school; looks like your perseverance has finally paid off." Tristan jutted a thumb over his shoulder as he pushed past his brothers and pulled a beer from the fridge. "Never mind the sparks between you two at the rehearsal and the wedding, and it's no secret she stayed out at the cottage with you last night. I'm betting you weren't playing checkers."

"No." Ronan smirked. "No board games."

"That's a bold move to go messing around with a woman who basically just got widowed."

"I'm not messing around with her," Ronan said, feeling defensive.

"Oh no?" Tristan's eyebrows lifted. "Then what are you doing?"

Silence hung between the three brothers, and Ronan didn't miss the knowing look the other two men exchanged.

"Taking the leap," Ronan finally said.

"Yeah?" Tristan snorted with derision. "Better you than me. Don't get me wrong. She's a fine woman. Hell, both Jordan and Maddy are. They're beautiful, sexy, and smart—"

"And taken," Ronan added.

Tristan's reputation with women was no less colorful than Ronan's had been. Maybe more so.

"I got it." Tristan rolled his eyes. "What I *don't* get is the idea of settling down with one person forever. Mom and Dad are the exception to the rule, but most married guys I know are miserable. Monogamy is an outdated concept. So is love. At least that kind of love."

"You live in LA," Gavin scoffed. "What do you expect? Most of the people out there are only faithful in their own zip codes. You'll see. One day some woman will knock you right onto your cocky ass and make you question all that crap you tell yourself. I just hope I get to see it."

"I'll second that." Ronan raised his beer.

"Ain't nobody gonna live that long," Tristan muttered. "But, hey, I'm happy for you guys. All I'm saying is that it's not for me."

Ronan nodded his agreement. Until recently he'd felt exactly the same way—but Maddy had changed everything. He couldn't imagine being with or wanting anyone other than her, and the thought of Maddy with another man? Hell, no! That sparked a dark surge of jealousy and tripped a deep primal instinct to protect what was his.

Jealousy? That was also a first. The whole "love" thing was definitely going to take some getting used to.

"Boys!" Their mother poked her head in the kitchen and smiled broadly. "We're going to give out the Christmas Eve presents now. I hope the little ones like the jammies I bought them."

His mother might enjoy Christmas more than anyone else on the planet.

"Be right there, Mom." Gavin grinned and shook his head. "Do you think she'll buy us Christmas pajamas for the rest of our lives?"

"Yup." Tristan arched one eyebrow and pointed at Ronan. "I can't wait to see Maddy's face when you open yours."

"Oh man," Ronan groaned. "I just hope they aren't matching sets."

When he came through the door, he was greeted by Maddy's smiling face, and any tension in his chest immediately eased away. She had a pair of red satin pajamas draped over her arm and stood by the fireplace, admiring the felt stocking with her name written in silver glitter along the top.

"I see you found your stocking," he said, then dropped a quick kiss on her cheek. "You like it?"

"Of course." Her blue eyes glistened in the firelight, and she folded her arms over her breasts. "It was so thoughtful of your mom to include me like this."

"Well, once she heard you might be staying for Christmas, and with the girls here... Mom didn't want to risk blowing the whole Santa thing," he whispered. He moved in next to her and slipped his arm around her waist, pulling her against him. "If you didn't have a stocking, where would Santa put your goodies? Gracie and Lily are sharp as tacks. They would've spotted it immediately if Santa didn't fill a stocking for you. So she made this one for you. Mom is crafty, on every level."

"True," Maddy said with a giggle. "And she got me these Christmas pajamas."

"*I* got you those. I picked them up in town the other day, just in case you decided to stay."

"Thank you," she whispered. "You really are full of surprises, McGuire."

"Ronan!" His mother hurried over with a small package and handed it to him. "This one is for you."

"Thanks, Mom." He looked at the gift warily and prayed that it didn't contain pajamas fit for a five-year-old. "Keepin' the tradition alive."

"That's what women do, dear." She patted his cheek before turning to Maddy. "Now, Maddy, I know yours isn't a knitted stocking like the others, but—"

"It's beautiful," Maddy exclaimed. She grabbed his mom's hand and kissed her cheek. "Thank you for welcoming me into your home like this."

"Are you kidding?" Carolyn waved her off, but

Ronan saw a hint of pride there. "That's what family is for, my dear. Now I have to hand out the rest, but this is the *only* present we do on Christmas Eve. All other presents come tomorrow with *Santa*!"

The girls squealed at the mention of the fat man's name, and Carolyn went right over to encourage the madness.

"She's amazing," Maddy murmured. She ran her finger over the stocking with the Christmas tree design and Ronan's name stitched on top. "Carolyn knitted all of these?"

"She did." He kissed the top of Maddy's head. "And she's been knitting her butt off since Jordan and Gavin got engaged to get four more done. Gracie, Lily, Jordan, and Claire all have Carolyn McGuire homemade stockings this year."

"I haven't had a Christmas stocking in years," Maddy murmured. She held Ronan's hand against her belly, and he noted the delicious way her body sank against his chest. "My mom had my old one in storage, but it got misplaced sometime between after she died and when we cleaned out the house. I never got a new one. Rick and I…"

Her body tensed, and she stopped talking.

"It's okay," Ronan whispered into her ear. "Tell me. He was part of your life for almost a decade. Go on."

"It's like I told you before. We didn't really have traditions like that. We didn't even get a tree. I'd make the pie but—" She spun in his arms, a look of panic stamped on her face. "The pie! Oh my God. I told your mother I'd make a pie for Christmas dinner tomorrow, but with the storm and the wedding, I forgot all about going to the grocery store. I am so embarrassed!"

A smile cracked his face. When she saw it, her expression shifted from total panic to mildly annoyed in a split second.

"Why does this amuse you?" She poked him in the belly, but he grabbed her wrists to stop her. "It's not funny, McGuire. After everything your mother has done, the least I can do is—"

"I have all of the ingredients in the cottage," he said calmly. "It's taken care of."

"What? How could you...?"

"You told me at Thanksgiving that your mom used that *Better Homes and Garden Cook Book*, the one with the picnic-table cover, right?"

"Uh...yes," Maddy said slowly. Her body relaxed, and he tangled his fingers in hers. "I did but..."

"My mom has the same one." He shrugged easily. "I took a gamble that I'd manage to talk you into staying for Christmas, and I wanted you to be able to make your pie."

"Are you serious?" Her voice was quiet, laced with a hint of awe. He liked that. "You really did that?"

"I did." He pressed a quick kiss to her lips. "So whaddya say we head back to the cottage and start cooking? It's about time for me to let Bowser out again anyway."

As he and Maddy said good night to the others, Ronan knew without a shadow of a doubt that everything would be okay. Gavin was right—all he had to do was give Maddy time. Hell, it had taken him thirty years to say it. If he had to wait that long to hear it from her too, then he damn well would.

—~~~—

The kitchen in the cozy little cottage was small and out-dated, and it didn't have state-of-the-art appliances like her place in the city. But as Maddy peeled the apples and cut them into slices, she noted what the cottage did have that her penthouse didn't.

There was heart here, and soul, and an unwavering sense of home.

A jazz version of *O Christmas Tree* played in the background, and Ronan sat on the island counter behind her tossing treats to Bowser. She'd originally wanted to listen to the news, but Ronan talked her out of it. Just as well, she thought. There was rarely anything good to report, even at the holidays. She had emailed Sharon earlier in the week to check on the party RSVPs and actual business updates, but she hadn't even looked yet for the response. The office was closed now for the holi-days anyway. Work could wait. Maddy shook her head, sprinkling sugar and cinnamon over the bowl of apple slices, along with some lemon juice.

Had she ever gone three or four days without check-ing on work?

The answer was a resounding no.

The best part, or maybe the worst, was that she didn't even care. In fact, she'd barely given work or the city or the recent ugliness there any thought at all. Sharon would have texted or called if there had been an emergency, but nothing had come in. And Maddy realized that she didn't miss it. Not the city, or the apartment showings, or the running around after her persnickety clients—and definitely not her cavernous, sterile apartment.

A pang of sadness fired through her at the notion of returning to all that. Maddy rolled her shoulder and stuck her hands in the bowl of apple slices. As she tossed the slippery mixture with her bare hands, she glanced over her shoulder. Ronan was using different signals to get Bowser to sit and lie down, and her heart melted at the sight.

Could the guy be any sweeter? No.

Ronan McGuire might have been one of the best-kept secrets in Old Brookfield. Who would have thought that a man like this lurked behind the cocky, self-assured hound dog? Certainly not her. Given his family and his career, she'd known he was a good man—all of the McGuires were kind, decent people. But she never would have pegged him as such a softie. His thoughtfulness rendered her practically speechless, to the point that she wasn't sure what to do with it.

So why was she holding back? She knew in her heart of hearts that she loved him. Somehow saying it out loud was more than she was ready for. If she wasn't sure of that last night, she certainly was after today. She had always known that the McGuire family life was idyllic, but she hadn't experienced the full force of it until today.

It was overwhelming and wonderful.

Except now Maddy wasn't only worried about hurting Ronan—she had his family's feelings to contend with too. They'd brought her into their home and treated her as though she had always been a part of it. After seeing Carolyn and Charles together, so loving and attentive with each other and their sons, it was easy to see why Ronan was such a good man.

He caught her staring at him and smirked.

"What are you lookin' at?"

"Nothing," she said innocently, turning back to her task.

"I smell a fib." Ronan tossed Bowser a treat and pointed toward the doorway that led to the hall and bedroom. "Go to bed, man."

The dog whined and sat down when Maddy looked back at him. He gave her a mournful gaze, and she couldn't help but laugh.

"She's not gonna help you." Ronan went to the sink and washed his hands. "Quit your whining."

"Sorry, buddy." She lowered her voice to a conspiratorial whisper. "But I'll sneak you some pie later."

"Bed." Ronan snapped his fingers after drying them with a dish towel. "Beat it."

"Good boy," Maddy whispered.

Bowser barked and trotted happily out of the kitchen.

"That smells good." Ronan sidled in behind her and settled a hand on the counter on either side of her, caging her in. "I don't know if I can wait until it's baked."

"You know," Maddy said with a sigh, "you could help me."

"I can be a taste tester."

He kissed her ear and pressed himself against her backside.

"Don't get ahead of yourself, McGuire," she murmured. "You of all people should know that taking it slowly makes the end result all that much sweeter."

She grabbed both of his hands and covered them with hers before diving back into the gritty, sugary apples. They massaged the slices, her fingers sliding over and tangling with his. Ronan made a groan of approval and nudged up against her, the quickly growing evidence of his arousal poking against her lower back.

Maddy let out a contented sigh as Ronan's strong

hands tangled with hers to work the apples over and over. She laid her head back against his chest and closed her eyes, reveling in the mix of sensations, the combination of his hard body against hers, and the gentle strength of his hands linked with hers.

Ronan nuzzled her hair off her neck and trailed butterfly kisses along the sensitive skin there. Maddy moaned softly and allowed her body to sag against him. She fleetingly recalled those trust exercises from a college drama class, the ones where she had to close her eyes and fall backward, believing the others would catch her.

She'd never been able to do that.

Until now.

What was it that Jordan had said? *He'll catch you.*

With that thought swirling through her mind and the searing heat of his body pressed against hers, Maddy was eager for more. She was ready to take the leap because this man, the one with the talented lips and devilishly gifted hands, was blessed with an exquisitely loving heart.

"I think the pie can wait," Maddy murmured.

She lifted her hands from the bowl and spun around, immediately capturing his lips with hers. Maddy linked her arms around his neck and clung to him, rising on her tippy-toes and trying to get closer. A growl rumbled in his throat and reverberated through the kiss, both of them reaching for something they couldn't quite get to. Ronan's arms curled around her like steel clamps, holding tight as though reinforcing the fact that he would never, ever let her go.

He slid his hands beneath her sweater, his sticky

fingers trailing over her back. He broke the kiss only
long enough to pull her sweater off over her head.
Maddy couldn't stop smiling between kisses. She
yanked his shirt open and sent buttons flying around the
kitchen. Where they went, she'd never know—but she
hoped they hadn't landed in the apples.

She pushed the shirt off his shoulders and grinned
wickedly at the glistening streaks her messy hands had
left on his chest. She pressed both hands on his belly and
walked him backward, licking the sugary bits from his
skin. Ronan grunted when he hit the edge of the granite
island behind him.

Maddy dropped to her knees, lapping the bits of
apple-flavored goodness off his belly as she went.
She made quick work of releasing him from the confines of his jeans and let out a moan of appreciation
when he was finally freed. Ronan swore and grabbed
the counter's edge when she curled her fingers around
his shaft. She dispersed the rest of the gritty, sticky
sugar over the length of him, first with one hand, then
the other.

She tugged his jeans down his legs, and he stepped
out of them as her hands settled on his narrow hips.
Maddy looked up at Ronan, then leaned in and licked
him from root to tip. She laved his steely shaft slowly
but surely, with long, wicked strokes, taking her time,
making it last. His body was tense and taut against her
when she finally took him into her mouth. She curled
her hand around the base and sucked him hard, wanting
to give back all the pleasure he had given her so many
times. When his hips began to pump, moving in time
with her, she knew he was getting close to the edge.

"Stop," he growled through clenched teeth. "I have to be inside you. Right now."

She rose to her feet, and within seconds, Ronan had pulled a condom from his pocket and sheathed himself. God love a man who's prepared. He stripped her jeans from her overheated body. He kissed her deeply, then picked her up and set her on the counter. Standing between her legs, Ronan hooked his hands under her knees and tugged her ass to the edge. Maddy reached back and braced herself, opening her legs wider. She needed him, wanted to take all he had to give but her hands kept slipping. Finally, she lay back, using her elbows for support as he brought her bottom to the very edge of the counter.

Maddy bit her lower lip and whimpered, wiggling her ass closer to him, but still he didn't give her what she wanted. What they both wanted. Her breasts bounced and carnal desire hummed beneath her skin as his dark, heated gaze skittered over every exposed inch of her.

"I want you, Ronan," Maddy whispered. She wiggled her hips again. "Please. Don't make me wait."

Ronan grabbed her hips with both hands and tugged her closer. The tip of his cock teased her swollen entrance. She might start begging in a minute. It was as though every single cell of her being was primed and ready to erupt. All she needed was *him*—no one else could possibly give her what she needed.

No one except for Ronan McGuire.

"You're mine, Maddy." Ronan's large hand curled around the soft swell of her hip, his fingers pressing deeper. "There's nothing I wouldn't do for you…or to you…to make you happy."

She gasped as he trailed the other hand over her belly and then lightly flicked her sensitive nipple. He dropped his hand back to palm her hip. Maddy was wound tight, and the beat of her own heart thrummed in her ears as she eagerly waited. The expression on his face wavered between lust and need, but beneath it all there was love.

"Then take me," she whispered. "I'm yours."

Cursing, Ronan plowed into her with one swift, powerful thrust. He buried himself to the hilt, and Maddy shouted his name as he touched a place deep inside, one she'd never known existed. Ronan started to move, still staring into her eyes. He pumped into her, slowly at first, and with each penetrating pass, the last remnants of the walls around her heart crumbled.

She had been so busy protecting her broken heart that she hadn't even realized it was already gone. Whether or not she'd made the conscious choice, she had already given it to Ronan. Or maybe he had stolen it. Did it matter? He loved her and she had fallen in love with him, one hundred percent. Ronan wouldn't hurt her or lie to her. He'd already proven that he would do everything in his power to make her happy.

No matter what happened between them in the future, she would never forget the damn pie-ingredient shopping. *Seriously? Who does that?*

As Ronan slammed into her one last time, their orgasms cresting together, Maddy sat up. She wrapped her arms and legs around his sweating, heaving body. She shuddered in his embrace. Her breasts pressed against the firm muscles of his chest, expanding and contracting in wicked little jags with each labored breath. With his body still buried deep inside hers,

Maddy pressed her cheek to his shoulder and held tight. Memories flashed through her mind, starting with the day of Lucille's funeral when Ronan had been waiting for her outside the church.

That was it.

That brief, beautiful moment was when Maddy had fallen. Tumbled off the ledge into the unknown. All this time, she'd been fighting something that had already happened.

And Ronan had been there, waiting to catch her all along.

Chapter 16

RONAN'S FIRM, NAKED BODY SPOONED AGAINST MADDY'S within the warm cocoon of the soft, thick layer of sheets and blankets. The room was dim, the early light of Christmas morning just beginning to break through and announce the day. An unfamiliar but welcome sense of peace greeted Maddy as she took note of each spot where Ronan's body met hers. She sighed and nestled deeper into his embrace, enjoying the weight of his leg as it draped possessively over hers. His chest hair rasped lightly against her back and his muscular arm tightened, pulling her even closer, his hot breath fanning across her shoulder.

"Morning," he murmured. Ronan pressed a kiss to her cheek and hugged her against him. "Merry Christmas."

"It certainly is," she whispered.

"Did Santa bring you what you wanted?" he teased. "Great sex with one of the NYPD's finest."

"Who says that's what I asked for?" She peered at him over her shoulder. "I did get a lovely pair of pajamas, but somebody kept me naked all night long, so I never got to wear them."

"Well, *I* wanted an apple pie, but *someone* got distracted and didn't finish it."

"Cut it out." Maddy giggled. "I can still bake it this morning before we go over to the main house. I did have enough of my wits about me last night to put everything in the fridge."

"I know." He tickled her belly. "I loved watching you walk around naked with only the moonlight covering you. I think you do some of your best work in the kitchen."

"If I recall correctly, you told me once it was your *second favorite* room in the house."

"After last night, the kitchen's moved into first place."

"You are too much," Maddy said, laughing.

She elbowed him playfully, but he pinned her arms and hugged her before blowing a raspberry against her throat. The silly gesture sent them both into a fit of laughter as he continued. She rolled toward the edge of the bed, trying to escape his tickle torture, but was greeted by Bowser's big, furry face.

"Get her, Bowser."

Before Maddy could protest, the bloodhound leaped up and licked her face in one big, slobbery pass.

"Hey," she said with a laugh. She wiped off his wet greeting and tried to push the overeager canine off the bed, but his big paws remained on the edge. "No fair. That's two against one."

Ronan, buckass naked, straddled Maddy and pinned her arms over her head. The sheet had fallen away during their tussle, leaving her breasts exposed to his hungry gaze. It didn't take long for the mood to go from teasing to tantalizing. Maddy arched her back, and Ronan's eyes widened as the rest of his body hardened against hers.

He leaned down to kiss her, and his cell phone rang. The loud noise interrupted the moment. Both of them stilled and exchanged a curious but concerned look. A phone call this early in the morning was never good.

"That's Gavin," Ronan said quietly. "It's barely light outside. Why the hell would he be calling now?"

He gently climbed off Maddy before snatching the phone off the nightstand and answering it.

"Gav?" He sat on the edge of his bed with his back to Maddy, his shoulders and back tensing up immediately. "What's going on?"

Maddy pulled the sheets over her breasts and propped herself on one elbow. The muscles in his back flexed and his shoulders squared, right before he shot to his feet and grabbed a pair of jeans from his duffel bag.

"Don't touch anything. She couldn't have gone far. I'm gonna need a good scent article—Gracie's hairbrush or the clothes she wore yesterday. That house is covered in different tracks, and I'm sure Gracie's been running all over. Yes, I—Gavin. We'll be right there."

The playfulness he'd exhibited only moments ago was already a distant memory. He threw the phone on the bed and started to pull on the rest of his clothes. Maddy's anxiety ratcheted up a notch when he grabbed the gun from the dresser and strapped the holster to his ankle.

"Gracie's missing," he said tightly.

"What?" Maddy tossed the covers aside and started getting her clothes on. "How could she be missing?"

"I don't know, but they can't find her and she's not answering them. Gavin said they've looked everywhere and it's been half an hour."

"Oh my God." Maddy tugged her sweater over her head and glanced out the window. "It stopped snowing. If she went outside, we should be able to see tracks or something, right?"

"Gavin said that there are no fresh tracks out any of the doors." Ronan's jaw clenched, and his face was tight with concentration. "Come on, Bowser. You're up."

Ronan went to a big, black bag next to the dresser and pulled out a leather harness and a long lead line. It wasn't the leash he used when they went running or even when he was in uniform. This one was easily three times as long and made of heavy, well-worn leather.

"Then she's got to be in that house." Fear and panic tightened in Maddy's chest. "But if she's not answering them…"

Maddy couldn't finish the thought. She couldn't even bring herself to say it out loud because the idea was too horrifying.

"We aren't going there, Mads." Ronan snapped his fingers and called Bowser, who came directly to his side. "She's fine, and we're going to find her because that's what we do. Right, boy?"

Bowser barked loudly, and the tension rose in the room as Ronan put the harness on his partner. It was like a familiar dance that both man and beast knew intimately. In that moment, the two were one. They moved with absolute precision and perfection, and for the first time, Maddy realized just how in tune they were with one another.

Maddy grabbed her coat with shaking fingers and put it on, not bothering with buttons. She followed Ronan and Bowser out into the frigid air and prayed for a Christmas miracle. It was brighter out now, and it was clear that the only tracks leading from the kitchen door of the main house were hers and Ronan's from last night.

Ronan stopped and Bowser shadowed him, almost mirroring Ronan's every move. Maddy hugged herself and hung back, not wanting to intrude or disturb the partners at work. The snow crunched beneath their feet, and the ocean crashed furiously beyond the bluff, creating an ominous soundtrack for an already tense situation.

"I don't see any tracks other than ours." Ronan pointed to the right and then to the left toward the ocean and the bluff. "Nothing coming around either side of the house. That's a good sign."

"It's freezing out here, Ronan." Maddy's teeth chattered, and she cringed at the mere idea of little Gracie trapped outside in this weather. "If she's lost in this…"

"Not going there, Mads. We need to stay calm and take it one step at a time." He gave her a reassuring look over his shoulder. "Let's get inside and give Bowser something to search for. This giant old house has more nooks and crannies than you can shake a stick at, and lots of tucked-away spots that a curious little girl like Gracie could get stuck in. Trust me, she's in there someplace."

His eyes, an almost stormy blue-gray, were sharp and kind at the same time, and somehow Maddy knew it would be okay. Gracie was going to be fine—because there was no way in hell Ronan would have it any other way. Confidence oozed from him. This was what he did.

Lily's weeping could be heard as soon as they stepped into the kitchen, and Maddy's heart clenched in her chest. The look of relief on Gavin's face when they came into the house was heartbreaking. He had his arm around Jordan, who looked terrified but was clearly trying to hold it together.

"I-I just don't know where she could have gone,"

Jordan said in a quivering voice. "She was so excited for Christmas morning."

"It's going to be okay." Maddy ran over and dragged her friend into the tightest hug she could muster. "They'll find her. She has to be somewhere in this house."

"Here." Gavin held out a little pair of green-and-red leggings, and his voice wavered as he handed them to Ronan. "She wore these yesterday."

"Good." Ronan nodded. "There are no tracks coming around the side of the house."

"None out the front," Tristan said, walking into the kitchen. He unzipped his coat and settled his hands on his hips, his expression as grim as the others. "I don't think she went outside."

"Then she's somewhere in the house," Ronan said calmly. "I need everyone to go into the family room. The fewer people we have walking around, the better. We want to have as clear a trail for Bowser as we can."

"Come on, Jordan." Maddy quickly took off her coat and boots, leaving them by the door. "It's going to be okay."

The festive, joyous atmosphere that had permeated the living room last night had been replaced by quiet tension. Lily was sniffling and sat on Claire's lap, her face red and swollen from crying all morning. Carolyn held Claire's hand. Bonded by their love for their grandchildren, the two women sat stoically, obviously doing their best to keep Lily calm. Jordan and Gavin stood by the fireplace, flanked by the other brothers, and the Christmas tree had a sea of presents spilling out beneath. Charles, the typically lighthearted patriarch, remained in the kitchen doorway watching over it all.

Maddy kept her eyes fixed on Ronan and Bowser.

"Okay, boy." Ronan squatted down and held the leggings to the bloodhound's nose. The dog startled snuffling and moving his snout around as though trying to soak up every single bit of Gracie's scent.

"Is Bowser gonna find my sister?" Lily's little voice, weak and teary, filled the room with gut-wrenching clarity. "She wanted to see Santa, but I told her that he was magic and wouldn't let her see him."

"He'll find her, Lily." Ronan rose to his feet slowly. "Bowser loves playing hide-and-seek. You ever play that game?"

"Uh-huh." She sniffled. Lily swiped at her red eyes and nestled deeper into Claire's embrace. "Lotsa times. Gracie likes it too."

"Well, Bowser is the hide-and-seek champ." Ronan winked and gave the little girl a reassuring smile. "He'll find her, kiddo. I promise."

"I'm coming with you, Ronan." Gavin kissed the top of Jordan's head. "It'll be okay, babe. I know the house is big, but she's got to be in here somewhere. We know she didn't go outside."

"Then why isn't she answering us when we call her?"

Gavin's jaw clenched, and he shook his head before kissing Jordan quickly one more time.

"Stay behind me, Gavin." Ronan leaned down one more time and let Bowser sniff the leggings before shouting, "Search!"

The dog's body tensed and then he was off like a shot, his nose to the ground and his tail in the air. Maddy went over to Jordan and wrapped her arms around her. They both held their breath as Ronan and his partner circled the room briefly before heading out into the front hall and up the stairs. The man was brimming with quiet confidence and once again in absolute control.

"He'll find her," Maddy whispered. "If there's one thing Ronan doesn't know how to do, it's quit."

———⁓⁓⁓———

"I don't think I've ever been this scared in my life." His brother's voice, tight and quiet, echoed behind Ronan as they climbed the sweeping staircase to the second floor. "This is crazy, man. Where the hell did she go?"

Ronan nodded but said nothing, his attention fixed on Bowser and his body language. When they hit the top of the stairs, Bowser snuffled along the carpet to the left and picked up the pace, his long tail bobbing like a sword. They passed three bedrooms, and Bowser paused for a second at the door of each one before trudging forward. Finally, they got to Gavin's old room.

"This is where she and Lily slept." Gavin pointed to the queen-size bed as Bowser continued his search and circled the room. The dog went to the bed, then around and around the space until he finally returned to the door. "Jordan and I stayed upstairs."

Then, as though the dog understood every word, he pulled a U-turn and followed a scent trail back out the door and down the hall. Right before they hit the main staircase again, Bowser turned sharply down the little hallway to the right. He paused in front of the bathroom door but then ran up the narrow stairway that led to the third floor of the house.

"You checked up here?" Ronan asked.

"Of course." Gavin's impatience was rising. "We

looked in every damn room ten times. The basement. Everywhere. Every closet. I even checked the cabinets in the bathrooms."

Bowser whined when they hit the third-floor landing. He trotted to the right and circled through the small bathroom with the old-fashioned claw-foot bathtub before quickly coming out and going back toward the stairs. He followed her scent into the bedroom where Gavin and Jordan had stayed.

"She and Lily were in here with us," Gavin said quietly. "We read *The Night before Christmas* before they went to sleep."

Bowser paused and stuck his snout in the air. For one painfully long moment, Ronan thought the trail was gone, and his heart sank. A split second later, the massive bloodhound stuck his nose back to the floral carpet. He pulled Ronan out to the hallway and took a right turn. He went to the creaky old door that led into the attic storage and barked loudly before nudging it open with his nose and trudging forward.

"We looked in here." Gavin's voice was edged with a hint of fear. "Three times. Oh my God. It's got to be below freezing back there. Gracie!"

The long, corridor-like space—one of the only sections of the massive old colonial that remained unfinished—had always been used for storage. The rough wooden floor and bare rafters gave it a dark and ominous feel. Old clothes and boxes filled with God-knows-what were stacked and strewn throughout the cavernous space. It was dark except for a faint shaft of light coming from the oval window at the very end.

Bowser moved faster and grew agitated—she was

back there somewhere. Behind a stack of boxes, maybe?
What the hell was she doing all the way up here? Ronan
just prayed that the little girl was okay. His partner
barked and whined, and when they reached the end of
the room, Ronan held his breath. It was freezing in here,
and if Gracie had been up here exposed for hours…

"Gracie!" Gavin shouted. "Gracie Ann McKenna,
answer me right now."

Then, just when Ronan thought he'd scream with
frustration, Bowser jumped up to the right and barked
loudly at what looked like a pile of blankets on top of a
stack of three or four storage boxes.

But the blankets moved.

"Got her!"

Before he could reach the little girl, Gavin pushed
past him. Ronan stepped back, giving way for his
brother. He squatted down next to Bowser instead and
ruffled the dog's ears, whispering words of praise. His
partner licked his face in between panting breaths.

"Gracie!" The relief that filled Gavin's voice was
music to Ronan's ears. "Baby, are you okay?"

Gavin pulled several blankets and coats off the sleepy
little girl. She had on three different winter hats and a
pair of mittens. She looked as surprised to see Gavin as
he was happy to see her. It was no wonder she hadn't
heard them calling to her all the way back here, nestled
as she was in her deep pile. Ronan was just grateful that
there were enough old comforters and sweaters for her
to keep warm and that she had been resourceful enough
to use them.

"What are you doing all the way up here?" Gavin
pulled her off the stack of boxes, out from under the

crush of old blankets, and into his arms. "Sweetheart, we've been worried sick and calling you all morning. Didn't you hear us?"

"I was tryin' to see Santa's sleigh." She swiped hair from her eyes and yawned before hugging Gavin and settling her head on his shoulder. "Lily said I couldn't 'cause he's magic, but I fought I could be sneaky and see him up here 'cause it's so close to the sky. But I fell 'sleep."

Ronan rose to his feet and exchanged a look of relief with his brother.

"Hi, doggie!" Gracie exclaimed as Bowser sniffed her sock-covered feet, dangling right near his nose. "He's ticklin' my toes." She giggled. "Nana Carolyn is gonna be mad that you're in the house. Maybe 'cause it's Christmas you can stay."

"Come on, kiddo." Gavin kissed her cheek and headed out of the attic. "I have a feeling Bowser's not going to be banned to the cottage much longer. In fact, I bet Nana Carolyn is going to set him a place at the table for Christmas dinner."

Ronan followed his brother out of the storage space with his partner, and they made their way back down to the first floor.

"We found her!" Gavin yelled as they reached the second floor. "Bowser and Ronan found Gracie."

They were greeted by shrieks of joy, lots of hugs, and plenty of happy tears from the entire family. Bowser even got a hug from Ronan's mom. Maddy ran over and wrapped Ronan up in her arms, holding him tighter than she ever had before. He pressed his hand to her back. The woman was shaking like a leaf.

"She's okay," Ronan whispered. He cradled Maddy's face in both hands. "A little cold, and annoyed that she didn't see Santa, but she's fine. Though I'm pretty sure my mom is going to put a lock on the storage door now."

"I know." Tears glistened in her eyes and she shook her head. "That's not it."

"Then what?"

"She's not the only person you found."

"How do you mean?"

"Me," she said with a shuddering breath. "You found me. No matter how hard I tried to hide, you kept on searching."

Maddy rose up on her toes and hugged her arms around his neck. She held on and pressed her lips against his ear, her body quivering against his.

"I love you, Ronan," she whispered.

It was like getting the wind knocked out of him, and he needed a second to catch his breath. He tangled his fingers in her long, silky curls and pulled back to look her in the face. Her blue eyes glittered brightly and one tear fell down her cheek, but a smile was blooming across her lips.

"I do." Her voice quivered, and she laughed. "I love you."

"Merry Christmas." Ronan pressed a kiss to her lips, gently and reverently, wanting to imprint this moment onto his memory forever. "I love you too, Mads."

Bowser barked loudly, interrupting them, and they both burst out laughing. Maddy rested her head on Ronan's chest, and he reveled in the feel of her body as it sank against his. He stroked both hands down her back before hugging her tightly.

Could his life get any better than it was right at this moment? It was perfect, and that was what frightened him. His joy was infiltrated by fear that slithered in like a snake. He'd never had so much to lose before.

And it scared the shit out of him.

His thoughts went to Gavin and the pure fear in his big brother's voice. He had heard that tone from plenty of other people when he was on the job—family members and friends who were worried sick over their missing loved ones. But he'd never truly connected with it or fully understood it until today. He'd always been an outside observer before.

"Come on, you two!" His mother peeked her head around the archway that led from the front hall and into the living room. "It's time to give these little girls their presents from Santa. Now, I know *we* don't need any because we have our Gracie safe and sound, but I might have something in here for both of you."

Bowser rose to all fours and whined.

"Oh fine," his mom huffed, feigning irritation. "I might have a little something for you too. I have some leftover steak in the fridge with your hairy name on it. After all, you are the hero of the hour."

Bowser looked at Ronan as though seeking permission, and he was happy to oblige. Ronan removed the harness and lead line from his partner and gave him another healthy dose of praise.

"Well, this certainly is a Christmas to remember." Maddy watched Bowser leave before turning back to Ronan. "But let's not make losing a kid a new tradition."

"Not a chance."

Ronan winked and released her hand as she headed

into the living room. No, he'd be happy without that addition. But there was one new aspect he'd like to continue. He wanted to wake up to Maddy's beautiful smile every morning for the rest of his life.

Chapter 17

MADDY TIPTOED OUT OF THE BEDROOM, CAREFUL NOT TO wake Ronan or Bowser, who was snoring and hanging off the edge of the bed by Ronan's feet. She dragged on the huge, navy-blue NYPD sweatshirt, one of Ronan's gifts to her, to cover her nakedness and stretched her deliciously sore body. Their lovemaking last night had been the perfect end to one of the most memorable Christmases she had ever had.

Once she was up, though, guilt tugged at her for ignoring work for the past week. Unable to sleep, and with her trip back to the city imminent, Maddy decided to catch up nice and early. That way, she and Ronan could enjoy their last day in Old Brookfield without a huge to-do list hanging over her head.

She slipped into the living room, far chillier than the bedroom, and pulled her cell phone from her purse. As she did, she caught a whiff of Ronan's warm, musky scent still clinging to her body. She smiled and pulled up the sweatshirt's hood. He'd kept apologizing that he didn't have anything better to give her and swore he'd make it up to her, but she couldn't have loved anything more.

It was like being wrapped up in Ronan.

What could be better than that?

After turning on the fireplace with the handy little remote, Maddy sat in the big chair and pulled her knees to her chest beneath the sweatshirt. The tie she had given him for Christmas, a blue one with white dog bones on it, was dangling precariously off the coffee table. Maddy giggled at the sight of the living room strewn with discarded clothing, thanks to yet another sexcapade in front of the fire.

She turned on the phone and prepared herself for the slew of emails she was certain were waiting for her. Ignoring work wasn't smart or savvy, but it had been necessary. She'd badly needed the break. The truth was, she hadn't missed work.

Not one little bit.

Two voice messages were waiting for her, along with a litany of texts. All of the texts were from her assistant, Sharon, and were mostly about the party. Updates on numbers, the caterer, and so forth. The voice mails were more worrisome. Sharon would only call Maddy on her vacation if there had been a major problem.

Panic flickered up Maddy's back. Had that asshole Drummond done something? Had a deal fallen through?

"Damn it," she whispered. "I know better than this."

Maddy pressed the phone to her ear and listened to the messages. A knot of dread coiled in her belly as Sharon's teary voice echoed over the line.

Two more women had been murdered, and Maddy knew both of them.

Patricia Teagan and Yolanda Baquero.

Both women worked at high-end realty houses in the city. Patricia was an executive assistant, and Yolanda was a seasoned commercial real estate broker. They'd been friendly acquaintances.

Not anymore. Now Patricia and Yolanda were

both dead. Killed by the same son of a bitch who had snuffed out the lives of Brenda and Lucille. What had Sharon said in her message? They were calling him the West Side Ringer. Maddy's stomach roiled at the sick name the media had come up with, all in the name of ratings.

Nausea flooded her, and she quickly grabbed the television remote, turning the set on and searching for the news. Tears stung Maddy's eyes as she cradled the phone in her lap and watched the morning report. Sure enough, an update on the West Side Ringer eventually flashed up on the screen. As the newscasters blathered on about the lack of leads on the city's latest serial killer, Maddy's thoughts darted back to the night of the wedding.

Ronan had taken a call from work.

She'd thought he was acting strange, and now she knew why.

"I'm sorry, Mads."

Ronan's deep voice rumbled behind her, and his hand settled on her shoulder.

"Is this why you didn't want to watch the news?" she asked, her voice thick with tears. "You knew about this! Why wouldn't you tell me?"

Maddy rose to her feet and turned to face him. He was shirtless and wearing only the paw-print-covered boxer shorts she'd gotten for him. His dark hair was tousled from sleep, but his body and expression were completely alert.

"I know you're pissed." He held up both hands and kept his voice calm. "But please hear me out."

"The call you got during the wedding—that was

about Patricia and Yolanda. Oh my God…" She backed up and pointed at him accusingly. "You lied to me. How could you do that, Ronan? I *knew* those women."

He blanched visibly, and his jaw clenched. Ronan dropped his hands to his sides, and the muscles in his chest flexed, but he didn't make a move toward her. His expression darkened to one she couldn't quite read, and he looked as though he was trying to figure out exactly what to say.

Maddy's head was spinning, and her heart hurt. Two more women she knew had been brutalized, and the man she loved had lied to her about it. He'd kept the information from her like she was a fragile, broken woman who couldn't possibly handle the truth.

"You treated me like a child," she said, seething.

"I'm sorry!" Ronan shouted. "You were finally *you* again, and I didn't want to do or say anything to change that."

"Really?" Maddy folded her arms over her breasts and stared him down. "So, *you* get to decide when I find out two of my colleagues have been murdered? *You* get to choose when I get upset? Is that it?"

"No." Ronan ran both hands over his face vigorously before letting out a growl of frustration. "Listen, Mads, with the wedding and then Christmas, I didn't want to dump news like that on you. I had planned to tell you about it today, before you left to go back to the city."

Maddy studied him closely. The earnest expression stamped on his face tugged at her heart. She knew, deep down, he was telling the truth. He'd tried to protect her because he cared for her, and yet she still found it unsettling. Was this what life with Ronan would be like? Would he constantly be judging what she should or shouldn't know about? Was the cop in him, the protector, going to be judge and jury, deciding what information she needed and when?

She tore her gaze from his and headed for the bedroom. "I have to pack my things and get back to the city."

Ronan's strong hand reached out and tangled with hers, preventing her from going any farther. Maddy stilled, their bodies wavering close and his warm, firm hand curled around hers like a blanket.

A conflicting storm of emotions swirled inside her. Grief for the women who had lost their lives dominated the swell, but there was more tangled within. Fear, however irrational, that Ronan's need to protect her would mean controlling her. But at the same time, there was immense love for the man who clearly put the feelings and needs of others ahead of his own.

"Please, wait." Ronan's voice was quiet but filled with strength. "Don't leave like this, Maddy."

"I trusted you," she whispered. She forced herself to look him in the eyes. "I know you had the best of intentions. I never would have wanted you to share that horrible news in the middle of the wedding. But you should have told me when we got back here."

"Maddy, I—"

"Wait." She shook her head and screwed her eyes shut briefly. "I love you, Ronan. I do. And I know you love me. But that does *not* give you the right to treat me like a pathetic, fragile creature who can't handle herself."

"Is that what you think?" His brow furrowed, and fury flickered in his eyes. "That I didn't tell you because I was worried you wouldn't be able to handle it?"

"Why else?" She tilted her chin, daring him to admit the truth.

"Because I knew it would hurt you." Ronan cradled her face with both hands. "Seeing you unhappy or in pain kills me, Mads. I was putting it off, and I'm sorry for not being straight with you. I don't think you're weak. In fact, I think you're one of the toughest women I've ever known." He let out a slow breath. "I was being selfish too. I'd waited so long to see that beautiful smile on your face… I didn't want to do anything that would make it go away."

She pressed her hands over his briefly, then tugged them down from her face and nodded her understanding. Maddy stared at her fingers, tangled with Ronan's, and ran her thumb over his. He would always try to keep her from harm's way, to protect her from anything or anyone he saw as a threat—even if it meant keeping the truth from her.

If she planned on being with Ronan, that was a fact she would have to accept. But could she? Maddy didn't want to fight. She would put this away and deal with it later.

"It's okay," she whispered. She rose on her toes and pressed a quick kiss to his cheek. "According to Sharon's message, Yolanda's wake is later today, and the funeral is tomorrow. I have to hurry. I'm sure traffic will be crazy, and it's going to take me forever to get back there."

She tried to leave, but he hung on to one of her hands.

"I'll go with you."

"No." Maddy looked over her shoulder at him and squeezed his hand. "You stay with your family like you planned. I'll be fine. Really."

Silence hung between them for three beats of her heart.

"Okay." Ronan released her hand, but concern edged his handsome face. "I'll give you a lift back to your car at the inn."

"Great," Maddy said with a forced smile.

Right before she reached the hallway, Ronan called to her.

"I'm never gonna change, Mads." His voice was serious and calm and edged with familiar arrogance. "I won't apologize for wanting to protect you."

She glanced over at him, and her stomach fluttered. His muscular body was taut and primed as though ready for a fight, and his fierce stare bored into her. Unmovable. Unshakable. Resolute. The man wasn't going to give an inch—not on this, or anything else he believed in.

She hugged her arms around her chest in an effort to quell the uncertainty that bubbled up. Unable to say a word, for fear she would start blubbering like an idiot, Maddy simply nodded and gave him a tight smile.

As she packed her bags, uneasiness simmered in her belly. She was going back to the city to attend yet another funeral, and all she really wanted to do was have Ronan hold her and tell her it was all going to be okay. But doing that would only confirm what he had been afraid of in the first place. No, there would be no pathetic weepiness or crumbling.

Maddy would soldier on and move forward and get back to work and her life in the city. She had been good at that before, being on her own. Keeping her head down and buried in work. This ache in her chest, the feeling of the earth shifting beneath her feet, this was exactly what she had been afraid of. For a fleeting moment, Maddy longed for the numb anonymity she'd had before letting Ronan McGuire into her heart and her bed.

Ronan's jeans fell off the bedpost when she dragged her suitcase to the ground, and a paper fluttered to the floor from the back pocket. Maddy bent to pick it up, but she knew what it was before she even unfolded the smooth square.

Her eyes filled with tears.

It was the page from the *Better Homes and Garden Cook Book*. She unfolded the paper with shaking fingers. The words on the page blurred, but she didn't have to read them to know what was there. She knew that the apple pie recipe covered the well-worn page, and Maddy's heart swelled with love.

How could she be angry with him for wanting to protect her heart? This was the same man who went grocery shopping for a pie he wasn't even certain she would be around to make.

She was being an idiot.

Ronan wasn't some asshole trying to control her. He was a loving, thoughtful man who had attempted to put her happiness above his own. Maddy spun around and found herself face-to-face with him. That fiercely intense blue-green gaze was pinned to hers, and his eyes glittered in the morning light that spilled into the bedroom. The stubble on his chin seemed even thicker than usual and accentuated the dark, dangerous side of him, the one that both attracted and frightened her. It was that piece of Ronan that had driven him to become a cop, fueling his innate desire to protect those he cared for.

He stood in the doorway with his arms at his side and

Bowser right behind him. Any anger Maddy had felt faded in an instant, like snow melting in the sun.

"I know you think I pulled a majorly stupid move by not telling you about what happened." He took one step closer. "I've had an incredible time since I've been home with you. The best of my life, in fact. I don't want it to end like this, with you pissed at me. I'm no good at relationships, Maddy, probably because I've never really been in one before.

"Get ready, baby, because I'm gonna screw up a lot more. So I'm apologizing, in advance, for the dumb shit I'm gonna do, because I'm sure there'll be *plenty* of it. But know this: no matter what I do or say, I love you, Maddy Morgan. For the rest of my life, I'm going to work hard to ensure that you know that, and I'll try to keep the dumbass moves to a minimum."

Overcome by love and gratitude, Maddy ran to Ronan. She latched her arms around his neck before burying her face in the comforting warmth of his throat. He let out a curse of relief as his arms curled around her, and he gave her a hug so tight that it stole the breath from her lungs.

"I'm sorry I got angry with you," she whispered into his ear. "What happened to Yolanda and the others is just awful, and I thought that you were trying to—"

"I'm the one who's sorry." Ronan pulled back and kissed her, brushing the hair from her forehead. "I'm no good at this relationship stuff."

"Are you kidding?" Maddy laughed through her tears and curled her hands around his biceps, shaking him playfully. "That pie-shopping thing should be put in a handbook. You know, *The Guy's Guide to Being an Awesome Boyfriend* or something."

"Boyfriend?" Ronan's eyebrow arched. "I like that."

"Well, yeah, I guess… I mean…yes," she sputtered.

"It's a start," he murmured. His smile faded, and he rubbed his hands up and down her arms reassuringly. "Are you sure you don't want me to go back to the city with you?"

"No." Maddy shook her head and hugged him, pressing her cheek against the firm muscles of his chest. She would never get tired of the feel of him. "Your family would be disappointed if you left early, especially your mom. I'll be okay."

"You sure?" He leaned back and eyed her warily. "This isn't one of those times when a woman says one thing but really means another, is it?"

"No," she said quietly. "And I'll make you a deal. I'll always say what I mean and mean what I say. No beating around the bush or trying to make you guess how I'm feeling. Life is too short to waste it on misunderstandings."

"Amen to that," Ronan murmured. He pulled her into another hug and smoothed his hands down her back. "I'm sorry as hell about what's happening to these women, Maddy."

"Me too," she whispered.

"And I want you to be careful. Remember what I said about trusting your gut."

"I will."

A shiver of apprehension shimmied up her back at the idea of going back to her empty apartment, but she shoved it aside. Selfishly, she *did* want Ronan to come back to the city with her, but she couldn't ask him to leave his family. Carolyn was so happy to have all five of her sons at home with her, and Maddy didn't want to do anything to disturb that. Especially after the warmth and hospitality the McGuires had shown her.

Ronan would say yes in a heartbeat if she asked him to come with her, because that's the kind of man he was. And it was precisely that quality that made her fall in love with him.

———

The silence that greeted Maddy in her apartment was deafening.

The funeral and the reception that followed were as sad as she had expected. Family and friends wept. The priest had spouted the typically reassuring words dripping with spirituality, and everyone spoke well of the woman they had lost.

Mother. Wife. Friend. Daughter. Professional.

Yolanda had been all of that and more.

Though the woman was gone, the ripple effects of her life remained, evident in the memories of the people she loved. It dawned on Maddy that for months after Rick died, she had existed without creating any ripples.

What the hell kind of life was that?

She tossed her keys in the little bowl on the sofa table and looked around at her empty apartment. She had always known this space wasn't her real home, but that truth was evident now more than ever. It didn't have a heart or a soul. There was no laughter here or even tears. No pain. No love. Nothing.

That was what she had needed, what she had *craved*, to survive losing Rick. But not anymore. All of that ended the instant she fell for Ronan McGuire.

"No pity parties, Morgan," Maddy said out loud to absolutely nobody but herself.

She let out a sigh of defeat, and her gaze settled on her laptop, which was sitting open on the dining room table. Maybe catching up on some of the emails she'd been ignoring would help her shake off the sadness from the funeral. She took off her coat and tossed it over the back of the sofa before heading to the computer.

Maddy sat down and went to turn it on, only to discover it was already running. Her brow furrowed. *That's weird*. She could swear she powered it down last night, but the little green camera light was glaring at her.

"Shit," she said with exasperation.

She and Sharon had done some business over Skype last night, and Maddy must have forgotten to close the program. When she tapped the keys, the screen flared to life, and Maddy's overflowing inbox glared at her accusingly.

"Jeez," she whined. "I left everything open? I have my head up my ass."

There were several unopened emails from one potential new client. The guy had sent six messages over the past week and seemed eager to work with Cosmopolitan Realty. Maddy read through them quickly before responding to the last one.

Of course she would be happy to work with him and apologies for the delayed response, but it was due to the holidays. Yada, yada, yada.

She hit Send.

Fourteen more unread messages remained in the queue.

Her fingers hovered above the keyboard. She didn't want to be doing work right now, any more than she had last night. Maddy settled her hands on the table on either side of the computer and stared at the list of messages through a narrowed gaze. A month ago, this kind of distraction would have been exactly what she wanted and needed, to dive into work until she couldn't think of anything else.

"What the hell am I doing?" She tossed her head back and let out a loud laugh that echoed off the walls. "This isn't where I want to be, and it sure as hell isn't where I'm supposed to be. Not anymore."

Maddy quickly closed out her email. She tried to get the computer to power down, but the damn camera remained on, and she had no idea how to shut it off. The green light blinked at her almost mockingly. Technology was *not* her thing.

"Whatever," she huffed before finally giving up and grabbing her coat from the couch. She fished her keys out of the bowl and headed for the door with a wide grin on her face. Ronan had texted her an hour ago to say that he had decided to come home early after all and was around if she needed him.

A smile tugged at Maddy's lips as she stepped into the elevator. She did need him, and for the first time, she wasn't afraid to admit it.

—◊◊◊—

When the doorbell of his apartment rang, Ronan was convinced it was his neighbor's kid trying to sell him more Girl Scout cookies. And if it was, he was going to lecture her again about going door-to-door without her mom. But when he yanked the door open, a far better sight awaited him.

Maddy stood in the hallway with a big bag of Chinese takeout in her hands and a wide smile on her face.

"You were scarfing down lo mein leftovers on Christmas Eve, if I recall correctly, so that's what I got." She kissed him on the lips and slipped past him into his apartment. "I might have to fight you for the extra egg roll, though."

Ronan shut the door and slipped the chain on before following her into the tiny galley kitchen. She wore a dark-blue dress and heels but had ditched her coat over the crappy folding chair behind her. The little café-size table for two was all that would fit in the kitchen. She was pulling out containers and chopsticks, and Bowser was already sitting behind her waiting for leftovers.

Her beauty, which always blinded him, shone even brighter against the dingy backdrop of his tiny kitchen. Ronan suddenly felt very self-conscious about the state of this place. He leaned in the doorway and folded his arms over his chest, wishing she'd called first so he could have at least picked up a little bit.

He glanced at the grease-stained slats of the white shade on the kitchen window. Yeah, he needed a cleaning crew to try to get this place in shape. She was too damn lovely to be hanging around in this dump. Hell, she was too good for this city. All he could think about was taking her back to the safety and serenity of Old Brookfield.

"What?" Maddy stilled, and her brows knit together as she sucked soy sauce from her thumb. Her eyes grew wide. "Oh my God. Should I have called first? I'm sorry. I thought you'd like a surprise. You're always doing thoughtful stuff for me, and I know you just got

home. I figured that you wouldn't have anything in the
house for dinner, so—"

"I love it!" Ronan grabbed her around the waist and
kissed her quickly. "Are you kidding? I'm thrilled to
see you but…" He lifted one shoulder. "I could have
come to your place. Wouldn't you be more comfortable there?"

"Nope," she said brightly. Maddy put the container
on the counter and curled both hands around the fabric
of his T-shirt, tugging him close. "I think you've ruined
me, McGuire."

"How's that?" Ronan slipped his hands down and
settled them on her backside.

"I was okay, you know?" Her voice was soft and
sultry, and her blue eyes were bright. "My world was
orderly and neat and safe. I could have existed that way
forever. And then *you* came along."

"Okay…" he said slowly.

"You ruined all that," she murmured.

She tugged his shirt out from his jeans and helped
him take it off, quickly tossing it aside. Ronan fought
the rising surge of lust as she trailed her fingertips over
his chest and down his stomach.

"How so?"

He unzipped the back of her dress and peeled it from
her body, leaving her in only her red lace panties, bra,
and heels. Ronan's cock twitched at the sight of all that
lovely skin exposed just for him.

"Because you brought *life* back into my life, and now
it's like a drug, Ronan." She flicked his nipple with her
tongue while she undid the button of his jeans. "I want
more. More of you. Your touch, your taste, and, most of

all, your heart. So you see, McGuire, you can't send me back to that empty, soulless apartment, at least not alone. I'd rather be anywhere *with you* than without you."

As he swept her up into his arms and carried her to bed, one thought went through Ronan's mind: How long did he have to wait before asking her to marry him? And would tomorrow be too soon?

Chapter 18

MADDY STARED OUT HER LIVING ROOM WINDOW AND BARELY noticed the caterers who were busily rushing around the apartment getting last-minute items set up for the New Year's Eve party. She had nothing but thoughts of Ronan on the brain. They had spent every night together since he returned from Old Brookfield, and Maddy felt like a teenager. She was giddy at the mere thought of seeing him, and every time she set eyes on the man, her heart tumbled in her chest.

She had almost canceled the party tonight, fearing it would be in poor taste to host it in light of what had happened, but Ronan convinced her to move forward. He reminded her that now, more than ever, they should recognize the gift of another year. Maddy eventually came to the same conclusion, but she made him promise to come to the party as her date.

He had been reluctant at first, to her surprise, but it hadn't taken much convincing to get him to accept. A grin curved her lips, and she sipped from the glass of pinot grigio in her hand. She'd never had such fun *persuading* anyone in her life. She'd even told him he could bring Bowser. He always seemed more at ease with his partner at his side.

"Maddy?" Sharon's voice pulled her from her wicked memories, and Maddy's face heated. "The caterer said everything is good to go. The bartender is all set, and the first guests should be arriving shortly."

"Thank you, Sharon." Maddy took the woman's hand and gave it a squeeze. "Not just for the party, but for everything. I really don't know what I'd do without you. You've been a lifesaver."

The doorbell rang, announcing the first guest of the evening. Maddy hurried to greet whoever it was, her heart racing with anticipation. Was it Ronan? She smoothed her long, red dress and checked her reflection in the foyer mirror before opening the door.

Five smiling people were waiting patiently on the other side. They quickly swept in and greeted her with air kisses. They were all clients that Maddy had known for years, summer beach renters who were now buying real estate from her in the city, and while she was happy to see them, none of them were the man she really wanted to arrive.

From that point on, the bell kept ringing and the guests continued to arrive, but Ronan wasn't among them. The booze flowed as freely as the music from the speakers set up around the apartment, and the servers passed the food exactly as Maddy had asked.

Almost two hours into the party, Maddy was beginning to think that perhaps he had changed his mind and wasn't coming after all. All of those fears were put to rest when Ronan and Bowser strode into the apartment.

The bell didn't ring, but why would it? He knew his way in to the apartment as well as he knew his way around her body. That moment she saw him standing there, filling the foyer as only Ronan could, was the first time her apartment felt like home.

Dressed in a dark suit, a crisp white shirt, and the tie she'd given him for Christmas, Ronan looked as gorgeous as ever. He was freshly shaven, and it looked like he had gotten a haircut. The man was stunning. He had even dressed Bowser for the occasion. The bloodhound had a silver bow tie around his neck and looked as pleased about it as one would expect.

"Excuse me," Maddy murmured to Mr. and Mrs. Weinstein. "A very dear friend has arrived. I'll be right back."

She wove her way through the crowd of people, a walk that seemed far longer than it should, until she finally reached Ronan's side.

"Hey," she whispered as he placed a kiss on her cheek. "I was beginning to think you weren't gonna show."

"Sorry we're late." He wrapped Bowser's leash around his hand, keeping his partner close. He seemed nervous or on edge about something, and he scanned the guests milling about with a professional eye. "I got hung up on a couple of calls."

"Work?" Maddy tightened her grip on the wineglass. "I mean, no one else is hurt, are they?"

"No." He shook his head and slipped his arm around her waist as that cocky little smirk curved his firm lips. "Not work. I promise."

"What are you up to?" Maddy's eyes narrowed.

"Nothing I can share at the moment." He kissed her quickly on the lips. "Soon, though."

"Okay, but don't think I'm going to forget about it." Maddy elbowed him and nodded toward the bar in the far corner. "Come on, let's get you a drink and then I'll introduce you to everyone."

With Ronan by her side, Maddy mingled through the party, and as she suspected, the man handled himself with all the confidence and charm he was capable of. The women were swooning, and the men were practically flexing muscles as they tried to keep up with Ronan's naturally dominating presence. Everything was going smoothly. Even Bowser had made himself at home and had disappeared into Maddy's bedroom.

To her surprise, Mr. Gregory had shown up, and at the moment, he was grilling Maddy about three new apartments that had recently come on the market. She nodded and smiled, reassuring him that she would pull the full listings for him first thing in the morning. As if anybody was going to be showing homes on New Year's Day! Ronan was a total trouper. He stuck by her, occasionally and discreetly rubbing her lower back, which was both a distraction and a comfort.

Gregory hardly paid any attention to Ronan. In fact, he was one of the only people in the room who ignored him. Maddy wasn't sure why that was, but she chalked it up to his arrogant nature. When Gregory finally finished his litany of requests, he flicked a quick look to Ronan before excusing himself.

Finally, she and Ronan had a moment alone.

"Now, *that guy* might win the Most High-Maintenance Client Award," she whispered. She leaned into Ronan's embrace and let out a contented sigh. "How long until midnight and all of them leave?"

"Not quite an hour, babe." His fingers settled on the curve of her waist in a delightfully familiar way. "How can you stand to spend time with these people? Some of them are okay but that last guy, Gregory? He's a cold piece of business."

"Be nice. His wife has been battling cancer, and I'm

going to help them find their new home, even if it kills me. In fact, I'm shocked he's even here. I thought she was coming to the city before the holidays."

"Well, shit. I'm sorry the guy's wife is sick, but he's still a piece of work. And if he's so concerned about his wife, why would he leave her alone on New Year's Eve and come to a party without her?"

"I know he's a little odd—"

"Odd?" Ronan snorted. "The second you told him I was a cop, it was like I became a nonperson. To high-powered men like Gregory, cops are beneath him. I'm like *the help*."

"Stop it." Maddy shook her head and waved him off. "That's ridiculous. As far as Mr. Gregory goes, you're right—he's difficult. But he's also my client. So play nice."

She turned to face Ronan and found his expression hard. His square jaw was set, and his eyes flashed with a hint of anger.

"What?" Maddy tilted her head and studied him closely. "What's wrong?"

"You don't get it, do you?" Ronan shook his head slowly, his eyes skittering over her face. "These people can buy and sell anyone and anything, and most of them would probably try. Did you see that one guy's face? What was his name? The one with the bad toupee."

"You mean Mr. Weinstein?"

"Yeah, when *he* found out I was a cop, I thought he was going to run away and wash his hands after shaking mine." Ronan tossed back the rest of his drink. "You would think a guy with all that dough would have a better rug. It looks like a ferret died on his head."

"Ronan!" Maddy said, barely able to contain her giggle.

"I'm sorry, Mads." He pulled one of her curls straight before letting go. "I don't gel with a crowd like this."

"Is this a money thing again?" Maddy tangled her fingers with his. "I thought we worked this out. You know I don't care about that."

"It's not a money thing," he said tightly. "It's a douche-bag thing. My family has money, but they don't act like they're better than anyone else. Why do you want to hang around with these people?"

"I don't," she said flatly. "This is a business event, Ronan. The only guest here on a personal level is you."

A smile bubbled up on Maddy's lips, but it was swiftly squelched when she spotted a familiar reflection in the window behind Ronan. Chris Drummond. How long had he been here? Maddy wasn't sure, but based on the drink in his hand, it had been a little while.

"What's wrong?" Ronan asked quietly.

"Remember the asshat that I basically got fired?" Maddy kept a smile on her face and her voice light. She sidled in closer to Ronan and nodded subtly toward Drummond. "That's him."

"Which one?" Ronan slipped his arm around her waist protectively. "The tall chinless guy with the brown hair? He looks like a weasel."

"Yes." Maddy stifled a giggle and elbowed Ronan. "Keep your voice down."

"The guy has balls to show up here."

"Well, Drummond is nothing if not bold."

The moment the words escaped her lips, Chris Drummond looked over and caught her gaze. A slow shit-eating grin slid across his face.

"Damn it," Maddy hissed. "He's coming over."

"I got your back, babe," Ronan murmured.

"Hey, Maddy." The unwelcome voice of Chris Drummond curled through the air, like a snake through the grass. "Sorry I'm late. I was making the rounds, you know how it is, and your little shindig was last on my list."

"Hello, Chris." She kept her voice even but couldn't hide the phoniness in her attempts at being pleasant. "I hope you're enjoying the party."

Why the *hell* hadn't she thought to put the front desk on alert and ban this guy from her building? Because who would be crazy enough to show up at the home of the woman who had recently gotten you fired?

The answer? An arrogant asshole.

Drummond narrowed his gaze.

"You and I may no longer work together," he whispered, "but you never rescinded your party invite. Free food and booze? Sounds good to me."

Maddy noted that he kept his voice low, a smile on his face, and his body language loose. If anyone looked over, they'd never pick up on the disdain in his voice.

"Most people would probably assume the invitation was no longer valid," Ronan said, his voice calm and strong. "You did get *fired*. Right?"

"No, I quit. Who are you?"

Maddy felt Ronan's body tense, but she answered before he could say a word.

"It's really none of your business, but my friend is right." Maddy gave Drummond a tight smile. "I think you should go."

"But it's not even midnight yet." Chris stopped the

waiter who was passing out hors d'oeuvres and waved his almost-empty glass in the air. "Yo, I'll take a Dewar's on the rocks."

The young man nodded but gave Maddy a nervous look before heading toward the bar. Maddy sucked in a steadying breath and fought to maintain her composure. How could she get Drummond out of here without causing a scene? She glanced casually around the room, but everyone seemed blissfully unaware of the tension between them.

Except for Mr. Gregory.

Damn it all. The man was standing by the bar and staring at Maddy with an expression she couldn't decipher, but it wasn't good. Did Drummond get hold of Gregory and tell his side of the story? A twisted version of the truth?

Shit.

Drummond was going to cost Maddy one of her biggest clients, and who knows what kind of damage he could and would do to her reputation? She had to do some major damage control.

And fast.

"Officer Ronan McGuire," Ronan interjected. He adjusted his stance and positioned himself between her and Drummond. "I'm with the city's K-9 unit, and I also happen to be Maddy's boyfriend."

"Boyfriend?" Drummond scoffed, catching Maddy's eye. "You're dating a cop? You turned me down for a civil servant? This guy isn't even in the same league. I bet your entire salary is less than I make on commission from one sale."

"Maybe, but it's obvious money doesn't buy

class," Ronan said in a calm, steady voice. "At least, not for you."

"Whatever." Drummond snorted. "She's not worth the trouble."

"I think you should leave," Ronan said flatly. "Now."

Maddy placed one hand on Ronan's arm. She noticed his hands were balled into fists, but to his credit, he didn't make a move toward Drummond.

"Ronan's right. I want you to leave, Chris." Maddy kept her voice as calm as possible, but even she could hear the slight quiver within it. "Now."

"Do as the lady says," Ronan said in a quiet but deadly tone.

"Or what?" Drummond scoffed. He slipped his hands in the pockets of his slacks and moved closer to Ronan, taunting him with their faces mere inches apart. "You gonna arrest me for coming to a party? What are you gonna do? If you put your hands on me, I'll sue your ass off." His voice was barely audible, and he shot an evil glance at Maddy. "Or maybe I'll sue her. This is her place, after all. You sure as shit couldn't afford it."

Maddy tightened the grip on her glass. People were starting to notice that Ronan and Drummond's conversation was less than pleasant.

"What?" Drummond taunted. "Are you going to arrest me?"

"I might," Ronan murmured. "Unless, of course, my partner gets you first."

Right on cue and with uncanny timing, a low, animal growl rose up between them. Maddy didn't know when that dog had come out of the bedroom, and she'd never heard that sound coming from him before, but at the moment she didn't care. The look on Drummond's face was priceless. The crowd of partygoers had made way for the massive dog and it was no wonder. With his head low and hackles raised, the sweet, lovable bloodhound with the floppy ears didn't look so adorable anymore.

Far from it.

He looked like he wanted to rip Drummond to shreds.

"Right." Drummond backed up, and sweat beaded on his forehead. "Look, I was only messin' around a little, Maddy. Jeez, does your boyfriend sic this dog on anyone who pisses him off?"

"Good-bye, Chris," Maddy said quietly.

The guests were staring at Drummond and he knew it. He smoothed the lapels of his jacket and laughed nervously as he backed away from Bowser.

"Your clients better watch out, or your cop boyfriend and his mutt will make trouble for you. That's *real nice*, Maddy. Cosmopolitan Realty has the NYPD in their pocket. Are you on the payroll, pal?"

"It's time for you to go," Ronan said. "I'm not on the payroll, but even if I were, I'd throw your ass out for free."

"Screw off," Drummond huffed.

He waved his arm toward Ronan, and a guttural growl erupted from Bowser. Someone in the crowd shrieked. Bowser lunged a foot closer and barked ferociously at Drummond, who looked like he was going to piss himself.

"Hold!" Ronan shouted. He held one hand out, with his palm toward Bowser. "Hold, partner."

The dog froze but kept his brown eyes intent on Drummond. The dog's upper lip lifted, and his mouthful of teeth was visible as a low growl continued to rumble in the air.

For a split second, Maddy feared that it was going to be a full-fledged brawl. Her fears eased back when Drummond mumbled something incoherent and left the apartment with impressive speed. A collective sigh of relief rose from the crowd, audible even above the music, when Bowser sat at Ronan's feet.

"Good boy," she whispered. Maddy scratched the dog's ears before giving Ronan a strained smile.

The beginnings of a mass exodus had already begun.

"I guess the party's over," she said quietly.

"You're better off," Ronan scoffed.

Maddy squared her shoulders and leveled an *Are you crazy* look in his direction.

"What?" he asked innocently. "You disagree?"

"These are my clients, Ronan." She kept her voice barely above a whisper. "Don't you get it? This scene with Drummond could cost me more than a blown party. I wouldn't be the least bit surprised to get emails from Gregory and others telling me they want to terminate their contracts with me."

"Would that be so bad?" Ronan rose to his full height and stared her down. "You don't need this crap, Mads. You're better than this city and these people. You deserve better. Is this really where you want to be for the rest of your life?"

"What are you talking about?"

"Shit. I thought maybe…" Ronan ran one hand over his face. "Forget it. This isn't the time to talk about it."

"Ronan…wait a minute."

"Your *clients* are coming for you." He snapped his

fingers and Bowser hopped to his feet. "Come on, man. Let's get some air."

As Ronan and Bowser made their way to the door, the Weinsteins came over and were the first to say their good-byes. Maddy put on her best smile and apologized profusely, but before long, everyone else was lined up behind them. Except for Mr. Gregory, who had made a stealthy exit right after Drummond.

So much for that client.

By the time everyone had left and the caterers had packed up, it was well past midnight and Ronan still hadn't returned. The apartment was emptier than it had ever been.

There was a better than good chance that her business was going to suffer a serious hit. Public displays of emotion like that were déclassé, after all. The community of the ultrarich in the city was small and incestuous, and the story of what happened tonight would spread like wildfire.

But she didn't even care.

All she could think about was Ronan, and the fact that he hadn't come back. Wrapping herself in her NYPD sweatshirt, Maddy curled up on the couch. She stared at the digital clock on the cable box, waiting for the merciful gift of sleep to claim her.

Her eyelids grew heavy, and before long, she could barely keep them open. Through the fog of impending sleep, she heard the sound of her front door opening.

Maddy smiled sleepily and nestled into the ultrasoft pillows of the couch. Ronan was finally home. She went to roll onto her back, but something sharp pinched her thigh, like the sting of a bee or a wasp. She yelped, swatting at her bare leg.

"What the hell?" Maddy squinted against the light from the foyer and saw only the dark silhouette of a man. "Ronan?"

Her vision blurred, and she rubbed at her eyes, but it didn't help. In fact, it only got worse. She could see just enough of the faceless dark figure to realize it wasn't Ronan.

It wasn't Ronan, and she wasn't just sleepy. Wooziness took over, and her limbs grew heavy. Then the darkness swallowed her.

Chapter 19

RONAN KNEW HE'D ACTED LIKE A PUNK KID, STORMING OUT of the party like that, but he'd had to get the hell out of there before he lost it and made things worse for Maddy. It was bad enough that he'd almost punched that asshole out, but then Bowser had practically gone Cujo in front of all those stiffs.

That was quite a party trick. Nice move, McGuire.

All he'd wanted to do was get rid of all those people and have Maddy to himself. He'd planned on proposing to her and starting the New Year off the right way. But as the night wore on, his insecurities had taken full hold. What if she said no? What if she realized he wasn't good enough for her and couldn't keep up in her circles?

Deep in his gut, Ronan knew it was nerves that had him on edge, not the stiffs at the party. It wasn't every day he decided to spend the rest of his life with someone, and he was feeling impatient. He wanted the rest of their lives to start as soon as possible, but instead, he'd flown off the handle and split. So much for his grand plan of proposing on New Year's Eve.

By the time he'd walked off his frustration, it was almost one in the morning. Going back to Maddy's place would only wake her up. The whole night was screwed, and all because he was so damn nervous he didn't know what to do with himself. He probably should have gone back, but he went home and sent her a text apology instead, promising a face-to-face grovel session in the morning.

When he woke up to find she hadn't responded, he wasn't particularly surprised. She was pissed at him and had every right to be. He had behaved badly and he knew it. Ronan owed her an apology, and he figured that donuts and coffee might help.

He rang the bell of her apartment twice, but there was no answer. That was odd. She didn't have to work today. Maybe she was still asleep? Bowser snorted his impatience and sat by the door.

"I know, buddy."

Ronan balanced the coffee tray and bag of donuts in one hand before trying the doorknob. To his dismay, it turned easily. The woman didn't lock her apartment? Ronan swore under his breath and opened the door, holding it so Bowser could pass. Even before it swung shut behind him, he sensed something was off.

The apartment was eerily quiet.

"Maddy?"

He strode into the living room but it was empty. Some remnants of the party were strewn on the counter, but for the most part, everything had been cleaned up. Ronan set the donuts and coffee on the dining table and kept calling her. She wasn't in the bathroom or the office, and her bed was made. Not only that, but her cell phone was plugged in on her nightstand.

"What the hell?"

Ronan went back into the living room and scanned the space carefully. Her keys were in the bowl on the sofa table, and her enormous purse still sat on the table in the foyer. He checked the hall closet and her coat was there. A feeling of foreboding crept up his back as he walked around the living room one more time.

"I don't like this, man," he said quietly. "Something's wrong."

Ronan grabbed Bowser's leash and went back downstairs. He checked with the doorman and the concierge. Neither of them had seen Maddy since they came on shift at seven that morning. With his concern increasing, Ronan took the elevator down to the building's parking garage and found Maddy's car parked in her assigned spot.

"Where the hell is she?" he whispered.

He went back up to Maddy's apartment and took yet another look around. Her wallet was there, and so were cash, credit cards, and an ATM card. It was like the woman had just disappeared without a trace, which didn't make any damn sense at all. The knot of fear in his gut started to tighten.

"No way." He shook his head and stared at Bowser, who looked as concerned as Ronan felt. "Maybe she went to our place?"

Even as he suggested it, Ronan knew it wasn't true. But with few other options, he and Bowser headed out. All the way home, he went over and over the evidence in his head. How far would she get without her ID, money, credit cards, car, and keys?

Ronan had been a cop long enough to know that time was the enemy when someone disappeared. Officially, he would have to wait twenty-four hours before filing a missing person report. But that didn't mean he couldn't look for her on his own.

As he'd feared, Maddy was not waiting for him at

his apartment. He called Sharon, and even Jordan, but they hadn't heard from her. Her offices were closed, and when he called, he got the Happy New Year message. The woman had seemingly vanished without a trace, but Ronan knew better than anyone—that didn't happen.

People don't disappear. They either leave, or they get taken.

There was no in between.

That was the problem.

By all the evidence, Maddy hadn't *left*.

With all of the rational possibilities exhausted, Ronan decided that he and Bowser would do what they did best. He gathered Bowser's search gear and headed back to Maddy's place. When the elevator reached her floor, he paused and glanced at 15B. Maybe the kid had seen or heard something that would shed some light on the situation.

Ronan knocked on the door and waited with Bowser at his side, but there was no answer. He rang the bell and knocked two more times, but still nothing. Maybe the kid had made a New Year's resolution and actually left the house?

"That's perfect timing," Ronan grumbled. "Where's a shut-in when you need him?"

He put a call in to the feds handling the West Side Ringer case, on the terrifying chance that Maddy's disappearance could be related. But with no proof and her disappearance only a few hours old, he had limited options. That asshole Drummond came to mind, but he didn't seem like the guy. He'd been a coward, a blowhard with balls when he was in front of a crowd, but once confronted, he'd shown himself for the chickenshit that he was. Besides, he'd ended up making a scene.

The West Side Ringer, and guys like him, didn't make scenes in public. They flew under the radar, and that wasn't Drummond. That jerkoff loved attention.

Ronan went back to Maddy's apartment and got the dress she had been wearing at the party. It was on the hanger on her closet door, and even as he took it down to use it as a scent article for Bowser, he fought to maintain some distance.

Panic, anger, and outright fear fired through his chest.

He simply could not lose her.

"Do the job, McGuire." Ronan squared his shoulders. "Cut the shit, and do your job."

A knock on the apartment door captured his attention, and hope fired through him. Dress in hand, he ran to the foyer, Bowser at his side. When he opened the door, it was only Vincent, the concierge.

"Hey, Vincent." Ronan nodded tightly. "Any news?"

"No, Officer." The concierge clasped his hands behind his back. "I spoke with the men who were on duty last night, and neither of them saw Ms. Morgan leave the building. All of her guests signed in and out, as per protocol, including the catering staff from her party. I'm sorry, sir."

"No, that's okay." Ronan stared at the dress in his hand. "That's more information that will help us. We know she didn't leave the building. Her car is still downstairs."

"And I checked the key-card records for the garage, sir." Vincent's mouth set in a grim line. "A resident has to swipe their key card to get in and out. Ms. Morgan's card hasn't been used since she returned from vacation."

"Alright. Bowser and I are going to do a sweep of the building, see if we can at least figure out what direction she went." Ronan's voice was tight and controlled. "No one, and I mean *no one*, is permitted on this floor. Do you understand me? And if anyone comes looking for Maddy, I want you to call me ASAP. You continue to make sure everyone signs in and out. I don't want anyone slipping past."

"Yes, sir." Vincent nodded quickly. "I have your card at the front desk."

"Good."

Ronan shoved his desperate frustration aside and squatted down, giving Bowser a good, long sniff of Maddy's dress. The dog snuffled away, and his tail wagged as he got a solid dose. After being sure Bowser had enough, Ronan placed the dress on the hall table and stood in the open doorway.

Vincent stood by the elevator and watched with a wide-eyed stare that told Ronan he was impressed and a bit scared of what was happening.

Ronan held the apartment door open for Bowser and gave him the command. The dog stuck his nose to the ground and moved out into the hallway and then back into the apartment before heading to the elevator.

"Okay, boy." Ronan patted Bowser's head, and the dog barked at the closed elevator doors. Ronan kept his voice calm and struggled to do this by the numbers. "That's a good start. We know she didn't go down the emergency stairwell but took the elevator. That narrows our search right away."

"What now?" Vincent hit the elevator button again, but kept his wary gaze on Bowser.

"Now we stop at every single floor." As Ronan wrapped the leash around his hand, fury settled in his chest. "We start at the roof and work our way down. Bowser will know when we find the floor where she got off."

Vincent came with them, and it all played out exactly as Ronan said. They stopped at every floor. But each time the doors opened, Bowser would sniff briefly before whining and going back in the elevator. Disappointment rose with each passing floor, and Ronan fought the tickle of panic.

There was no sign of her.

Until they got to the garage.

When the doors opened, Bowser touched his nose to the ground and then took off like a shot with a bone-chilling howl. Nose to the ground, tail in the air, and hackles raised, he had picked up her scent, and it was strong. Ronan ran with him, and Vincent followed, though he lagged behind. They rounded a corner by a large pillar until they came to an empty parking space, and Ronan's heart sank. Bowser howled and barked, agitated by having reached the end of the trail, and Ronan didn't blame him.

"Whose parking space is this?" Ronan shouted. He snapped his head around and glared at Vincent. "Whose is it?"

"Um...I'm not sure, but I think it belongs to Mr. Reinhold." Vincent swiped at his sweaty brow and left a dark stain on his gray jacket sleeve. "Thomas Reinhold. He's Ms. Morgan's neighbor in 15B."

"Son of a bitch," Ronan whispered. "The computer guy?"

"Yes," Vincent sputtered. "He invented some kind of security software. I-I'm not sure. I mean, I don't know about that sort of thing, sir."

Rage surged as Ronan recalled the conversation with Jenkins about the perp using technology to cover his tracks. Holy shit.

That dorky kid with the glasses was the West Side Ringer.

And Maddy was his next victim.

—∿∿—

The thick smell of damp air and mold assaulted Maddy's senses as she emerged from the fog of the blackout. Her entire body ached like she had run a marathon through a sea of molasses. She was sitting on a cold, bare, wooden floor. Her head felt heavy, as if a blistering headache was brewing. She blanched and squinted against the sunlight that streamed in through the partially covered window. From what little she could see of the faintly amber light, Maddy got the impression the sun was setting. A black or brown curtain riddled with holes kept out most of the light, but there was enough for her to get an idea of her surroundings.

Fear crawled beneath her skin when she realized her wrists were tied to an old, rusty radiator. Maddy lifted her head and whimpered as a wave of nausea came over her. Panic threatened to consume her, but she knew that would get her nowhere.

How long had she been here? Hours? Days?

Calm. She had to stay calm and look at her surroundings.

She was still wearing the sweatshirt and her bra and

underwear. A thin, musty green blanket had been placed over her legs but had started to slide off, allowing the damp, cold air to creep over her. The room looked like it was in an old cabin of some kind, and other than a small chair by the door, it was practically barren.

This couldn't be real. She was still asleep on the couch, and this was only a nightmare. *Wake up, Maddy. Wake up.* She tugged on the nylon ropes that bound her wrists, but they wouldn't budge. Pain shot through her hands. She swallowed the scream that began to bubble up when the realization struck home.

This was not a nightmare. She was awake and in trouble.

Wind whistled outside and snow flew by the window, but the light seemed to be fading by the minute. Maddy could see branches bouncing amid swirls of white, but that was it.

It all started to come back to her.

She had fallen asleep on the couch waiting for Ronan, but a man had been in her apartment. The spot on her left thigh tingled, a twisted reminder of the stinging pain that had awakened her. That man, whoever he was, must have drugged her and brought her here.

But where the hell was she?

She thought of Lucille and Brenda, Yolanda and Patricia, and a sob escaped her lips. Maddy tugged again on the ropes, but they wouldn't budge. Her skin stung from the ties scraping mercilessly against her.

It was no use.

The sound of something—or someone—moving on the other side of the crooked door made her freeze. Footsteps, faint at first, grew closer, and she thought she heard someone whispering. Or maybe that was her imagination?

Sweat broke out all over her body. She shivered and bit her lip, fighting the urge to scream. What good would that do her? They must have been miles from any other cabins. Otherwise her kidnapper would have gagged her, wouldn't he? Screaming wouldn't help, and if this son of a bitch hurt women, then he would probably get off on hearing Maddy in pain.

Her heart thundering in her chest, she squirmed against the restraints, but there was nowhere to go. Nowhere to hide. No way out.

The man who intended to kill her was on the other side of that door.

Maddy was going to die, and all she could think of was Ronan.

As the door creaked open slowly, Maddy squeezed her eyes shut and prayed for the strength to fight. She fleetingly thought of self-defense classes she had taken in school, but with her hands tied, there was little she could do. She could kick or bite her abductor, but that would probably only enrage him, making her situation worse.

Heavy footsteps and the sound of something being dragged across the floor filled the small room. A chair? The little wooden chair she saw in the corner by the door. Was that it?

Maddy squelched the scream and tried to stop her body from shuddering, but it was no use. Pure unadulterated fear and adrenaline coursed through her like an electrical current. Even her teeth chattered. She could feel him, whoever he was, getting closer, and she instinctively pulled her knees to her chest and scooted closer to the wall, trying to get away from him in whatever way she could, no matter how small.

"Good, you're awake." The male voice was soft and mild and vaguely familiar. "Now we can begin."

Maddy's heavy breathing and her heartbeat thundering in her ears were the only sounds in the room. She flexed her hands, opening and closing them, hoping against hope that she could free herself from the ropes. It was no use. Digging deep for even an ounce of bravery, she sucked in a shuddering breath and opened her eyes.

It was the computer guy from 15B.

"Tom?" Her voice was shaky and barely above a whisper. "What the hell is going on? Why are you doing this?"

"Oh, *now* you know my name?" he asked flatly.

Confusion spiraled through her, and she shook her head. Maybe she could reason with him? Appeal to some shred of human decency that might be lurking beneath that cold, disconnected exterior? He was bigger than she thought she remembered, and slim but obviously not weak. He wore a Captain America T-shirt and khaki pants. His Clark Kent glasses completed the image of a computer nerd, but obviously someone far darker lurked beneath.

"Please," she whispered. "Just let me go. I won't tell anyone what happened."

"Yes, you will." He pushed his glasses up his nose before resting his elbows on his knees and studying her intently, like she was a bug under glass. "The others said the same thing. That's always what they say, but it's a lie."

Maddy swallowed the bile that rose in her throat.
The others.

"It was you," she whispered. "You killed Lucille and
Brenda…"

"Practice makes perfect," he said, his voice void of
emotion. "I wanted to be sure that it was exactly right
when I got to you. It's not easy to strangle someone,
you know. It takes real power. And I didn't get to take
my time with them. Not really. But you and I will have
plenty of that."

Maddy's brows knit together, and she squelched the
hysterical laugh that threatened to bubble up and boil
over. He was *bragging.* The little sicko was trying to
impress her with his strength? That was it. That was her
opening. Maddy flicked her tongue out over her dry lips.

"I-I know," she rasped. "I won't fight you. I know
you're too strong for me. Just tell me what you want,
and I'll give it to you. You don't have to hurt me."

"You," he said simply. Tom waved his hand toward
her in a bizarrely casual gesture and leaned back in the
chair. "I wanted you from the first time I saw you. People
aren't like computers, you know. They're much more
complicated. Unless, of course, you just take what you
want. I got tired of women treating me like dirt, using
me and then tossing me aside. Helping them with their
papers back in school. Carrying groceries. Whatever.
People take what they need and leave the rest behind.
That's all I'm doing. Taking what I need."

"I would have helped you," Maddy whispered. "I
would have—"

Tom jumped from his chair. It tumbled backward as
he lurched forward and screamed in her face.

"You didn't even know my fucking name! I was in your apartment, fixing your computer, and you called me *Tim*. My name is TOM!" His calm exterior faltered, and his fair complexion flushed bright red. "So don't tell me what you *would* have done."

Maddy squeezed her eyes shut and shrank from him, bracing herself for whatever came next. His breath was a mixture of sweet and sour, like old soda and stale mints, and it fanned over her in disgusting little waves. Her body was tensed to the point of pain, but she didn't dare move.

A small whimper escaped her lips when he trailed one finger over the exposed flesh of her thigh, but a sound outside made him stop. It was probably just a falling branch or an animal, but whatever it was, Maddy was grateful for it.

"Be right back," he whispered. "And don't bother calling out for help. We're in the woods. Nobody will hear you. Besides, the sun will be down soon, and I always do my best work in the dark."

Revulsion roiled through her at the clammy press of his wet lips against her cheek, and Maddy bit the inside of her mouth to keep from screaming. Tom left the room. Once the door closed behind him, she let out the breath she'd been holding, and it escaped in a heaving sob.

All she could think about was Ronan. Why hadn't she followed him after the party? She could have stopped him. She could have told her clients to wait a damn minute, but she didn't. It would prove to be the single biggest mistake of her life.

What was it he had wanted to talk to her about?

Maddy squeezed her eyes shut and pictured his

handsome smiling face. She replayed their best moments together like a movie in her head. If this was going to be her last night on earth, then Ronan would occupy her final thoughts. Not the crazy person who had brought her here, or the horrible fate that likely awaited her.

It was not supposed to end this way.

"No fucking way," Maddy rasped through a shuddering breath.

She shook her head and grunted as she tugged on the ropes again. She would not die here. Not like this. Maddy flicked a glance at the closed door and began pulling at the knot with her teeth. She would get out of here and get back to Ronan or die trying.

———

Ronan and Bowser crouched behind a huge pine tree, but the dog was restless. He had picked up Maddy's scent before the cabin even came into view. The bloodhound shivered as he leaned against Ronan, his large furred body tense and ready to pounce. Ronan didn't blame him one bit. The son of a bitch who had taken Maddy was just arrogant enough to think they wouldn't find him. He had no idea that Ronan, along with several feds and some of the local cops, now had the small cottage surrounded.

With his gun drawn, Ronan nodded to the three men positioned on the other side of the driveway. Snow drifted over them, but the two snipers in the brush remained stone still, waiting to take their shot. The windows were covered, and there was no way to see inside. Ronan couldn't think about what might be happening to Maddy because it would paralyze him. He slammed his mind shut to anything but getting her out.

He didn't have the luxury of letting the fear in.

This was search and rescue. It was his job. That's it.

Even as those words rushed through his mind, Ronan knew it was a lie. This wasn't just *any* job and the woman held captive within those walls wasn't just *any* woman.

Get it together, McGuire. Ronan gripped his gun tighter and let out a slow, steady breath through his nose, attempting to slow his racing heart. *Focus*.

Sanderson, the lead investigator for the feds, captured Ronan's gaze and gave him the signal.

Game time.

All four men moved in swiftly and as silently as possible. Bowser kept his nose to the ground and ran a few feet ahead of Ronan. The sound of leaves and gravel beneath their feet sifted through the air. As they got closer to the rickety front porch of the dilapidated cottage, Ronan's heart thundered in his chest.

The feds were supposed to take point. That was the plan. But Bowser didn't get the memo. When the door burst open and gunshots erupted, Ronan dropped to his knees by the railing of the porch, attempting to get cover, but his partner leaped in front of him.

A howling wail of pain filled the air, and Bowser fell onto the steps like a stone.

—◈—

The sound of gunfire and shouting filled the air, and Maddy froze. A dog barked savagely, and the sound was immediately followed by several more shots, a howling, haunting wail, and then…silence.

Had she imagined it?

Maddy's body shook with fear and adrenaline

following the noise, and the horrifying quiet surrounding her. Then the footsteps came, moving fast and getting closer, echoes thundering through the cabin. Maddy held her breath, and a split second later, the door of the room burst free from its hinges and clattered to the floor.

For a minute, she thought she was hallucinating.

Ronan McGuire stood in the doorway like an avenging angel. He was in uniform, and his badge glinted in the fading light that streamed through the window, like a beacon of safety telling her everything was going to be okay. Wild-eyed, blood smeared on his cheek, and with his gun drawn, he looked ready to rain havoc on whoever got in his way. Perhaps he already had.

The fierce expression of concentration stamped into his features flickered and dissolved into one of desperate relief when he saw her. The man looked haggard and drawn, like he hadn't slept in weeks.

"Maddy." Her name fell reverently from his lips. "Thank God."

Ronan ran to her and tumbled to his knees by her side. He quickly undid the ropes around her wrist while raining kisses over her face. She sat up, and sobs loudly racked her body. She wrapped her arms around his neck and held him tightly.

"I thought I was going to die," she whispered. "You found me. Thank God you found me. How? How did you—"

"That's what we do, Mads." Ronan held on to her as though he would never let her go. "And you know how I love surprising you," he murmured.

In spite of the ordeal or maybe because of the

incredible relief that it was over, Maddy laughed and buried her face in the comforting warmth of his throat. It took her a moment to realize someone was missing. And she had heard a horrible howl.

Bowser.

Red and blue lights strobed outside, and another officer appeared in the open doorway. He was wearing a beige-and-brown uniform that looked more like the ones she had seen on state troopers than on NYPD.

"McGuire, they're taking him in now." The older man looked at Maddy briefly. "Do you need the ambulance?"

"Yes."

Maddy started to argue, but Ronan shot her a look.

"Yes, she needs to be looked at first. You guys can get her statement later."

"Ronan?" Maddy gripped his arms and looked past him to the open doorway as he helped her to her feet. Her legs shook, and she feared they might give out on her. "Where's Bowser?"

"He took one in the chest. Stupid damn dog ran right in front of me." Ronan's eyes watered, and he shook his head curtly before scooping Maddy up into his arms. "Doesn't look good. They're taking him to the local animal hospital."

"You should be with him," Maddy whispered.

Ronan strode out of the room, Maddy safe in his arms. She averted her gaze when she spotted Tom's lifeless body on the porch. A shiver of dread swept up her back when she thought about what could have happened. But it didn't, because of Ronan and Bowser.

"I need a blanket here," Ronan shouted as they approached the front door of the cabin. "Now!"

An EMT ran over and draped a black blanket over Maddy.

"Ronan," Maddy said gently. "Let's go be with Bowser."

He stopped by the ambulance but didn't put her down on the gurney.

His dark brows furrowed and the hardness in his eyes softened, bringing down some of the defensive wall she knew he'd put up to keep it together. She pressed her hand to his cheek, the scruff rasping against her palm.

"I'm okay, I promise," she whispered. "But I wouldn't be if it weren't for the two of you. So let's go."

Chapter 20

MADDY SPRINKLED THE BOILED GROUND BEEF OVER THE bowl of white rice and mixed it thoroughly. Satisfied it had cooled off enough, she poured the concoction into a big dog bowl printed with *Bowser* in bright-red letters. Ronan was watching the game on the couch in the living room, and his newly retired partner sat right next to him. Maddy's white couch was quickly becoming a dingy gray.

She didn't care. That big dog and his gorgeous partner were her family. What good was a fancy, white couch if she couldn't share it with them?

"Come on, buddy." Maddy brought the bowl over to Bowser's special spot by the dining room table and set it down. "Dinnertime."

The enormous bloodhound whined with appreciation before gingerly getting off the couch and making his way over to the food. The stitches would be removed soon, but the poor dog had a limp that would likely be permanent, and the injury was bad enough to force him into retirement.

"You know," Ronan said, "you're spoiling him rotten. He only needed that diet the first week after the surgery. It's been three weeks, Mads. He can have regular dog food."

"No he can't," she said in a silly voice. Maddy rubbed Bowser's ears before leaving him to his dinner. "Bowser saved my life and got shot in the process. The least I can do is give him a decent meal every day."

"What about me?" Ronan grabbed her hand and pulled her onto the couch with him. "What do I get?"

"Me." Maddy kissed him quickly before snuggling against his chest. "I still can't believe that you two got to me before…"

"Hey." He kissed the top of her head and wrapped his arm more tightly around her. "It's done. You're safe and he's dead."

"I know," she said shakily.

"The little sicko wasn't that smart." Anger punctuated his words. "With all his fancy Internet tricks, he failed to hide that property he owned upstate. Besides, the creep hardly ever left his apartment, but the days he *did* leave just happened to coincide with the dates the women went missing. He was arrogant and never thought a bunch of dumb cops would catch a smart guy like him."

Ronan put his sock-covered feet up on the mahogany coffee table and played with her hair as she nuzzled deeper into his embrace. She felt safe with him and she always would. No matter where they were.

"It makes me sick to think how long he'd been spying on me." Maddy shuddered and snuggled deeper into Ronan's embrace. "Using my GPS to track me and watching me through my computer camera. Creepy as hell."

"I know." Ronan kissed her cheek, and his arm tightened around her. "But it's over, and the feds triple-checked your apartment but didn't find any bugs or cameras."

"That's a relief." Maddy sighed. "And tell them they can keep the computer. I'm getting a new laptop. I don't want that other one anywhere near me."

"Agreed."

A comfortable silence fell between them, and Maddy rested her head on his shoulder. She giggled when Bowser belched loudly after finishing his food.

"Nice, buddy," Ronan said through a laugh. "See? You're spoiling him. If you keep it up, he's gonna weigh three hundred pounds."

"Bowser's really retired now?" Maddy asked. "There's no way he can go back on duty?"

"Nope. He's gonna miss it too." Ronan's voice was quiet and edged with a hint of sadness. "But he's going to stay with me for the rest of his life. Most K-9s retire around eight years old anyway, and Bowser's going to be seven soon. It's just a little early, really."

"So now what?" Maddy asked quietly. "For you, I mean? What *ever* will you do with yourself?"

She grabbed the remote and turned off the television before straddling Ronan on the couch. A lusty smile spread across his face, and his hands settled on her hips, tugging her against the quickly hardening evidence of his desire. Maddy braced both hands on the cushions on either side of his head and rocked her hips.

"I'll think of something," he murmured. "I'm still a cop. But I'll have to switch departments unless I want to train with another dog."

"You're a one-dog kind of guy, huh?" she asked playfully. "I hope that goes for women too."

She leaned down to kiss him, but Ronan grabbed her face with both hands and held her there. His lust-filled

gaze shifted to one of serious concentration as he studied her intently.

"What is it?" she asked gently. "What's wrong?"

"Hang on."

Ronan took her by the arms and carefully helped her
off his lap before he disappeared into the bedroom. A
funny feeling settled in the pit of Maddy's stomach at
the way he'd shifted gears so quickly at the phrase "one-
woman man." Maybe the bloom was off the rose, and
Ronan had decided that being in a relationship wasn't
for him after all. Was that it? Was that what he had
wanted to talk to her about at the party? Maybe he had
been waiting until things settled down to break it off
with her.

"Oh shit," Maddy whispered.

Unable to sit there and simply wait for him to deliver
the bad news, Maddy hurried into the kitchen. She still
had to clean up from making Bowser's dinner, and that
would give her something to busy herself with. She
pushed up the sleeves of her sweater and flipped on the
water, waiting for it to get steaming hot.

"Shouldn't you wear gloves when you wash dishes?"

Ronan's deep male voice cut into the kitchen, but
Maddy kept her gaze fixed on the rising dome of bubbles.

"I don't know," she said quickly.

*Dishes? He wants to talk about freaking dishpan
hands? Jeez. Just dump me already and get it over with.*

"Well, I think I heard that all that grease and dish
soap isn't good for your rings and stuff."

"I don't wear any rings, Ronan," Maddy said with
more than a little irritation.

"But what if you did?"

The steam that started to rise wasn't from the water but her waning patience. Maddy slammed the faucet off and spun around, expecting to see Ronan standing behind her.

Only, he wasn't standing. He was kneeling.

On one knee, to be more specific, and he was holding out a black velvet box with a stunning ruby-and-diamond ring inside. The bright-red stone sat in what looked like an antique setting and was surrounded by glittering diamonds.

It was absolutely exquisite.

Maddy's hands flew to her mouth, sending water and soap around the kitchen, which only made the satisfied smirk on Ronan's face grow wider.

"Is that what I think it is?" she whispered through her fingers.

"Madolyn Morgan, will you do me the honor of being my wife?"

"You're proposing?" she asked through a laugh. Maddy dropped to her knees in front of him and punched him in the arm. "I thought you were breaking up with me!"

"No way, Mads." Ronan shook his head and took the ring out of the box. "I'm not letting you get away. Why would you think that I was going to break up with you?"

"That night at the party, you were acting so weird and talking about what I deserved, and…just now…I said something about being a one-woman man…"

"I was gonna *propose to you* that night, but I freaked out when Bowser made a scene and you got so upset."

"That's why you were acting all nervous!"

"Yes. And proposing to you on the kitchen floor is

not what I originally planned. I can promise you, my other idea was way more romantic." He grabbed her hand and held up the ring. "I love you, Maddy, and I want to spend the rest of my life surprising you. Will you be my wife?"

Maddy smiled broadly and drew in a deep breath. "On one condition."

"Uh, okay." Ronan's grin faltered but he remained composed. "Anything."

"Let's get the hell out of this city." Maddy linked her arms around his neck and kissed him. "Take me home," she murmured against his lips. "Can we do that? Move back to Old Brookfield?"

"I thought you'd never ask," he growled.

Ronan slipped the ring on her finger, and Maddy only had a brief moment to admire it before he hopped to his feet and tossed her over his shoulder. She let out a shriek mixed with laughter and Bowser barked, joining in with the fun.

"What are you doing?" Maddy giggled and smacked his backside as he carried her toward the bedroom. "Ronan! Was this part of your proposal plan?"

"Taking you to bed?" He held her knees against his chest and whacked her butt playfully. "You bet your sweet ass it was."

"Why am I not surprised?" She laughed.

Ronan spent the rest of that night showing her over and over again just how much he loved her. In between lovemaking, they talked about the possibilities for the future. Ronan had already looked into transferring to the Old Brookfield police department, and Maddy shared her dream of buying the inn from Imogene and Bob.

With plans in motion and her head spinning with possibilities, Maddy lay in bed, exhausted and sleepy, her nude body draped comfortably over Ronan's.

The ring, a family heirloom, glinted in the moonlight that streamed through the window. It was perfect, and she couldn't have asked for anything better. The steady, familiar sound of Ronan's breathing surrounded her like a security blanket.

She was leaping into the great unknown once again. But when Maddy stepped over the edge this time, she would have Ronan by her side. Bowser snuffled loudly from the foot of the bed. Maddy stifled a giggle.

Ronan, and a big, hairy bloodhound.

Acknowledgments

I must extend special thanks to the Westchester County K-9 unit but especially to Officer Tierney and his partner, Saratoga. They were kind enough to let me into their unique world, and I will be forever grateful to them for taking the time to share their extensive knowledge and experience. Officer Tierney and Saratoga provided wonderful inspiration for Ronan and Bowser's relationship.

About the Author

Sara Humphreys is a graduate of Marist College, with a bachelor's degree in English literature and theater. Her initial career path after college was as a professional actress. Some of her television credits include *A&E Biography*, *Guiding Light*, *Another World*, *As the World Turns*, and *Rescue Me*.

In 2013, Sara's novel *Untamed* won two PRISM awards: Dark Paranormal and Best of the Best.

She loves writing about hot heroes and heroines with moxie, but above all, Sara adores a satisfying happily ever after. She lives in New York with her husband, their four amazing sons, and two adorable pups. When she's not writing or hanging out with the men in her life, she can be found working out with Shaun T in her living room or chatting with readers on Facebook.

For a full list of Sara's books and reading order, please visit her website at www.sarahumphreys.com.

May the Best Man Win

Best Men

by Mira Lyn Kelly

USA Today bestselling author

Four friends. Each a best man at a wedding. One chance to get it right.

Jase Foster can't believe his bad luck. He's been paired with the she-devil herself for his best friend's wedding: Emily Klein of the miles-long legs and killer smile. She may be sin in a bridesmaid dress, but there's no way he's falling for her *again*.

They can barely stand each other, but given how many of their friends are getting married, they'll just have to play nice—at least when they're in company. Once they're alone, more than just gloves come off as Jase and Emily discover their chemistry is combustible, and there may be something to this enemies-to-lovers thing after all…
